WELCOME TO POTTER'S BLUFF.
A NEW WAY OF LIFE.

That's what the sign said. But for some, Potter's Bluff had become a new way of death.

DAN GILLIS. He was the law. And he was terrified. At first he was puzzled by the epidemic of murder. Then he was angry. And then his anger turned to fear. Gut-wrenching, cold-sweating fear of what was about to happen . . .

JANET GILLIS. What was her link to the murdered stranger? Was she hiding something that would soon be buried?

WILLIAM DOBBS. The mortician's mortician. His business was death. And business was better than ever.

It's good to know that
the truth will out—even if it's
DEAD AND BURIED
. . . or maybe it would be better
never to know the truth at all!

Also by Chelsea Quinn Yarbro

Cautionary Tales
False Dawn

Published by
WARNER BOOKS

Screenplay by

Ronald Shusett and Dan O'Bannon

based on an original story by

Jeff Millar and Alex Stern

Novelization by

Chelsea Quinn Yarbro

A Warner Communications Company

This is a work of fiction. No person, location or event depicted represents or is intended to represent any actual person, location or event.

WARNER BOOKS EDITION

Warner Books, Inc., 75 Rockefeller Plaza, New York, N.Y. 10019

A Warner Communications Company

Printed in the United States of America

First printing: August, 1980

Reissued: July, 1981

10 9 8

For Donald:
craft for art
and a Toyota

Acknowledgments and thanks to:
Ron Cobb
J. R. Thompson
Sandra Procopio

Prologue

Sea gulls were coasting on the brisk wind off the ocean, their high cries lost in the growl of the surf. Sunlight so intense, so white that it seemed to shatter as it hit the water, flooded the empty beach. Slender, high-arched impressions appeared to come out of the sea where the incoming tide washed away a solitary trail of footprints leading toward the distant town of Potter's Bluff. At the edge of the high tide mark lay driftwood looking like dark, twisted creatures who had crawled out of the depths of the water to die in the air.

That was the way the beach looked when the photographer found it: a bright, vacant expanse under a wind-scrubbed autumn sky—isolated. The houses of Potter's Bluff were just far enough away to make the deserted beach look lonely.

He pulled his vintage Volkswagen bus to the side of the road and got out, jumping down from the high seat. Then he stood for a few minutes, his hands lifted to shade his eyes as he studied the beach. His concentration was broken when the shadow of a sea gull passed over him, darkening his vision.

"Yeah," he said to himself as he reached into the van, pulling his camera off the front passenger seat. The name stamped on the leather was George LeMoir. He had to slam the car door twice before it closed, and after giving the matter a second's consideration, decided not to lock the door. Why bother? He had not seen more than four cars on the road in the last hour and there was no one on the beach. Pocketing his keys, he started down the steep slope to the crescent of sand.

He walked quickly, his eyes moving restlessly as he searched out bits of seaweed and driftwood. Occasionally he stopped to examine a promising collection of flotsam at the edge of the water, but nothing caught his attention enough to make him take his camera from its case.

Then he came upon a knot of seaweed where the spent waves foamed around a dead sea gull. With a tingling of excitement, he stopped to examine this. What photographer in the world could pass it up? The arrangement and rearrangement was more promising than a Rorschach test. He went down on one knee, hardly aware of the wet.

The sea gull was waterlogged and drab, its feathers resembling the seaweed fronds that held it so gently. As the waves lapped and licked at it, the mass continually changed shape, like abstract sculpture. As he watched, all the possibilities began to take form in his mind. The photographer began to breathe a little faster. This was *it!* Fumbling with his camera case and swearing at the shoulder strap, he at last pulled the camera from its red felt nest. He remembered his light meter, and made a hurried check before he began to snap pictures.

He was on his second roll of film and had stopped to set up his tripod when she spoke.

"Hi."

At the first shock of interruption, the photographer turned to see who this interloper was, prepared to send the person on with a few brusque words. His scowl was replaced at once with an oddly bashful smile as he caught sight of the girl. "Hi," he returned.

She was no more than twenty-two, pretty in an unaffected way. Her skin was starting to redden on her shoulders and knees, though she was honey tan. It was chilly on the beach but this did not seem to bother her—her cutoff jeans were faded and sandy and her halter top was skimpy enough for the photographer to find it slightly embarrassing to look at her. Her mouth turned up at the corners, and she came a little closer, sure of her welcome. "What're you taking pictures of?"

He made a flustered gesture toward the sea gull. "That." As an added explanation, since he saw she did not understand, he said, "The sort of boring stuff you see in *Popular Photography*, you know."

Her nod was supremely neutral, but her eyes twinkled. "I've been watching you." She thrust her hands into her jeans pockets and grinned at his sudden nervousness. "You really work at it, don't you?"

The photographer got to his feet and

brushed his knees to get off most of the damp sand, discovering that his jeans were soaked from the knees down. "I've got patience. You need patience for good photography . . . and a lot of film."

"You're a professional photographer?" She raised her hand to wipe her long, sun tawny hair out of her face. The movement was subtly provocative.

He reached out to steady his tripod, finding reassurance in this practical movement. "Uh . . . no, but I'm trying. That's why I'm here. Getting up a portfolio. I'm on vacation, really, but I'm hoping that if I get enough really good shots, I won't have to fill out any more quality control reports." His voice sounded as if the admission were startling to him. He hurried on. "If I get some fantastic pictures of driftwood and sea gulls, and those strange tracks . . . are they yours?"

"No, not mine." She gestured toward the beach. "There's plenty driftwood around here, and you've already got the sea gull." Now she was faintly amused.

"Well, if my pictures are good enough, then maybe the oil companies will be convinced I can take fantastic pictures of flanges and valves and pumps, and things like that." He gave a shy snort of laughter to let her know how ridiculous it was. His self-effacing manner was rather unexpected; the awkwardness he revealed was that of a man younger than his thirty years. He was of medium height and build and his features were regular, pleasant without being striking or handsome. Only a small, crescent-shaped scar just below his left eye made his face memorable.

"Is that dead sea gull all you're going to shoot?"

He shrugged. "I don't see anything else as interesting . . . not meaning any offense, but . . ."

She pointed northward. "I saw some more driftwood down that way."

"So did I. There wasn't a thing worth photographing. Driftwood's hard to do well. Everyone tries it." Once again he steadied his tripod.

"Then let's try the other way." Her hands in her cutoff jeans drew the denim taut against her skin, outlining her hips.

"Okay." The photographer bent to take his camera off the tripod after carefully wiping his hands on his sweater. "Show me where."

"This way." The girl set off to the south, squinting a little in the sunlight. She walked with long easy strides, her lithe young body temptingly near. "You from around here?" she asked when they had gone a little way in silence.

He shook his head. "No. I'm from St. Louis."

"That's a long way. You visiting anyone?" The wind snapped through her hair, but she ignored it, giving him her flattering, undivided attention.

"Nope. I wanted to look around—find new places, you know?"

"And you found Potter's Bluff. You staying there?"

"Yeah, at a hotel." He felt he ought to add something in case she lived there, which, he admitted, seemed likely. "It's a nice town. Not too touristy. Real friendly people."

The girl nodded, and paused to let a spent wave run over her bare feet. "I came down here about six months ago and just *loved* it so much I decided to stay." The wave retreated and she resumed walking, pointing toward an arch through one of the rocks. "Let's go through there. There's a great cove on the other side."

"What do you do here?" he asked.

"I work in town. I was a waitress in Galveston, so I figured I might as well get out and find a place I really liked. This way, I can spend my nights on the beach and have an easy job during the day."

"Sleep on the beach?" The photographer looked around quickly. "Where?"

"Just out here. I sleep out here about every third night. Now that winter's coming on, I'll have to spend a little more time indoors, I guess, but during the summer it was great." Her pace slowed a little, and she moved nearer to him. "Are you here by yourself?"

"Yeah." His smile was unconvincing. "Nobody to bring with me. You know how it is?"

Her grin was impudent, tantalizing. "Maybe you'll end up staying here. I did." She stepped into the dark arch of the rocky outcropping. "Come on."

"Who knows?" He wished he had nerve enough to ask her name. After all, why shouldn't he? He kicked a beached jellyfish out of the way and followed her through the arch.

"You shouldn't have done that," she said as he came up to her.

"What?"

"Kicked the jellyfish. Those things can be dangerous," she said, then was quiet as she walked on. Once she glanced back over her shoulder as if looking for something. "Didn't I see your van on the cliff? Isn't it a red Chevy?"

He did not know why he felt relieved. "No. I've got a VW."

Again she gave him her tantalizing smile. "Maybe you can tell me. Something I've always wondered about. Where do men keep their car keys when they're wearing bathing suits?"

"Well, I put mine in that little pocket in the front with the button on it. You've seen them. Not all suits have them, but mine does." With unusual audacity, he asked, "Where do girls keep theirs?"

She laughed, tilting her head back so that the light glistened on her upturned face. "I'm not telling you." She went on, walking a little faster, smiling with satisfaction. "Didn't I tell you this was a good place?"

The cove was small and private, the walls of the cliffs cupped around the beach protectively. Waves tumbled over the outcropping rocks on either side of the cove and rushed up the beach in confusion.

"It's great," the photographer said.

"It *is*," she insisted, grinning at him as she went toward the steep rise of the rocks. "See?

There's all kinds of driftwood here." She lifted up a gnarled branch with a shell caught in it.

"Yeah." He was looking for a place to set up his tripod, and then, while he wasn't looking at the girl, asked in a rush, "How about letting me take your picture?"

"I thought you'd never ask," she answered eagerly. "I love having my picture taken." Gleefully she tossed the driftwood aside. "O-kay. What do you want me to do?"

Now that he had her consent, he was at a loss. "I'm not sure. I don't know. God, there's not a single way you can pose a girl on a beach that hasn't been done before." He said the first thing that came into his mind. "How's this? You can climb up there on those rocks and let the wind blow your hair around."

"There's too much salt in it," she warned him mischievously as she started to make her way to the ledge he had indicated.

"It's fine," he told her as he began to fix his camera to the tripod.

On the rocks, the girl had struck a pose, arms braced straight behind her, head tilted back, her breasts thrust forward with nipples standing out against the thin cloth of her halter. The light angled across her, so that she was cut in half by it. "How's this?"

His tongue felt like flannel in his mouth as he looked at her. There was nothing new in the pose but the girl, and for him she was enough. "Not bad," he said with the hint of a stammer. He checked the light meter and adjusted his shutter speed. "I wish the wind would veer around. Your hair keeps whipping across your face. Turn a little, will you? To the right?" He waved one arm, then held up his hand when he was satisfied with the pose. The camera clicked again.

"Have you ever done any nudes?" She was holding her pose well, hardly moving at all, and her question startled him so that he jarred the camera as he took the shot.

"No. Never have," he answered in what he hoped was a disinterested voice. The very idea of seeing her naked was distracting him—getting to deal with the reality was more than he could wish for.

The girl tossed her head as the shutter clicked. "It's supposed to be every woman's secret desire to be photographed in the nude."

"I've heard that," he said after a moment. He had heard a great many things about what women wanted from men, but they did not seem to want those things from him.

"Why haven't you?"

"Why haven't I what?" He was avoiding the questions and both knew it.

"Why haven't you asked a woman to pose for you in the nude?"

The photographer laughed nervously. "Never had the guts, I guess. It isn't something you just go up to a girl and suggest."

"Isn't it?" From her place on the rock the girl regarded him. There was something predatory in her smile as she leaned down toward him. "So ask."

"What?" This could not be happening to him. The scar below his left eye turned darker. "Do you mean that?"

"Sure." She was almost haughty in her confidence.

"You really want to?" He could not say to her how much he hoped she meant it.

As if she knew his thoughts, the girl pulled her halter off, watching the photographer with a measuring eye. She knew that her body was attractive, and that the stark white contrast of her breasts against the tan would hold him. He was hers now, caught by the promise of her sun-burnished flesh. She turned provocatively, her thumbs hitched in the top of her cutoff jeans on either side of the zipper, her nipples hardening in the ocean wind. "Well? Do you like what you see?"

He was afraid to answer. "I . . . I'm just studying the light, you know?"

"Want me to take these off, too?" she asked, her hands on the zipper.

"Uh . . . not just yet. Let me . . . get some shots of you that way . . . first." His palms were slippery.

Her laugh was gently mocking as she took a more outrageous pose. "How's that?"

His eyes roamed over her. It was happening, he thought. At last it was really happening to him. A gorgeous woman was going to take all of her clothes off and let him photograph her. And if he could do that, what else would she permit him to do? "You're wonderful," he said sincerely, and added with relish, "In fact, I don't think I'll ever take pictures of dead sea gulls again."

"That's for sure." Her tongue flicked over her lips. "Tell me . . . how you want me. Like this?" She struck another pose, this one almost innocent, dreamy. She half reclined on the rocks, her expression remote, her eyes languorously closed. She heard the shutter of the camera click below her.

"Fine. That's fine." He took the camera off the tripod for greater mobility. As he took his pictures, he started to move closer to her.

Abruptly she changed position, crouching with her back to the rock, her attitude both defensive and challenging. She looked down the beach and saw a dumpy woman in a faded pink-flowered housecoat and pom-pom slippers coming toward them through the stone arch. The girl smiled in anticipation. "Is this okay?"

"Great. Just great. Tilt your head up a little."

Now the girl could see other figures moving toward them. There was a tall man in his sixties with heavy glasses, in proper tweed trousers and an old cardigan sweater with suede patches at the elbows. Beside him walked a boy in his teens dressed in track shorts and a Potter's Bluff High School athletic jacket. A young woman in a red cocktail dress was having trouble with her high heels in the sand, but she did not remove them. Another woman walked next to her, a woman in her early forties, dressed in a severe business suit, her gray-streaked hair gathered into a knot at the back of her neck. They came on steadily; what little noise they made was covered by the slap and hiss of the waves.

"Stand up and put your arm over your head, like you're reaching for something," the photographer said. He was much closer to the girl. "That's it. Can you turn your hips a little? Tilt them? Hold it. That's fine." He took three more shots, and there were only four more left on the roll. He wanted to make the most of them before he changed film. He was afraid that once he paused, she would find an excuse to stop.

"What about both arms up?" she asked, turning toward the rock and looking back at him over her shoulder.

There were more people coming through the stone arch. One man in a mechanic's overalls carried a five-gallon gas can in each hand. A freckle-faced redhead in a mint green shirtwaist dress followed the mechanic. To her right was a tall young man in a Coast Guard uniform. Behind them came a thin old lady in a dark dress with a lace collar.

"Lean back a little," the photographer said, and moved very close so that he could get the arch of her breasts in the frame. "That's perfect . . . just like that. Yeah. That's beautiful." He used up the last shots in a rush, then looked up, startled, as a few loose pebbles clattered down from above. A shadow fell across the two of them.

The girl giggled.

"Uh . . ." The photographer shaded his eyes and saw a man in a black suit and a minister's collar. "There's a guy up there." He waved uncertainly, lowering his hand when the man did not return the courtesy. He suddenly felt guilty—at least for being caught—for photographing a woman with naked breasts. What would have happened if the girl were completely nude? Carefully the photographer stepped back. "I've got to change film," he said to the girl. His voice came out wrong and he cleared his throat. "It might be better if . . . maybe on another part of the beach." He gestured tentatively toward her discarded halter. "Maybe . . . you know . . . Don't you think you'd better, uh, cover up . . . ?"

The girl looked down and giggled again.

He took another step backward, motioning to the girl to follow him. As he turned, he saw the others.

The middle-aged woman in the pink housecoat was quite near him, and the man in the tweed trousers was not far behind. The others straggled out along the beach, but were moving closer. The man in the minister's collar started to climb down the rocks clumsily, as if unused to such activity.

"Hey!" The photographer turned to the girl, his face a little wild. "Who are these people? You're from around here, you say. Do you know who any of these people are . . . ?"

Again the girl giggled, though this time there was no mirth or mockery in the sound.

Anxiety and irritation turned suddenly to fear as the photographer registered for the first time how strangely, how inappropriately they were dressed. "What's going on?" He expected no answer and got none. "Oh, God," he whispered as the silent people closed in around him. He turned toward the girl, trying to protect her. "We'd . . .we'd better get out of here." He stepped toward her, his hand out to her, offering support.

She moved swiftly, savagely. Her hands clutched the photographer's arms, and her face, turned up to his, was expressionless—no anger, no fear, no lust, nothing.

""What . . . ?" He tried to break away from her, nearly lifting her off her feet, and found that he could not break her grip. "Jesus God!"

The girl released him, but only to take his camera out of his hands. "There's film in the case," she said evenly, and watched while the dumpy woman in the pink housecoat came up to the photographer and opened his case.

"Wait a fucking minute . . ." the photographer began, his arms flailing out in desperation. The woman avoided him, passing the container of film to the girl before stepping back a pace or two. The girl ignored the photographer while she changed the film, casually tossing the exposed roll away toward the surf. The photographer lunged toward her. "Don't!"

She put her hand out and forced him back. "Say cheese." The shutter clicked.

"You're crazy!" he protested, but his voice was going higher now, and his eyes were bright with fear.

The girl stuffed the camera into the top of her jeans, the lens a bizzare parody of an erection as it protruded above the zipper.

Although there was no signal, the people on the beach began to close in around him, forcing him back toward the rocks where the girl had posed for him. The only sound was the percussion of the waves and the muffled tread of their feet.

"What are you people going to do? Why are you here?" The photographer looked from one vacant face to the next, his questions becoming shriller. "I didn't do anything wrong. Look, will you tell me what's going on here. I didn't touch her. Ask her. I just took a few pictures! What do you want!" He stumbled and almost fell, and in that moment of menacing silence most of his hope left him. They were hostile and indifferent at once.

The man in the minister's collar reached into his pocket and pulled out a small home-movie camera and began to film the photographer. The camera whirred, almost inaudible against the sound of the waves.

"Oh, God, God, God, God." The photographer had reached the rocks, and the people were all around him.

"Who are you? Why are you doing this? What have I done?"

No one touched him. No hands reached out to restrain him. The photographer raised his hands to protect his head from blows, but none fell.

"What do you want?" he shrieked.

The girl pulled the camera out of the top of her cutoff jeans and took his picture once more.

A few of the people moved aside and the man in the mechanic's overalls came forward and stopped a few feet from the photographer. He set down one of the five-gallon cans of gasoline and began to open the other. Every movement was efficient. The young woman in the red cocktail dress came up and began to open the second can.

The smell of gasoline hit him. "Christ! What are you doing!" Panic clogged his throat and what should have been a shout was little more than a croak.

Gasoline splashed onto the photographer's head and shoulders, soaking into his hair and sweater, running into his eyes, blinding him. Retching, he felt the second can drench him—and heard the click of the camera. Dropping to his knees, he rubbed desperately at his eyes. As his vision cleared he screamed.

The young woman in the red cocktail dress was lighting a match. With a slight, well-mannered, almost apologetic smile, she let it fall onto the photographer's gasoline-soaked clothing.

The air compressed and then billowed, black smoke rolling up from red and orange flames.

The girl with the photographer's camera took another picture.

Chapter 1

Just at the edge of town, a fire was blazing where an old Volkswagen bus had overturned in the ditch that ran beside the road. Flames lit the night with an intense, ruddy glow, so that the billboard that marked the city limits, and read

WELCOME TO POTTER'S BLUFF
A NEW WAY OF LIFE

took on the same baleful cast as the fire. The rotating red beacons of two old fire trucks sent their own bands of light across the billboard.

Sam Evans, the fire chief, sat in the cab of the larger fire truck and watched the gauges showing the rate of flow through the hoses. He had been dragged away from a card game not quite twenty minutes ago and was still cursing his luck.

A tow truck came barreling down the road, and braked to a stop twenty feet from the fire trucks. It showed signs of age although the engine had the contented sound of constant and expert care. Leaving the motor idling, the driver, a heavy, middle-aged man in mechanic's overalls, got out of the cab and ambled over to the nearer fire truck. "How's it going?" he asked sociably.

The young volunteer fireman shrugged and continued to direct the stream of water over the Volkswagen bus.

"Shit," said the mechanic, shaking his head in disappointment. "Look at that thing. Not enough left for decent scrap. That's not Jem Williams, is it? He's got a van like that."

"Naw, his is blue. It's gotta be taken away, Harry. You know that."

"Sure, sure, but nobody's gonna make money on this one." Harry Clemens sighed and braced his thick, square hands on his hips. "Where's the Sheriff? I thought he'd be here by now."

"On his way," the fireman assured him. "The Sheriff's office said that he was out at the Preston ranch, checking out a complaint."

"Huh." Harry stared at the flaming wreck. "You don't suppose that anyone got out of that VW, do you?"

The firemen shook his head. "No way."

"Crap. It means I gotta wait for the coroner. I'm gonna be out here all *night!*" He turned and strode back to his truck, grumbling as he went.

A police car skidded up to the fire trucks, its siren just starting to fade as the car came to a stop. The door swung open at once and a rangy, dark-haired man of about forty got out. He wore his uniform well, an air of diffident strength about him.

"Evening, Sam," he said.

Evans turned. "Hello there, Sheriff. A little late for you to see the best of the fireworks, but we couldn't wait for you."

"That'll keep the taxpayers happy," he said, pulling out a notebook. "What can you tell me about all this? Any indication of what caused the accident?"

"Not a hell of a lot to tell you, Sheriff," Sam answered wearily. "The fire was going when we got here. I checked for skid marks, but there aren't any. No sign of impact that we can see on the bus, though even if there were, I doubt we could find it. And no license plates."

"Anyone besides the driver in the bus?" He was looking down at the paper, making notes as he listened. This was the part of being sheriff that Dan Gillis hated.

"Can't tell. We haven't been able to get close enough." Sam raised his hand to indicate the dying fire. "You want to have a look for yourself, go right ahead."

Dan gave a brief, unamused smile. "No, thanks. I'll pass. Are you willing to come by the office tomorrow and give me a statement on the accident?"

Sam nodded fatalistically. "It'll have to be in the evening. I've got a full day tomorrow and I don't think I'll be clear until after four."

"Fine. I'll look for you then." He started back to the squad car, but paused as Sam Evans called after him.

"You're going to need Dobbs's report more than mine, Dan. This thing's in his department."

"Gotta have 'em both. You know how the county is about forms. I've got to have the report on file, or there'll be more hassle. That's one thing that Dobbs is good about—he always gets his damned forms done and turned in."

Dan Gillis got into his squad car and reached for the radio microphone. "Hello, Betty. Hello, Betty."

The distorted voice sounded tinny in the car. "Unit one, Betty here. Go ahead."

"Betty, I'm out at the wreck. The Fire Department is still on the scene, Harry's got his tow truck here and we're all waiting for Dobbs to show up with his meat wagon. You did handle the call to the funeral home, didn't you?"

"Ten-four, unit one. I reached the funeral home almost twenty minutes ago. Dobbs said he'd come over just as soon as he could, only he has a service this evening and he doesn't have anybody to drive his . . . ambulance out where you are."

The billboard that welcomed travelers to Potter's Bluff was fading into darkness as the fire died. Now only the rotating red emergency lights flashed across it, making the friendly words hard to read.

Dan sighed with impatience. "Well, maybe you'd better call him again, and tell him to hurry it up. The fire's almost out and nobody can go home until he gets here. There's at least one guy in the wreck."

There was a slight hesitation on the other end of the radio and Dan could imagine the irritated expression Betty was wearing. In a tone that was a little too precise, the radio asked, "Unit one clear?"

"Yeah, sure, Betty," Dan said in exasperation. "Unit one clear." He set the microphone back in its cradle and thrust his pencil into his breast pocket. He would have to say something nice to Betty tomorrow, to make up for the insult she had decided he had given her. Dan endured her idiosyncrasies only because she was willing to put in long hours and organize the endless paperwork of the office. And because there was no one else in Potter's Bluff who was willing to do Betty's tedious job.

"Hey, Dan, how's it going?" Harry asked. He had come over to the squad car and was leaning on the door of the passenger side, his face thrust in the open window.

"Okay. Betty and her toys. There's nobody else to talk to on that damned police channel and she can't even call me by my name. 'Unit one.' Who the hell else does she think she's going to pick up? TV cop shows do that, Harry. Betty's heard the jargon for so long, she's disappointed when she doesn't get to use it."

Harry shrugged. "Yeah, I guess so."

Dan saw the headlights shining suddenly in his rearview mirror, and stopped Harry before he could launch into one of his discourses. "Hold it. That's probably Dobbs coming now."

Harry straightened up and grunted a confirmation. "That's him, all right. He didn't have to hurry—the guy is definitely gone."

"Is it just one, or is there a passenger?" Dan asked quickly.

"Sam told me one. Barker went down and had a peak in the window as soon as he could get near enough. He says there's one guy, or what ought to be a guy. Wait until you get a really good gander at his face. Barker said it was enough to make him toss his cookies." With this parting shot, Harry strolled away from the squad car.

Reluctantly Dan got out and walked between the two fire trucks to the edge of the ditch. Sam had switched on one of the floodlights of his truck and the stark light fell on the Volkswagen bus.

"You can go down closer, Sheriff, if you want to," the young fireman named Barker said without enthusiasm.

Dan nodded and started toward the overturned VW. The ditch was slippery; he almost lost his footing. He pulled his flashlight from his bent and shone it in the front window of the wrecked bus. The beam flickered over the man inside for a second or two, and Dan felt his skin turn cold. "Oh, Jesus," he murmured as he turned away.

"Hey, Sheriff," Harry called out from the cab of his tow truck. "Dobbs is here."

Dan shielded his eyes against the glare of the ambulance headlights as he climbed out of the ditch.

Strains of Mozart's Eine Kleine Nacht Musick drifted sweetly through the night from the stereo system in the ambulance as Dobbs emerged. He was a small man on the downslope of middle age, with something of the neglected look of a child's stuffed animal left too long in the attic. His eyes were button-bright and cold. He extended a beautifully manicured hand to Dan as the Sheriff walked up to him, and was not offended when Dan did not take it. "G. William Dobbs, B.S., M.S., M.D., etc., etc., etc., at your service."

Dan glared at him. "You could drive a little faster, Dobbs. That's what the siren's for. If this guy had been alive . . ."

Dobbs ignored the barb. "Sirens wear out. The ambulance, you may recall, is eight years old," he said affably but without warmth. "Our city's taxpayers would frown upon the purchase of a new one. And Betty said this was a DOA, anyhow."

Involuntarily Dan looked back toward the wrecked van. "If he wasn't dead when the car went off the road, he is by now. Much longer, and I doubt there would have been enough to get out of the bus and bury." The memory of the charred face flashed through his mind again and he winced inwardly, knowing that it would be quite a while before that sight was gone from his dreams.

"Can't be helped, Sheriff. I'm a busy man. And at the moment I'm just about a one-man operation. My so-called assistant has an algebra exam tomorrow and is off cracking books. Reverend Gower carried on longer than usual over Mr. Simmons, and there was no way I could leave gracefully." He nodded in the direction of the wreck. "Well, let me get to work."

"Dobbs!" Sam Evans yelled from his seat

on the fire truck. "If you need torches to cut him out, Harry's got some. We've got wrenches, crowbars and that equipment."

"Sure thing!" Dobbs said loudly as he picked his way over the hoses that were spread out on the road. He had a bit of difficulty getting into the ditch. "Somebody lend me a flashlight," he called when he had got his footing in the six inches of water at the bottom of the ditch.

"Here." Dan Gillis tossed his flashlight to Dobbs. "I can get another one from Sam if you need it."

Dobbs caught the flashlight and turned it on. "Son of a bitch. That's what I call well-done."

Dan came to the edge of the ditch. "Well, Dobbs, just offhand, as Potter's Bluff's distinguished coroner, B.S., M.S., M.D., etc., etc., etc., what would you say the cause of death was?"

Dobbs's grin was not pleasant. "Offhand? I'd say it was complications arising from pneumonia, and perhaps a touch of food poisoning. That's only an educated guess, mind you."

Harry had come out of his cab and lumbered down the side of the ditch. "He's a mess," he announced as he jabbed the coroner in the ribs. "Won't give you any trouble, Dobbs. Except maybe when you try to pretty him up. This poor bastard's gonna be a *real* challenge in that department."

Dobbs was silent, but contempt radiated from him like a dark halo.

Harry warmed to the subject. "Will you *look* at that guy."

Dobbs frowned. "Well, there's not much point to this, but the book says I must."

"Must what?" Dan asked.

"Do a routine check for life signs." Dobbs wiped the muddy hand on his trousers in an oddly finicky way. Then he peered closer and when he couldn't reach either of the man's wrists, decided instead to check for pulse signs by pressing the man's carotid artery, in his neck. He reached through the broken front window of the van and touched the blackened skin with the faintest trace of distaste.

A bloodcurdling scream from the depths of hell itself assaulted their ears . . . and it came from what was left of the mouth of the burned man.

"Jesus H. Christ, no!" whispered Dan. All stared in awe into the wrecked VW.

• • •

It was well past midnight and the resident was tired. He ran his hands through close-cropped limp brown hair and loosened the neck of his greens. "I don't know, Sheriff," he said to Dan. "The way he looks, there's no way to tell if he'll last the night. By all rights he should be on a slab at Dobbs', not here. And the repair—I don't know how much of his face can be rebuilt, and after so much damage it's questionable if grafts will take at all. You remember the way old Mr. Shearman looked, white patches all over his face?" He drew a rickety chair forward and dropped into it.

The Potter's Bluff Community Hospital was quite small, having a total of twenty-two beds. The emergency room was down the hall from the single operating room, the X ray facilities were crammed into a space not much larger than a good-sized clothes closet, and the lab, only slightly more sophisticated than the chemistry room at Potter's Bluff High, was in an alcove off the lobby. The administration offices were opposite the laboratory, and at this hour, they were closed and dark. Only the night receptionist, intent on a torrid-looking paperback, waited at the desk between the emergency room and the lobby. One of the three night nurses had come to get a cup of coffee from the percolator before taking her place at the station.

"Should he be transferred?" Dan asked, covering a yawn. Now that the excitement was over, he was beginning to feel his fatigue.

"No, too risky. In a couple of days, if his condition stabilizes, we'll see. Dr. Vanderbury will take over his case tomorrow morning. He's already been called about it. One of the first things he'll do when he gets here is check all the monitor graphs and records from tonight. That will give him a little better idea of how extensive the damage is. With the guy on oxygen and filled up with half the drugs in the pharmacy, there's no way we can tell right now. Burns are hellish. Anything can go wrong with them—infection, inflammation, man, you name it. I'll have to talk to Dr. Tolliver tomorrow about putting an extra nurse on duty for the guy. He's going to need someone with him all the time. Tolliver won't like it. But it has to be done." The resident rubbed his stubbled chin. "Sometimes I think I'd rather talk to Dobbs. At least he'll tell you what he really thinks and the hell with you if you don't like it. Tolliver thinks life takes place on a golf course, all smiles and hail-fellow-well-met, and the best kinds of scotch for the best kinds of people."

Dan agreed. "You let me know if you want me to arrange a transfer. We can work around Tolliver if we have to. If the request goes into the county from my office, they'll give it emergency priority, and they might be willing to make room for the guy in a hurry. Tolliver's afraid that if anyone's transferred out of here that it's an insult to his hospital." He ended with a shrug. "You keep me posted, Ed, and I'll talk to Vanderbury as soon as possible."

Ed Thurston lifted a clipboard from the white-enameled rolling table where blood-tinted gauze sponges lay in a heap. "The orderly will clear this away before morning," he muttered and looked over his few, hasty notes. "You say that when you arrived, the guy's van was burning. Both fire trucks were there."

"Yeah. Harry had his tow truck there, too, and Sam Evans was in charge of the Fire Department." It had been little more than two hours ago but the experience already had the unreal feeling that distant events had.

The resident shook his head. "It's fantastic, his getting out alive. Most guys burned this badly don't last long. Shock, dehydration, smoke inhalation—they get you if the burns don't. This is amazing."

"If he doesn't make it, it's probably my fault, and Dobbs'," Dan said. "Nobody thought he could be alive, and we wasted a fair amount of time getting him out because we didn't think we had to hurry."

"Um." Ed Thurston put the clipboard aside. "Well, I'll have one of the secretaries type this up for you and send it over to your office first thing in the morning. It's probably a good idea to have it in your files. No telling what might happen to this guy, and you may need my report to help identify him."

"Thanks." Dan put on his hat and walked through the glass doors at the back of the hospital.

There was a brisk, salty wind blowing and Dan welcomed it as he strode to his waiting squad car. He glanced down at his watch—2:38. And he'd meant to be home at a decent hour tonight. He'd promised Janet they could have a little time together. She would not complain, but he could not help visualizing the pinched expression she wore when he came in at such an hour. She always insisted that it was because she feared for him, but he knew that was only part of the reason. Janet was a woman who demanded a lot because she gave so much. He fished his keys out of his pocket and got into the car.

Main Street was almost deserted. There were a few cars parked in front of shops, but only those with apartments above them. Further out, near the gray bulk of Potter's Bluff High School, a couple of kids in a raked Mustang crept by him. Dan waved, trying to put them at their ease, but he remembered how little these kids approved of cops of any sort. At last he made a right-hand turn into a quiet residential street and in a bit drew up in front of his own modest house.

Dan let himself in the kitchen door, as he always did when he came home late. Janet had a light burning over the stove, and there was a note in the middle of the kitchen table in her firm, easy hand.

> Dan, irritating, annoying LATE man that you are:
>
> There are two sandwiches in the fridge for you, and some milk. Also beer, if you insist on it. I've probably fallen asleep correcting papers, and so I'd appreciate it if you'd take time to make sure the lights are out and the heat turned down. Betty called me and said you'd be late, and though I was less worried when you weren't home at nine, it was no thanks to you. When will you learn that you're very important to me?
>
> Enjoy your snack.
>
> Love and kisses (that's all you get, since it's late)
>
> Janet

He picked up the note and chuckled, mildly embarrassed and tremendously smug. After twelve years, he still thought he was the most fortunate man alive to have found a woman of Janet's quality. That she had married him still astonished him. She was a very intelligent woman, who had had a promising academic career, and had gladly given it up for her life with him in Potter's Bluff. At first he had thought she would resent the isolation, the lack of stimulation, and would come to think of her marriage as a bad bargain. Yet it had not turned out that way. Janet was truly content with him, and he was deeply, irrevocably in love with her.

When he had read the note for the third time, he folded it and stuck it in his pocket before opening the refrigerator and staring into its white, glaring interior. Sure enough, the sandwiches were on the first shelf, two thick, tasty helpings of roast beef between dark wheat bread and a veritable salad of additions. He took the sandwiches out, reached for the milk, then changed his mind and had a beer. Though he hated to admit it, Dan Gillis was more shaken over the events of the evening than he had thought at first. Accidents always bothered him, but the guy he'd left at the hospital... He opened the beer and drank deeply, the sandwiches untouched before him. He finished the drink and took a second can from the refrigerator.

Finally he ate the sandwiches, but they had little taste to him. His mind was stubbornly fixed on the burned man. A stranger in a Volkswagen van with no license plates overturns in a ditch and by all rights should be dead of burns. Dan felt an odd prickling at the base of his skull, that premonitory sense almost any cop develops. He had not had that feeling in a long time, and he knew that it boded ill.

When the sandwiches were little more than crumbs on his plate, he took his beer—the third can he'd opened that night—and wandered into the living room. Janet had, as usual, put the newspaper by the worn leather chair that had been designated his since the first year of their marriage. He sat down and reached for the paper, opening it first to the sports page. Potter's Bluff High School track team was featured, in anticipation of a day of track and field events being held next weekend. The enthusiastic write-up for once did not hold Dan's attention. He put the paper aside, finished his beer and got out of the chair. As he walked down the short hall toward the larger of the two bedrooms, he unbuckled his belt, removed it, and buckled it again so that he could hang it within reach on the bedpost, the holster toward his hand. For all the years he had been doing it, he had felt slightly foolish, more like those paranoid cops in the tough parts of big cities than the Sheriff of a quiet seaside town. Tonight he was reassured by this familiar ritual, and as he got into bed, he reached out to be certain he could grab the pistol. He had never taken that extra precaution before, and it bothered him.

Janet was fast asleep. On her nightstand was a neat stack of papers, most of them torn from binders, all written in young hands on lined sheets. He noticed that the paper on top was about Potter's Bluff at the turn of the century when it had been a bustling, expanding town. He looked at the name at the top of the paper. Roberta Andrews, it said. That had to be Horace Andrews' daughter—Horace, the town's justice of the peace, published the *Potter's Bluff Sentinel,* as had his father and grandfather before him. Dan wondered what Horace would say about the accident and the unknown man lying in the hospital.

Dan Gillis dreamed that night, but, fortunately, he did not recall what it was he had dreamed in the morning.

Chapter 2

The Potter's Bluff Cafe was located at the halfway point of Main Street. To the north were the more prosperous businesses—a clothing store owned by the second most successful family in town, a bank with a pseudo-Roman facade, a general grocery and the Post Office. South of the Potter's Bluff Cafe there was a hardware store, a ships' chandlery which serviced the few boats sailing out of Potter's Bluff harbor, a lumberyard, a service station, and a boatyard. The cafe itself was, in the truest sense of the word, neutral ground. Farmers, fishermen, bankers, secretaries, haberdashers, mercers, even G. William Dobbs, could come into the cafe without feeling out of place.

From 12:00 noon until 12:45 the Potter's Bluff Cafe bustled with lunchtime traffic, but by 1:00 P.M., it was almost deserted except for those stalwarts who made the cafe their headquarters. Today only two men lingered over their coffee and pie. One was Phil Preston, in town to pick up a few new sprinkler heads for his farm. The other was Herman Ewing who worked half-days at the lumberyard.

Dan Gillis removed his hat as he came in

the door, hanging it on the old bentwood rack by the cash register. The room was warm enough that he unzipped his jacket, but decided against taking it off. He started toward his accustomed place at the counter, then turned as one of the two men called out to him.

"Over here, Sheriff," Preston said, waving. "No reason to sit over there all by yourself."

"Oh, hi, Phil . . . Herman." He pulled a chair from one of the nearby tables and sat down with the two men. "I came by here half an hour ago, but . . ."

Phil shook his head. "Couldn't've got a seat if you tried then. Poor Penny, she gets herself run ragged every day." He cocked his head toward the kitchen door. "She's back there now. I'll call her, if you like."

"No, not yet. I can wait till she's finished." Dan had been coming to the Potter's Bluff Cafe as long as Penny had worked there. The hour of his arrival might be anywhere from ten thirty in the morning to three in the afternoon, but the essential pattern did not vary.

"I thought I might stick around until the bar opens," Herman said dreamily, paying no attention to the cold coffee in his cup. "I like seeing that red outfit she wears at night."

The waitress, Penny Strickland, worked in the Potter's Bluff Cafe during the day, but in the evening changed into a cocktail dress and served drinks in the bar of the Bowie Street Hotel. Both the Potter's Bluff Cafe and the Bowie Street Hotel were owned by Gerald Bass, who was president of the Chamber of Commerce. Everyone called him Tubby.

Phil nudged his companion in the ribs. "Mighty fine body that girl's got on her. Just enough of everything and in all the right places. Like someone built her special."

"Shame about Tubby's no-touch policy," Herman said as if to himself. "That's one broad I wouldn't mind passing a little time with." He put his coffee cup down hard. "Yeah, that's some kinda woman."

The door to the cafe opened again and Harry Clemens strolled in. He was in working overalls with a grease-stained Windbreaker jacket zipped over it. His jowly face was in need of a shave. "Hi, Sheriff," he called out cheerfully. "You find out who that burned guy is yet?"

Dan was about to answer when Phil said, "I heard about that. Car just went right off the road, no reason. You'd think there'd be a way to find out who . . . What about the license? Was the van stolen?" His tired eyes were greedy for scandal.

"No license plates on the car, and if the guy was carrying ID, it got burned in the fire," Dan responded.

"And somebody filed off the engine number," Harry said with satisfaction. "This is one guy who doesn't want to get found."

"Maybe somebody did it to him?" Herman suggested.

"A guy in a VW bus? Probably some left-over hippie looking for grass or trying to find one of those communes they used to talk about. Who else rides around in VW buses, anyway? You know how those turds are—they think it's a great thing to hide out. They change their names and live in tepees on money their folks send them. *I* know how it is." Harry dragged up a chair. "Hey, Sheriff, that guy still alive?"

"He was an hour ago." Dan sighed. "Until we know how the accident happened, it might be a good idea to keep a lid on this."

"What'd you mean, how it happened?" Harry demanded. "A guy in a VW bus goes into a ditch and burns. There's nothing to figure out about it. Just a damned hippie stoned out of his mind. No big thing. Is it, Dan?" He waited for the Sheriff to confirm his opinion.

"I don't know, Harry. Nobody does. That's where the trouble comes from." Dan pushed back from the table. "There's not a thing to go on. I've been checking all morning. Called as far as Greentree, and couldn't get any information. What do you do with a guy who has no ID, no license plates, no luggage, no wallet, no face, and no fingerprints? The doctors won't try to get dental impressions because they've got him all wrapped up. He's in a coma, and there's no telling when or if he'll come out."

Harry smiled at Dan and winked at the others. "Why, Sheriff, I thought this was the wonderful E-lec-tronic age. How come you can't turn a computer loose on this bastard?"

"You have to have something to give the computer," Dan explained patiently. "You have to start somewhere. And this guy's got nothing to start with."

"Well now, it seems to me," Phil drawled, "Dan, ol' buddy, for that fancy salary the city of Potter's Bluff sees fit to pay you, and all that money the state spent getting you educated in all those E-lec-tronic gadgets Harry mentioned . . . why, you oughta be able to find some clues, fingerprints or no fingerprints."

Harry was truly enjoying himself. "If you can't solve a crazy traffic accident, with only one car, what're you gonna do if a real crime happens?"

Dan wanted his coffee. "Very funny."

"Come on, now, boys," Harry said as he saw Dan's discomfort. "You better not ride the sheriff here too hard. He just might leave town. Never can tell. An educated man like Dan, well, I tell you, we're lucky to have him. Yes, sir. Why, just last Sunday, in the paper, I was reading about the problem the rural areas are having—this ought to interest you, Phil, you being a farmer and all—with all them children growing up and going off to college and then not bringing their skills back home like Dan here did. Yeah, I'd say we're mighty fortunate. Here's Dan, with all those fancy degrees and things, sittin' down with us just like he was nothin' special."

"Shit, Harry, I don't know about wanting kids back. I sent my boy off to college and all he came back knowing was how to grow his hair long and shout dirty words." Herman gave a jeering laugh and held up his coffee cup.

Harry was not yet through with Dan. "Here's this fine boy. He's an expert in criminology . . . All the big cities are just *dying* for a fancy cop like this one, who can take care of their criminals, and he turns 'em down and comes back to his own hometown to help us plain folks out. Real noble of you, Dan-boy. Don't know where we'd be without you."

Dan stared at Harry a few seconds. "You're right. You're damned lucky people." He raised his voice a little. "Hey, Penny—can I get some coffee?"

The three men took the hint, and it was Harry who asked the first serious question. "That guy we cut out of the car—could the hospital give you any idea when he might come to?"

After a moment, Dan said, "They're not sure he *will.*" He felt a light hand on his shoulder and looked up at Penny Strickland.

She was carrying a tray with four cups on it, but she stared down at the sheriff as if there were no one else in the room. "Is that right? He might not wake up at all? I heard about the guy from Betty this morning. They really don't know if he'll make it? Oh, God, that's terrible. To go through a thing like that . . ."

Dan reached up and took a cup from the tray. "It sure is terrible." He did not want to talk about the man in the hospital anymore.

"And nobody knows who he is, or where he comes from?" Penny went on as she placed the other three cups in front of the other men, then took a small jug off the next table and handed it to Phil. "He's probably got family somewhere who are worried sick about him. And he's all alone. That's awful." She smoothed her apron and gave Dan a long stare. "You need any cream, Sheriff?"

"I've got plenty, thanks," he said, more brusquely than he had intended. He saw her distress and against his better judgment, added, "Thanks, Penny."

"Any time." She looked once around the table. "The rest of you guys okay?"

"Sure," Herman said, and watched as Penny walked away toward the kitchen.

"You need any cream, Sheriff?" Herman mimicked lewdly, chortling to himself. "That's a new word for it—cream. Except maybe for jeans."

Phil winced. "Harry, shut up."

"Sorry, but I have things to do. You'll excuse me?" Dan said.

"Go ahead, Dan-boy," Harry said.

He did not bother to drive the two blocks to the Bowie Street Hotel, but walked over past the Fire Department and a couple small stores.

Bowie Street crossed Main Street one block north of the Potter's Bluff Cafe. The hotel was close to sixty years old, a low, rambling, nondescript building with unreliable air conditioning in the summer and insufficient heat in the winter. The paint on the front had faded and the whole building could have used sprucing up. But it had reasonable rates, a tolerable bar, and Potter's Bluff's two service clubs held their meetings in the mezzanine function rooms.

The manager, Ben Collier, was behind the desk when Dan came in. He smiled at the sheriff; but then, he always smiled. "How're you doing, Dan?"

"Okay," Dan answered as he came up to the desk.

"Anything I can do for you?" Ben's tone became a shade more formal. He was always wary of the police, no matter how friendly and soft-spoken. "Something wrong?"

Dan gave his best reassuring expression. "Just hoping you might be able to help me out, that's all. You probably heard we've got a mystery on our hands." This part of the speech came out automatically. He had already said it four times that day. "You have anyone here recently who left without paying? Someone who just . . . disappeared? Maybe didn't even pack?"

Ben smiled determinedly, his guard still up. "Well, this is kind of irregular, and I don't want to embarrass my guests . . . You know . . ."

Dan was growing exasperated. "I'm not worried about anyone's bedroom antics, Ben. If you got some misters and missuses that don't add up, I'm not going to pay any attention. That has nothing to do with what's on my mind."

"Okay, okay," Ben said hastily. "Now that you mention it, there was one guy. He checked in three days ago. He wasn't from anywhere around here. I hadn't seen him before. He said he was going to be here for a while—not a long time, but more than a week, probably. He paid the week in advance, and it isn't up yet."

"Where is he?" Dan asked, cutting the recitation short.

"I don't know," Ben admitted helplessly. "I haven't seen him since early yesterday. One of the maids said his suitcase is still in the closet in his room, so—"

"What's his name?"

Ben's expression turned sheepish. "Look, Dan, you know how things are around here. I don't always get a registration right off. And the man said he'd be here for a week, so . . ." He opened his hands, palms forward. There was a sheen on his forehead.

Dan sighed. "Ben, Ben. One day that's going to get you in a lot of trouble. I guess we'd better go check his things."

"But—" His protests stopped. He came out from behind the desk and reluctantly led the way toward the stairs. "You think he's the guy who got burned, that it?"

"I'm afraid so," Dan said as he followed Collier to the second floor.

"Oh, God," Ben muttered to himself, realizing that it was worse than he had thought. He reached the landing and said loudly enough for Dan to hear him, "I hope that no one knows about this. I mean, I'm sorry for the man, whoever he was, but I hope that it wasn't anyone staying here. You know how people talk. It's a jinx. Things like that, they scare away business. Kills the tourist trade . . ."

"I didn't know we had a tourist trade," Dan said coldly.

"You know what I mean. Folks around here . . ." Ben's voice trailed off as he started down the hallway.

"Yeah, I do know," Dan said.

Ben stopped by one of the doors. "Well, here's the room." He made one last effort. "I just hope that when the guy comes back here, you'll explain about this to him. You really ought to have a search warrant, Sheriff. You know it."

"And you really ought to have a registration card, Ben. You know it," Dan countered. "Open it up, okay?"

Ben shrugged. "Whatever you say, Sheriff."

The room was on the west side of the building and there was a slice of sunlight from the windows striking the old flower-patterned carpet on the floor. A boar-bristle hairbrush was on the dresser and a jacket was hung across the back of one of the two chairs.

"Doesn't look as if he's left," Dan said pointedly. He touched the jacket as if the material might reveal something to him. Then he went through to the little white-tiled bathroom. On the drainboard of the large sink there was a leather shaving kit, and beside it lay a toothbrush. Whoever the man who occupied this room was, he had not intended to leave town just yet.

"There's a suitcase in the closet." Ben's voice came from the other room. "Two shirts on hangers, an empty flight bag and the suitcase. That's it."

"Open the suitcase," Dan said as he came out of the bathroom.

"But—"

"Open it, Ben." He waited while the hotel manager brought the suitcase from the closet.

"It's locked." His face creased in an ingratiating smile, but the edges of it needed shoring up. "I haven't got a key."

"You've got a pocket knife. Open it." Dan went and peered into the closet. Sure enough, there were two shirts on hangers, both fairly good quality, one a cream color, the other a tan stripe. The flight bag was made of nylon, the same sort as the suitcase, though they did not match. Neither was lavish, but they were not the cheapest goods, either. Dan picked up the flight bag and looked into it for an identification tag, but there was nothing.

"It's open, Sheriff," Ben said, his hands dropping to his sides as if he wanted to disown them. "Go ahead and look."

Dan put the suitcase on the bed and tugged at the zipper, lifting the side of the bag when it was freed. This was the part of his work he truly disliked. It was so demeaning, this rummaging in the privacy of other people's lives. "What—?" he said, startled. Half of the suitcase was packed with clothes—a camel-colored blazer, three sweaters, a white shirt, two rolled-up ties, a pair of good shoes, underwear—but the other half had large manila envelopes and a stack of brochures in it.

"Something?" Ben asked, growing more apprehensive but smiling with grim tenacity.

"I don't know." Dan took the large manila envelopes out of the suitcase and opened the first one of them. "Photographs," he said, holding out the rest of the envelopes to Ben.

"What kind of photographs?" Ben did not take the envelopes and his eyes grew shifty.

In spite of his irritation, Dan laughed. "Not dirty pictures, if that's what you're afraid of. There's some shots here of a leafless tree, and some of tracks in the snow, and one of an old hanging bridge. You know—arty stuff. Take a look for yourself. They're pretty good."

Ben accepted the envelopes with reluctance. "I wonder if the guy took them, or what?" He looked at the first set of photos with slight interest. "That's a pretty nice picure of a broken-down barn. But why photograph that?"

Dan finished looking through the suitcase, then sat on the end of the bed. "I don't think I'll find anything much here." He picked up one of the brochures. " 'Focal Point Photographic Services,' " he read. "Maybe he's some kind of salesman or agent." He slapped his hands on the bed and the mattress bounced a little. "God damn it all to hell, someone must have talked with him while he was here!"

"What?" Ben put the last of the photographs back into their envelope and suddenly his expression changed. "Well, Dan," he said in a professionally soothing voice, as if he were talking to one of the older ladies of the Potter's Bluff Garden Club, "don't get me wrong, but maybe you ought to ask your wife . . . I think she knows him."

"My wife?" Dan turned to look at Ben. "What do you mean?"

Ben's smile was automatic, conciliatory, guilty. "Well, you see, I just remembered. Truly. It had completely slipped my mind. Really, Dan. The maid, Edna Jo—she said your wife dropped over here to see this guy day before yesterday, right after he checked in. Yeah, that's it. I didn't think of it until now. I've had other things on my mind."

"Yeah?" Dan's face was closed. "What else did Edna Jo tell you, Ben?"

"Hey, nothing. Not a thing. Don't get me wrong. It was in the middle of the afternoon, right after school. It wasn't anything secret. She asked for him in the lobby."

"This was day before yesterday? You're sure?" He had not been home too late, and Janet had said that nothing much had happened to her that day. She liked to keep him posted on what was going on at the high school. "Are you sure it was day before yesterday? Are you sure it was Janet?"

"Sure, I'm sure," Ben said indignantly. "I've seen your wife at every one of those teachers' meetings they hold in the Tudor Room on the first Thursday night of the month. A very pretty lady, Mrs. Gillis. And I mean a lady, not like some of those biddies. That biology teacher—just like someone out of the Gestapo—I had a run-in with her last time, and you wouldn't believe the fuss she made, all because the speaker system was hooked up wrong—"

"Did Edna Jo say how long Janet was here?" Dan interrupted. He had not been listening to Ben's complaints.

"I didn't ask. Probably not long. Ask her, why don't you?" He hesitated, then leaned toward Dan to confide in him. "Don't worry about it, Sheriff. There wasn't anything going on here, if you're thinking about that. Edna Jo would know if there was."

Dan turned sharply to Ben. "What do you mean, Ben?"

Ben's smile stayed fixed. "Edna Jo changes the sheets. She didn't . . . notice anything, if you get my meaning."

"I get it." Dan stood up quickly. "That's not what was on my mind, Ben, but I guess in your business . . ." He was too ashamed to admit, even to himself, that it was precisely what he was thinking. If only Janet had said something, if he had found out about this visit some other way. He did not want to have Ben there watching him with that smug pity in his eyes. "It slipped her mind, Ben. She's had a lot of things going on at school. You know what kids are like now." He took a hasty step toward the door. "I'll send someone over to pick up this stuff if the guy doesn't come back in the next couple of days. Thanks for letting me have a look at it."

"It's nothing," Ben said, coming to the door with Dan. "I just hope that this guy is a skip, Dan. Skips I can live with, but guys burned up in cars, that's something else."

Dan stood in the open doorway and stared down the hall. "I know. It's bad for business. For all those tourists."

• • •

All that day, right up to the moment he arrived at his own driveway, Dan was consumed by doubts. Rationally, there was no reason to suspect Janet of anything. They had a long, solid marriage. She knew a number of men in town, and often had coffee with them. But those were teachers and administrators at Potter's Bluff High School, men she saw almost every day, not a stranger who breezes into town and has her up to his hotel room. Janet was not the sort of woman who did that. The trouble was, Dan reminded himself, that he had never trusted his luck where Janet was concerned. His feeling now had to do with his own insecurity, not with his wife's conduct. He knew Janet, and had real faith in her. She would not indulge in clandestine affairs. If someone else were in her life, she would not hide it from Dan. But none of this reflection brought him any solace. Only one thought comforted him: if Janet were to have an affair, she was much too bright to have it at the Bowie Street Hotel, or at the Hide-Away.

Janet's five-year-old Duster was parked in front of the house when Dan pulled in. He looked at the car as if it were an ill omen, then made his way to the kitchen door, half hoping that Janet would be next door, talking to Sally Webber.

She was in the laundry room off the kitchen, folding the last of her ironing when Dan came in the door. She was an attractive woman, four years younger than her husband but with an air of self-possession that made the difference in ages appear to be less. Though her prettiness was quite real it was the least arresting thing about her. Janet Gillis had a presence about her which often startled her colleagues and awed her students. It often humbled her husband. She put the shirts aside and smiled at Dan. "You're home on time, for a change."

"I'm home," he echoed, tossing his hat onto the kitchen table.

"Goodie." She came across the room and wrapped her arms around his waist, her head pressed against his shoulder. "I've missed you. We haven't had much time together the last few days."

"Yeah." Dan could not let himself succumb to her. He had to have an answer that would still his doubts.

She felt his lack of response and looked up. "Uh-oh." Her large eyes met his. "What is it? Are you mad about something? Have a run-in with one of the boys today?"

"I don't know." He broke away from her and busied himself with taking his pencils, pens and notebooks from his pocket.

She sat down at the kitchen table. "What's wrong? Are you still trying to find out who that man in the hospital is?"

"Yeah." This was going to be more difficult than he thought, and although he had not intended to, he simply blurted out his question. "Who's the guy you know at the hotel?"

Janet laughed and tossed her hair. "I was warned against marrying a cop. You can't keep anything secret."

Dan let his breath out unsteadily. If Janet joked about knowing that man, there was probably nothing to it. " What kind of secret?"

"Oh, come on, darling. I'm kidding. There's no secret. Who can have secrets in a town this size, even if they wanted to?" She could see he was still bothered. "The guy at the hotel is George What's his name, who sells photographic supplies and equipment to the school. He comes by about once a semester."

"Did he come to the school? Did you see him there?" Dan asked, and wished he had not been so obvious.

"Naturally he came to the school. He always does. I had a couple of questions I wanted to ask him about a class project we're doing. He left before we could talk, so I went to the hotel..." Her face changed: for the smallest part of a second there was anger and steel in her, and then it was gone. "What happened? Did Ben Collier tell you that I'd been in a man's room at the Bowie Street Hotel? Is that what this is all about?"

Dan attempted a smile. "I *was* startled when he told me about it, since you hadn't mentioned it. But there are other things on my mind."

"Such as a man in critical condition at the hospital."

"That's him." He relented: "Coming on top of the rest of it, I guess I leaped to a few conclusions. I know you're not like that, but..."

Janet's face darkened. "You thought that I was out with George What's his name? Good God, Dan, if I wanted to have an affair, I wouldn't pick the Bowie Street Hotel in the middle of the afternoon. I might as well get laid in the middle of Main Street. Give me *some* credit. That's like hiring a brass band and a speaker system."

The bone-deep relief Dan felt made what he had to say next more difficult. "Janet, how well do you know this George guy?"

"Not well enough to remember his last name, right off," she said, still edgy. "Why?"

"Well, it could be—mind you, I'm not saying it is—that the man who was in the accident, the one who got burned, is that guy."

Janet was genuinely shocked. "You're joking."

"I'm afraid I'm not." He ached to be kind to her. "Is he a friend of yours, at all?"

"Not really. He's in town for one or two days twice a year. He seems nice enough. Oh, that poor man." She had taken a step away from Dan, but now sought his arms. "It's just that . . . well, this is the sort of thing that happens to other people. No one we know can get burned in a car wreck."

Dan held her close.

Her arms grew tighter, but from frustration, not desire. "What *is* his last name? It's worse not remembering, if he's the man in the hospital. Being burned so badly, and no one knowing who you are—" She shuddered.

"Would someone else at school remember? What about Mrs. Harris? You said she remembers the name of every student she's had since nineteen thirty-three." The gloom that had held Dan was starting to fade. He wanted to follow this new line of inquiry.

"LeMoir," Janet said suddenly. "George LeMoir. That's his name." She broke away from him, looking for the scratch pad where she made her weekly shopping list. "Capital *L*, small *e*, capital *M*, then *oir*. Pronounced Lee-MOY-er, not Le-MAWH." She found the pad and printed the name carefully.

"Do you know anything else about him? Is he married? Where does he live? Where was he going next? Things like that." Dan took the sheet of paper she offered him, folded it carefully and tucked it into his pocket.

"I don't know." She put her hand to her face. "If he *is* married, his wife must be worried sick. He never said. I never asked. I thought he came from the Midwest somewhere, but I'm not certain he ever mentioned the place."

Dan shrugged. "We've got a stack of brochures. We'll see what comes from them. I put a request for information out on the wire this morning." Whether the man in the hospital was George LeMoir or not, Dan was convinced that this would be the break he needed. If LeMoir had not gone on to the next town, then he had missed appointments. Unbidden, a remark of Ben Collier's returned to him. Ben had said that the man who was missing from the Bowie Street Hotel had paid for a week in advance, but Janet had indicated that the man selling photographic equipment never stayed long in town.

"How long did you say LeMoir usually stays here?"

"I haven't the vaguest notion. He comes out to the high school for half a day. He probably isn't around for much more than forty-eight hours." She came close to him again. "Can I have a hug, Danny?"

Resolutely, he set his doubt aside as slowly, luxuriously, he put his arms around Janet, holding her tightly.

Her chuckle was low and provocative. "Oh, Danny, Danny."

"What's so funny?" He loosened his hold on her just enough so that he could look down into her face.

"You were jealous, weren't you?" Her eyes were bright with amusement and a subtle satisfaction.

It was not easy to admit it. "Well, if you put it that way . . ."

She freed an arm and touched one finger to his lips to silence him. "I love you, Dan. I really love you."

"I love you, too." He kissed her tenderly and all other thoughts faded from his mind.

Chapter 3

There were very few pleasure boats in the Potter's Bluff Boatworks yards. Most were commercial fishing boats, crotchety with age. A small, lopsided tug was drawn up next to a sagging timber barge which, from the look of it, had not been in the water for more than a dozen years. Two sailing boats, one a forty-foot ketch, the other an ancient schooner with a hole under the port bow and a broken mainmast, were drawn up at one side of the yard in splendid isolation from the motor-powered craft.

Fog drifted in from the ocean, not so thick that the world was obliterated, but so that every object took on an uncertain outline, like things seen in a dream. The few lights on tall poles made halos for themselves in the fog, but their luminescence gave little useful brightness. The night was chilly and the damp air took the cold through a person's bones.

Nils Uhri had been a fisherman for most of his life. The sound of surf was as much a part of him as breathing or the beating of his heart. From his twelfth year on he had spent more time on the decks of boats than on land. But the last three or four years had been slow in Potter's Bluff, and the boats did not go out to sea as they had done. Larger, faster boats owned by packing companies were inexorably driving private fishermen off the ocean. If Potter's Bluff were a busier city, a place where tourists or artists flocked, then it might have been possible to convert to party-boat expeditions and picturesque excursions along the coast. But things had not turned out that way. So Nils spent most of his time in the boatyard helping Tony Chapman work on the old hulls and engines, and serving as night guard.

Tonight, as most nights, Nils had a bottle for company, and he sat on a large packing crate that contained a rusting engine. He made it a point to do his drinking in the boatyard, not in the shed at the back of the workshop. Guards should be on the job. Nils had rolled up the sleeves of his greasy, shapeless sweater, having reached the stage of drunkenness that creates a spurious warmth. On his right arm was a cross-anchor tattoo, his only souvenir of the three years he had spent in the Navy during the Second World War.

"Time to make the rounds," Nils told his bottle, and hugged it to his chest as he began to make his way through the rows of dry-docked boats. He spoke to them as he went, for he knew them all, and in a very real sense they were his last friends. "Hey, there, *Lady Alice*," he said as he patted the peeling hull of an old fishing boat, "'member the time we had out by the Blue Point, with the ocean bucking like a half-broke colt? That was some day, that was.

Billy Peterson got swept overboard and it took more'n an hour to find him, and the fucker was still alive. And talk about *mad* . . ." He chuckled to himself and moved to the next boat which listed forlornly in its mountings. "Don't you worry, *D. G. Hatton,* we'll have you back in the water any day now. A good paint job, the brass all shining. You'll be swell." He could not recall how long it had been since the boat had been pulled onto land and set on supports. He and Tony Chapman had not spent much time on the fishing boats these last few months—or years.

He stopped and took another swig from the bottle, letting the fire of cheap rum spread through him. He squinted at the two sailing boats looming like tenuous castles out of the night fog. "You two old dowagers. Think you're too good for this place, don't you?" He made a choking sound. "You're probably right. All the great boats are gone. They're gone. Used to be, when I was a kid, you'd still see the old tall sails headed out to sea. Not anymore." He lapsed into maudlin silence as he finished his rounds and once again wove his way toward the packing case.

It may have been a trick of the fog that kept him from seeing the people approaching him in the corridors between the boats.

The first figure he saw clearly was a middle-aged woman in a faded pink housecoat, with pom-pom slippers on her feet. Nils Uhri stared at her and shook his head. "What is—? Who—"

A sound to his left caught his attention. He

turned and saw a pretty young woman in a skimpy red cocktail dress. That was more like it! If Nils was going to have the DT's, he said to himself, let them be of pretty ladies. He took an uncertain step toward her, then realized that there was a man behind her, about sixty, wearing heavy glasses and an old cardigan sweater and tweed trousers. Something about that man was familiar, but Nils could not think clearly enough to place him. Another woman came behind them, this one in her forties, dressed in a neat, tailored suit. By the look of them, not one of them belonged here.

Nils stared at the silent, blank-faced people, and could make no sense of it. He was still sufficiently drunk not to be frightened, only bemused, and so he took another step toward them.

"I don't know what you folks are doing here," he said, slurring a few of the words in spite of his effort to speak clearly. "I wasn't told anyone was coming. Tony didn't tell me." He had to admit that Tony Chapman might have mentioned visitors, and he would not have noticed, not if it was past three in the afternoon when he had his first cozy rum fire kindled inside him. He rubbed the bottle he held. "Anyone want a drink?" he asked, because at that moment, he needed one badly. After a few seconds, when nothing was said, he helped himself to the rest of the rum, then cast the bottle away. It left him feeling oddly naked.

A tall young man in a Coast Guard uniform came through the crowd, and after him, an older man in mechanic's overalls carried two five-gallon gas cans.

"Hey . . . wait . . ." The alarm which had been muffled awakened at last in Nils. "Who are you people?" he demanded, turning belligerent. It was his job to guard Tony Chapman's boatyard, and these people, he realized, should not be here now. "You all gotta leave!"

There was no response, though the people continued to come nearer. In the fog their faces were unclear, but Nils had the impression that they were all like sleepwalkers, hardly aware of what they were doing, and not concerned with their surroundings. A woman in a housecoat, for Chrissake! Nils made a tremendous effort to shake off the intoxication holding him and reached for a rust-crusted wrench.

"I said that you all gotta leave! I mean it! *Now!*" He wanted to bolt for his shack, but as he turned, he saw a redheaded woman in a mint green shirtwaist dress walking toward him, and with her, holding a flashlight, a teenaged boy in track shorts and a Potter's Bluff High School athletic jacket.

The mechanic was opening one of the gas cans and the woman in the red cocktail dress stood next to him, waiting. There was a book of matches in her hand.

A man in a minister's collar reached into his jacket pocket and pulled out a home-movie camera.

Still another figure approached, this one rounding *Lady Alice*'s bow; a pretty girl in her early twenties wearing a halter top and, incredibly, given the weather, cutoff jeans which bulged in front where she carried a camera.

Nils struck out with the wrench, but by now it was much too late. The smell of gasoline was strong in the air, so strong that Nils did not realize how much of it came from his own old sweater. The wrench hit the temple of the young man in the Coast Guard uniform, smashing into the bone and tissue, so that the skull crumpled like a bashed fender. The young man did not fall, and no blood dropped onto his shoulder. He continued to stand patiently.

"Oh, Christ, no," Nils gibbered, and stared about as a sudden, intense light hit him.

"Smile," said the girl with the camera as the flash went off, masking the smaller, deadlier scrape of the match.

Flame roared skyward and the strange, leaping shadow within the fire reached for the familiar hull of the nearest boat, bequeathing his death to the rotting timbers as a last, loving, destructive gesture.

Sam Evans was on the scene ten minutes later, his face haggard, his clothes thrown on hastily. He directed his three men in an oddly disinterested way until Tony Chapman, who owned the boatyard, showed up.

"What happened?" Tony demanded as he strode toward the blazing wreck of his business. "*Look* at that!"

"We're doing everything we can," Sam said without apology, giving a sidelong glance at Tony. "It seems like it just went up, all at once."

"But *why?*" Tony had pulled his raincoat on over his pajamas, and his face still had that softness that is part of sleep.

"Hard to tell, until we get in there. Which we aren't going to do for a while yet," Sam answered. "Offhand, I'd say it looks like petroleum started it." He gave Tony an inquisitive stare, not at all commiserating.

"Gasoline? What are you talking about? The pumps are down at the pier." He rubbed his hair, trying to become fully awake.

Sam shook his head. "It's been a slow year for you, Tony, hasn't it?" His eyes were hard and expressionless as pebbles.

"What?" Tony stared at Sam.

"It's a solution—at least, some people think it is." He folded his arms and waited, openly daring Tony to contradict him.

It took a while for Tony to speak. "Are you suggesting I had this done? To my own business? What kind of shithead do you think I am, Evans? Well?" His voice had risen and the three men handling the hoses gave their chief uneasy glances.

"Desperate, maybe," was Sam's cynical, laconic answer.

"Not that desperate." Tony placed his large, sausage-fingered hands on his hips. "If I hear another word from you that sounds as if you think I started this fire, I'll sue you for every cent you have, and every cent you'll ever make."

"Maybe you didn't," Sam said with no trace of apology. "What about that rummy who hangs out with you?"

"Nils?" Tony blinked. "You think he did this?"

Sam did not relent. "Could be. He knows how things are with the business. Could be he took it into his head to help you out. Rummies aren't very smart." Again he waited for a response.

"Why don't you ask Nils?" Tony shouted. "Go on, ask him! His room's at the back of the workshop."

Sam shook his head. "I've already been back there. It's empty. He's nowhere around." He rocked back on his heels and regarded Tony through narrowed eyes.

"Not there? You mean he's . . ." He looked toward the fire in renewed horror. "He's there?"

As if in punctuation there was a crash from the boatyard and sparks rose in a fountain in through the flames.

"One of the boats, I'd guess," Sam said to Tony. "I doubt we'll save any of them. The fire's too far along."

Tony took several impetuous steps toward the fire, but Sam caught his arm. "Let me go! Goddamnit, Evans, get your hands off me!" He wrested free of Sam's grip. "There's a man in there, an old man. Get him out!"

"Of that?" Sam asked quietly. "If he's in there, Tony, the only way he'll come out is in a sack." As an afterthought, he added, "I'm sorry, if he is."

"Sorry?" Tony repeated. "When Nils could be burning to death?" He looked back toward the conflagration, then turned away.

"You don't know for certain he's in there,"

Sam pointed out. "Okay, you think he's in there, but I think he cleared out. I'll bet we find him tomorrow afternoon down by the pier with another bottle, head up, feet dangling, and asking your thanks for what he did." He walked back to the larger of the two fire trucks.

Tony hurried after him. "And if he's not?"

Sam's answer was lost as the sheriff's squad car skidded to a halt less than ten feet away. The siren died and the red light stopped its whirling glare. Dan was out of the door at once. "What is this?" he shouted, pointing to the fire. "Are we having an epidemic?"

"Fires give people ideas," Sam said evenly.

"Sheriff," Tony interrupted, shouldering past the Fire Chief, "Sam's hinting—hell, he came right out and said—that he thinks I had this set. Well, I didn't. I can't get through to him. *I didn't set this fire!*"

Sam sighed. "I'll buy that. But I'm telling you that this is too neat. You'll find out that I'm right when you talk to the rummy."

Tony turned on Sam. "His name is Nils Uhri, damn you!"

"Calm down, Chapman," Dan said, putting a hand on Tony's arm. "Sam, this isn't the time to make irresponsible accusations, and you know it."

Both men glared at Dan but Sam spoke first. "When is the time? When nothing's happening?" He turned on his heel and strode away.

Tony was breathing unevenly as he watched the fire chief. "He won't even look for Nils. Just keeps calling him 'the rummy.' So

Nils is a drunk. He sure as hell isn't the only one in town."

Dan saw that the flames were dying, though they still towered over the boatyard and made a sound like the sea in a storm. During his years as sheriff, Dan had come to know the rhythm of fires, and this one had ceased building, was falling back into itself, devouring itself. He looked at Tony Chapman. "No, he's not the only drunk in town."

"And he wouldn't do this to the boatyard. He *loves* those boats. He talks to them; I've heard him. Not just when he's drunk, either."

Although Dan could not recall any time in the last two years when he had seen Nils Uhri sober, he agreed with Tony. "Men who go to sea are like that. Boats are like family."

"And he doesn't care how business is going," Tony went on. "It doesn't mean anything to him. What matters to him is the boats. That's all he cares about. The rest of it means nothing. Oh, shit!" Tony put his hands to his face. "He said it was a gasoline fire."

Dan tried to steady the man. "So it was a gasoline fire. You've got cans of it, don't you? What about machine oil? It couldn't take much to get a fire going with so much dry wood around. Some of those old boats probably still have a little gas in the engines, or a little oil." He said the first things that came into his mind, and was not sure that he believed any of them. Two fires could be coincidence. In the Army, Dan had heard that old military saw from his major: once is happenstance, twice is coincidence, three times is enemy action. He dreaded the possibility of another burned man.

Sam Evans trudged back toward Tony and Dan. "It's gonna be a while, Sheriff. Do you want a cup of coffee? Or you, Chapman?" It was as close to an apology as Sam would ever come..

"Sure," Dan said with false heartiness. "You, Tony?"

From the set of his jaw to the brightness of his eyes, it was plain that the last thing Tony wished to do was accept this offer from the fire chief. But he caught the warning tone in the sheriff's voice, and said, "Why not?" The alternative was to stand there and watch his business burn.

• • •

Dobbs's Mortuary was close enough to the center of Potter's Bluff to be regarded as an eyesore by some and a landmark by others. It was an old frame building resembling a church, but instead of being topped by a steeple, there was a carved, white-painted statue of Father Time scything off the hair of a young woman seated in front of him. Over the years, the statue had spawned a number of tasteless jokes.

The reception area was surprisingly attractive, if somewhat simple. Two rooms flanked it, each with its formal draperies and padded folding chairs. Behind one of these reposing rooms was the salesroom—though no one was so crass as to call it that—where the various caskets available were on display. Behind the other reposing room was the working part of the mortuary, where G. William Dobbs plied his trade.

As Dan Gillis came though the door, he saw Dobbs's assistant half rise in the chair behind the old rolltop desk. Jimmy Baker had good reason to react that way, for he had had more than one run-in with the sheriff.

"Relax," Dan said, raising one hand. "I'm here to see Dobbs."

"What about?" Jimmy asked truculently.

"That's none of your concern. Just tell him I'm here."

Jimmy gave him a look designed to pierce heavy armor, then pressed the key on the rather outmoded intercom on the desk. "Mr. Dobbs? Are you busy?"

Strains of Beethoven's Pastorale Symphony came through the intercom as Dobbs answered. "Of course I'm busy. Why?"

"There's someone to see you," Jimmy said, smiling insincerely at the sheriff.

"Who?" Dobbs sounded preoccupied.

"Sheriff Gillis." He added, "He says he wants to talk to you. I don't know what it's about."

Dobbs's unpleasant chuckle mixed with Beethoven's rich harmonies unpalatably. "Ah, Jimmy, he *says* he wants to talk to *me*. In truth, you are the object of his interest. Without doubt. He's in pursuit of an immodest amount of that curious weed you and your school chums find so fascinating and of which, rumor hath it, you are the town's leading merchant. If it weren't for certain irregularities in the attitude of the authorities, you would doubtless occupy a suite of offices over the bank. However, let him in, let him in and fear not. I shall never tell that you keep what he seeks in one of the reposing rooms, under a stiff."

"He's in a good mood," Jimmy muttered. "You go back along that hall there—"

"I know where it is," Dan said as he went past the desk.

In contrast to the front of the mortuary, there was little that was soft or cushioned or reassuring in William Dobbs's workroom. There were three enamel-topped tables, one with a large sink attached to it; two rolling trays on tall legs with equipment that seemed more appropriate for an operating room than a mortuary; nearby, a large toolbox stood open, filled with enough makeup to outfit a good-sized troupe of versatile actors; beyond that, a pair of speakers continued to fill the air with the liquid Second Movement of the Pastorale.

Dobbs himself was bent over the second table, minutely examining the withered, pale face of an old woman. A sheet covered most of the body, and when Dobbs touched it, he used fussy, little gestures, as if he were afraid of disturbing the corpse. He hardly looked up at all as the sheriff came through the door. "Good afternoon, Sheriff Gillis. I hope you don't object to my using you as the object of a little lighthearted banter with my assistant? I'd offer you a chair, but . . ."

"He probably didn't think it was so light-hearted," Dan said without a trace of a smile. "I've caught him with grass more than once."

"Going to turn him in, are you?" Dobbs asked. "When he gets out, I'll give him his job back, though doubtless by then he will be a hardened criminal. Never let it be said that I'm not an equal opportunity employer. Working with the dead does it. Death is very democratic."

"I let him go. Sorry to ruin your good deed for the year, Dobbs. Both times he had about a matchbox full—enough for three or four joints, but not much more. He shares with his friends, I hear, but he's hardly a dealer. All things considered, he's a good kid. You're lucky to have him." Dan did not like this room, or the man in it.

"Certainly, certainly. Also, he is a minimal conversationalist. Have you noticed that the young ones are often like that? Either they gabble constantly about next to nothing, or else they communicate in a series of profound grunts. But then, I probably shouldn't complain. He's the only person I could find in this town whose attitude toward dealing with the dead has progressed past 1590 A.D."

Dan was fairly certain that part of Dobbs's comment was aimed at him.

"And before you lapse into your hometown chauvinist posture," Dobbs went on merrily as Beethoven welled around them full of babbling brooks and nightingales, "let me agree with you in advance that yes, people back home in glorious, stodgy old Providence have the same benighted attitude as Potter's Bluff does toward the mortuary sciences."

"Yeah, I'm sure."

"And you must forgive my distraction, Sheriff. It's necessary, believe me. I'm dealing with a rather tricky problem here. Mrs. Collins, predictably, given the sort of fractious woman she was, has been a little more difficult than I had anticipated."

Dan looked down at the old woman. He had had a few run-ins with her and remembered that she had the temperament of a Prussian general. "How could Mrs. Collins be any trouble now? If she was still alive, that's one thing. And she died in her sleep, didn't she?"

"Yes, she did, which is remarkable in itself. I always expected her to go out in a burst of spleen." He chuckled again and patted the cold cheek of the old woman. "No, it was not her personality that created the difficulty. Lividity, Sheriff—that was the problem, and quite a nasty one it was. Mrs. Collins passed into rest a good ten hours before her demise was noted by that sad little waif of a niece who's been visiting her every day for two years, doubtless expiating hideous unknown sins, since there's no other way to account for her fidelity. Mrs. Collins, when she departed this vale of tears, was lying face down. In the elderly, the blood vessels are very fragile, particularly those in the face. With all the blood pooling wherever gravity drew it, many of those blood vessels, the fragile little capillaries, distended and burst. Naturally, the face was severely influenced, but so was the torso, the arms, the hands, the whole abdomen, the knees and the feet. Mrs. Collins looked as if she had been hit by a truck, or been worked over in a vicious fist fight." Dobbs grinned and indicated the old woman with pride. "Would you guess, looking at her now, that her face is leaden blue?"

This disclosure, though not unfamiliar knowledge to Dan, bothered him. "So you put a lot of makeup on her. Great."

"A lot of makeup, for your information, Sheriff, would only be appropriate for the final viewing of a streetwalker. The deceased, termagant that she was, nevertheless was a retired music teacher."

Dobbs continued fussing with the corpse. "It seems a simple matter at first, doesn't it? Make a stiff look presentable, make them look better than they ever did in life, so that when the bereaved come to see them, they will be comforted and reassured rather than see the final rot that awaits us all. Let them think that they can stave off the end, be fresh and attractive." He was rambling, and obviously enjoying it. His button-bright eyes lit up puckishly. "Oh, Sheriff, the tricks I've played. This is child's work, believe me. A novice could have achieved fair results with Mrs. Collins. There was little to challenge me. But there have been others who required true ingenuity. I've replaced missing eyeballs with sawdust and glued the lids together, with just enough mascara on the lashes so that the glue was hidden and the lashes cast gentle shadows. I've used bent aluminum combs for dentures. I've taken the back part of the deceased's scalp and brought it forward when the front was . . . missing. I've folded one hand over wadded up newspaper because the other hand had no fingers. I've used wax to fill out shrunken cheeks. I've taken desiccated limbs and padded them out with cut sections of foam rubber . . ."

Dan had made an effort to block out this rhapsodic boasting.

"I know what's on your mind, Sheriff. You needn't think to spare my feelings. I've heard it before, oh yes, many times. There are hundreds, thousands, probably millions of good, honest men and women out there who feel as you do, who are disgusted by the sight of the dead. You think that all this"—he gestured, indicating all of his shiny tile workroom and its various appliances—"is obscene." He drew the word out, paying no attention to Dan's attempt at polite denial. "It sounds to you as though death is a cheat and a cruel trick. But it's our bodies, don't you see, that betray us; life that cheats us. Death is patient, and so utterly loyal." He reached out and lifted the head of the old woman off the table. "Look at her. Look at the work I've done. Mrs. Hester Collins hasn't looked this good in more than a decade. Art! It's an art. I am an artist. And tomorrow, Sheriff, this beautiful work of mine will be put in a box, the lid will be closed and nailed down, the box will be lowered into the earth and buried. And all the work I've done will be lost forever. Even a good cook has a longer time for appreciation than I do." Dobbs was indignant now, and he met Dan's eyes fiercely.

He walked around the table and looked

down at Mrs. Collins. "Who would have thought that she had such pretty features, really? She was always so annoyed and demanding that most everyone forgot that her mouth is quite lovely, and her brows arch perfectly." He pointed these things out to Dan with every sign of satisfaction. "I think of myself as a matchmaker between the bereaved and their lost loved one. I give them their very last look. That final memory, last rendezvous. With skill it can be serene and natural. But a botched job—and I have seen some horrendously botched jobs in my time—can ruin the moment."

"Why not close the casket?" Dan asked.

"Close the casket?" Dobbs said, accompanied now by Beethoven's robust and musical storm. "What can you remember about a sealed box? Now, that *is* obscene. It's the death of both the loved one and of the memory of them." As he spoke, he reached down and tenderly patted one of Mrs. Collins's wisps of hair into a wave. "For the dead more than the living, the cosmetologist gives birth. We restore life, or the illusion of life. If you wish to be trivial, you might say I make souvenirs."

"Bring one home for the kiddies?" Dan suggested. "Or maybe keep them on display next to the china."

"It might not be such a bad idea," Dobbs mused. "It would make it easier for a lot of people to accept death." He came out of his throughts. "In any case, Mrs. Collins, I think, can now be pronounced a success." He reached over to his intercom and depressed a key. "Jimmy? When you have a moment, Mrs. Collins is ready to be dressed."

"You're going to have that kid put clothes on a corpse?" Dan asked, strangely shocked. He was not certain whether it was a matter of the person's being dead or her being female that distressed him more.

Dobbs gave no indication that he had heard Dan. "Put her in reposing room number two. I think the dress will look better with the blue draperies than it would with the brown ones."

"I'll be there in a couple of minutes. I'm finishing my French homework," Jimmy's voice said.

"Excellent. *Très bien, mon brave.*" He released the key and turned back to Dan. "I've rattled on unconscionably, haven't I? And this is not a social call, is it, Sheriff? No, of course not. So perhaps you should tell me precisely what it is I can do for you?"

Now that Dobbs had asked him, Dan was forced to admit, "I'm not sure. You were the first person to see the guy . . ." Dan stopped, knowing that he was grasping at the most tenuous of straws. "I'm trying to make sense out of that wreck. There was no reason for it to happen. And that fire at Chapman's last night hasn't made it any easier. Two unexplained fires, with nothing to go on except that they shouldn't have happened."

"And Nils hasn't been found yet?" Dobbs asked.

"They're looking for him. Sam's convinced

he'll show up with the hangover of the decade and a sheepish expression, but I don't know. He wasn't on the pier this morning and no one, as far as I can tell, has seen him since sunset yesterday when he picked up a bottle of rum at Jason's store."

"One, possibly two people badly burned in separate fires in as many days," Dobbs said quietly. "Not on the normal curve, as the statisticians would say. Challenging."

"Is that the way you see it?" Dan inquired evenly, striving not to offend Dobbs. He had to keep in the coroner's good graces if he intended to ask the man for help. "You've seen that poor bastard we found in the car. You've probably heard that he had no ID on him, and that the plates weren't on his car. Now, I don't know about you, but this suggests to me that there was more going on than a tragic accident."

"A young man may have reasons for wanting to disappear permanently. But I will concede that if he had wanted to do that, all he had to do was walk into the ocean. If it was suicide, it was a most flamboyant one. But that is not what you're getting at, is it, Dan?" Dobbs made a steeple of his fingers and stared at Dan over the tops of them. The effect should have been friendly, but it wasn't

"No, not exactly." He hesitated. "Dobbs, you had a chance to look at the man in the car on the way to the hospital . . ."

"Hardly a thorough examination, and his condition did not encourage tampering," Dobbs protested dryly.

"But you had a look at him." Dan paused, then continued, "From what you saw out at the crash site, is it possible that the guy we pulled out of the ditch could have been hurt somewhere else, before the wreck, in some other way? That he was put into the car and the car driven into the ditch and set on fire to cover up something?"

"What?"

"I don't know!" Dan burst out. "I'm going around in circles on this thing. I can't see how the accident happened, and so I'm beginning to wonder if it was an accident at all. If the man were killed, who would be the wiser?"

Dobbs had given Dan's questions his consideration. "Anything is possible, Dan. You should know that better than I do—you see the process, I only see the results. I didn't observe any broken bones, but that doesn't mean a great deal. If he was beaten and nothing broken, his burns are too severe to show mere bruises. And, assuming I had found bruises, which I did not, there would be no way to determine easily if they were a result of the car overturning or some other injury, provided that injury had occurred shortly before. Now, had there been an obvious indication of abuse, such as indications of torture, that would be one thing, but in this case, I haven't any real basis for suspecting anything other than a freak accident." Dobbs shook his head and rubbed his hands together before dropping them. "I was truly looking forward to working on that man. Damage so extensive—well, it's an opportunity that comes rarely in my profession."

"Opportunity?" Dan did not trust himself to ask more.

"Oh, yes, my disgruntled young friend, most certainly an opportunity. Most of the time my work is confined to jobs like Mrs. Collins here, who are routine cases, about as exciting as keeping house. A deft hand with makeup, a few minor adjustments, and she's a delight to look upon, But a man who has been burned, whose face is like a mess of overcooked steak, whose skin is broken and charred, that is a real test of art. All that's missing from him is mangled limbs." Beethoven's folk tune expanded in sonority through the room, underscoring Dobbs's new fascination. "Think how he could have been rebuilt, reconstructed. So much restoration would be needed. The veterinarians came up with a stuff called tissue cement. Wonderful material! It hasn't been medically cleared for use on people, or at least not live ones. I have a fairly large supply of it. If there hasn't been too much damage, sinew and muscles can be glued back together again. Naturally, I've made some modifications in the compound. Corpses and racehorses have different requirements."

Tissue cement, Dan thought. Muscles reglued. Torn bodies patched together. The images jumbled through Dan's mind. "Dobbs, could a man be beaten and then . . . pasted back together again. Enough so that it wasn't very noticeable?"

"You mean a dead man or a live one?" Dobbs demanded. "A live man might mention it. A dead one—well, if there was an autopsy, it would be found out soon enough. But could a dead man be made to look . . . okay enough to pass casual inspection? Probably." Dobbs whistled the violin line of the Pastorale through his teeth. "I gather that you think this may have happened to the man in the car. That's pretty farfetched. And I expect, since he's in the hospital, that one of the good doctors over there might have found evidence of . . . tampering, if that were the case."

Stubbornly Dan pursued the matter. "Okay. But how many people know about this tissue cement stuff? Who might have it?"

"Vets know about it. They're the ones who use it. Out here, with the farms and ranches around town, I'd imagine a few of the larger operations have it. Phil Preston probably doesn't keep it on hand, but Howard Cranston may very well have some, since he's got sixty head of dairy cattle. *I* don't know, Sheriff. Why don't you ask them?" Dobbs beamed at Dan, delighting in the sheriff's perplexity. "It will sort itself out in time. Everything does."

"Where could I find out who has access to this stuff?" Dan was not convinced that this had any bearing on his investigation, but clues sometimes came from strange sources. One time he had stopped at a small farm to inquire about the children of the family who had been absent from school for more than a week without explanation, and discovered three stolen automobiles in the yard.

"Call the vets in Smiths Landing. They're the closest. I get my supply from there." He was about to say more when the intercom buzzed and Jimmy said loudly, "Is Sheriff Gillis still in there with you, Mr. Dobbs? There's an emergency phone call for him."

Dobbs pressed the intercom key. "He's still here. Put the call through to my phone, Jimmy." He pointed to the extension that was sitting on a phone book beside the nearer speaker.

Dan picked up the receiver. "Gillis here. What is it?"

Dobbs hummed along with the last chords of the Pastorale.

"What?" Dan very nearly dropped the phone as he listened. "What in Christ's name—? I'll be right there." He was about to hang up when Betty told him the rest of it. "Okay," Dan said firmly, confident now that he had new information to work with. "Yes. I'll be at the hospital in twenty minutes. Let them know I'm coming. I'll go by the boatyard on the way." He hung up and signaled to Dobbs. "You'd better follow me. They found Nils Uhri's body."

"Burned?" Dobbs's face lit up with hope.

Dan cast one uneasy glance at Mrs. Hester Collins as he hurried out the work room.

Chapter 4

The bow of the *Lady Alice* had broken as she burned and much of the planking had fallen forward on top of Nils Uhri. His body had been discovered accidentally fifteen minutes before by one of the Fire Department volunteers who had been shoveling the ashes to be certain that nothing still smoldered. When the blackened, brittle wood had not lifted easily, the young man had probed and found a calcined hand. After he was sick, he notified Sam Evans of his discovery.

"This way, Dan," Sam said as he made a path for the sheriff through the small gathering of curious villagers. He had to ask Agnes Whitestone, for once wearing street clothes, to move. After turning a blank face toward him, she wandered away, and Sam shook his head. "I don't know what brings 'em," he said in an undertone to Dan. "Every time there's a disaster, even a little one like this, there are gawkers. Why do they want to see it? What do they get out of it?"

"Immunity, maybe," Dan said.

The young volunteer fireman had not left his place beside the ruin of the *Lady Alice*. His face was pale and had the waxen pallor of shock. As Sam came up to him, he moved his hand as if he intended to salute but had changed his mind. "He's . . . uh . . . here."

The tarpaulin was slightly darker than the ashes around it, and in the hazy sunlight it gave off a dull shine. It was the shape of what was under it that made Dan Gillis walk the last few steps more slowly.

Sam went down on one knee. "We don't have a positive identification, but, given the circumstances and the location, we'd have to say this is Nils, all right." He lifted the edge of the tarpaulin, revealing a leg so burned that blackened bone showed through the remnants of flesh. "The rest of him is like this, too."

"The poor son of a bitch," Dan said as he looked down. Nils Uhri would certainly provide G. William Dobbs with the major challenge he wanted.

"There's one other thing," Sam went on, reaching under the tarp. "We found this." He held up a melted, whitish blob from which Dan almost recoiled until he recognized it.

"A flashcube. Where did it come from?"

"Right beside the body," Sam said, fixing Dan with a hard look.

"But. . ." Dan knelt beside Sam and took the flashcube from him. It was irregular, pitted and scarred like a bit of the moon. He held it up, turned it in his fingers. "Beside the body, you say?"

" 'fraid so." Sam got heavily to his feet. "There's no way of telling how long it's been there, but most times when used flashcubes sit out in salt air, they discolor pretty fast. Maybe the heat of the fire did it, or maybe . . ."

"Maybe this is connected with the fire," Dan finished for him. "You said you don't think this fire was an accident. Nils' death is manslaughter at the very least. I can't see calling this misadventure. Not with all the damage that was done. Not with this"—he tossed the ruined flashcube up and caught it—"here. Unless you've heard of someone taking pictures of boats . . ." His voice trailed off. The man missing from the Bowie Street Hotel was thought to be a photographer. There might be a connection.

"Who'd want pictures of—" Sam began, then stopped as he saw Dobbs shouldering his way through the crowd.

"Under there, is he?" the coroner called out in happy anticipation.

"He's all yours, Mr. Coroner," Dan said as he got to his feet. "If you discover anything interesting when you look at the body . . ."

"A formal autopsy, Sheriff?" Dobbs asked apprehensively. "On a body in this condition. If there's a tarp over it, then the damage is quite extensive. Most of the time a sheet is enough. Under the circumstances, I think we can stipulate that the cause of death was burning." His cold, shrewd eyes flicked to the shape under the tarp, then back to Dan.

"It could be murder, Dobbs." Dan's tone was sharper.

"Isn't there something in law about probable cause? Don't you have to have a reason to assume that there was intent, or something of that nature before you can, willy-nilly, say it's murder?" Dobbs smiled beatifically.

Dan looked away from Dobbs and said to the fire chief, "I'll leave the rest of this to you, Sam. And I'll call you when I'm through at the hospital."

"Running off again, Sheriff? Well, if there's no rest for the wicked, I suppose that it follows that the officers of the law don't get a great deal of rest, either." He was about to kneel down to the tarp when Dan spoke to him quietly.

"Dobbs, two men have been in unexplained fires in little more than two days. Think about it." He did not wait for any comment, but made his way through the crowd to his squad car.

A haze hung between the earth and the sky, making smudges of shadows and creating just enough glare that driving without dark glasses was uncomfortable. Dan guessed that the glare would thicken to heavy fog by nightfall. The light was deceptive. Buildings emerged from it like mirages, and faded into the glowing air. All the weathered stores along Main Street took on a glamour in the haze, like another age, for a moment reborn. The hospital, as Dan drew up in front of it, loomed in the light like a stark Spanish fortress, then changed back into the slightly run-down, utilitarian structure it was.

The hospital had only two private rooms and two small intensive care facilities. The man who had been in the overturned bus was in one of the latter, lying in a specially constructed bed with a water-filled mattress. He was almost totally wrapped in bandages and a number of soft restraints held him immobile. Over his head a television screen displayed his heartbeat, and beside his bed, a stylus traced out his breathing on a long roll of slowly moving graph paper. The IV stand by the bed was hung with so many bottles and plastic bags that it looked like a grotesque Christmas tree. All but two of the various solutions fed into one tube which led to an undamaged part of his inner thigh. A heavy band of adhesive tape held the long steel needle in place.

Dr. Clark Vanderbury was forty-nine and had looked in need of a good night's sleep for the last twenty years. He was a tall man who often was assumed to be short because of his stooped posture. He studied the cardiac monitor, then watched the tracing on the graph paper.

Three nurses shared the intensive care duty, when it was required. One of them waited near the glass door for the doctor's instructions. Her hair was colorless and her plain face was impassive.

"The lungs are still lousy," Clark Vanderbury said quietly. "I don't know how much we can do about it. Heart action is holding steady, fairly strong, no indication of shock fibrillation. Not too bad, taken as a whole. Temperature patterns are within tolerable ranges. Better give him 50 cc's now, and see if there's any clearing of the lungs. I don't want to have to resort to Adrenalin for his breathing when we've got everything else almost balanced."

The nurse nodded. "50 cc's. Yes, Doctor." She drew the required amount from the sealed vial into the syringe she held. "Shall I inject in the leg?"

"Yes, in the leg. Look at the rest of him. Where else is there?" He studied the tracing a while longer. "Well, it's steady. You go off duty shortly don't you?"

"Within the hour. I'll check on the patient before I go, if you like. The orderly will be outside at the station all the time I'm not here." She gave the injection to the still figure on the bed.

"You or your replacement. He should be checked every fifteen minutes. I don't have anything against orderlies, but this man needs the regular attention of a nurse. Once the breathing stabilizes, we can ease off. Smoke and heat. It's astonishing that he can breathe at all, after what he's been through."

Dan Gillis tapped on the glass door and waited for Vanderbury to turn.

"Um?" The doctor looked up and there was a slight lessening of tension around his dark blue eyes. "Oh, Dan. It's all right. Come in." He gestured to the nurse. "We've got three of them keeping an eye on our mystery patient here."

"One of us will be back shortly," the nurse said just before she left the room.

"God damn," Dan said softly as he came to stand by the bed. He had never seen anyone so encased in bandages.

Clark Vanderbury was still at the lung monitor. "Exactly. It's very difficult, as you can imagine. If we stimulate his lungs too much, so that he can breathe easily, we might put him back into shock. At the same time, it is necessary that we get air into him. We had him on oxygen for most of the night, but I don't want to keep him on that too long. What worries me is the possibility of brain damage. His breathing was heavily impaired for the better part of an hour, and it might have caused part of his brain to become oxygen-starved. There's no way to tell yet."

Looking at the still figure in the bed, it seemed impossible to Dan that there was any chance for recovery. He said, not quite believing it, "I had a call from Betty. She said Dr. Tolliver told her this guy's come out of his coma."

"He has. But no," Dr. Vanderbury said, voicing Dan's reservations, "he doesn't look as if he has. There has been a change—a dramatic one; if you'd seen the monitors two hours ago, you'd know how dramatic. However, don't make the mistake of thinking that he's out of the woods. It's very much touch and go. We might pull him through, but . . . even if we do, there's not going to be a great deal of help for him. He'll need the *best* plastic surgeons, and there won't be much they can do."

Dan had a sudden, vivid impression of the burning Volkswagen in the ditch. "Why? Too much harm done?"

"Essentially, yes. You saw him when they took him out of the van. You know what his face is like. We've lost the right eye. There was no way to save it. The left, you notice, is unbandaged. There's some damage to it but the eye itself is still functioning. We discussed the matter and the consensus here is that it would be better for him to be able to see a bit when he regains consciousness, if he ever does. To wake up in terrible pain, unable to move, breathing with difficulty is bad enough, but to add blindness to it seems a great deal worse." The doctor left the monitor at last, and put one hand on Dan's shoulder. "You have some questions and I'll do my best to answer them now. Don't expect any wild revelations."

Dan hesitated. "Clark, do you think there's any possibility he'd be able to talk to me? You say he's out of the coma. That means he could regain consciousness. I know it would have to be brief, but if I could have five minutes . . ."

Clark Vanderbury shook his head. "Dan, I'm afraid it's impossible." He went out of the glass-walled room, pointing the way down the hall toward his office.

"But why? I've got to find out what the hell really happened to that van. There weren't any skid marks, the evening was clear, traffic was light—"

"Dan—"

Something else occurred to Dan and he did not let Clark go on. "What about the nurses? If they hear anything, can't they tell me about it?"

"I doubt it." Clark opened the door to his office and glanced inside as a way of avoiding Dan's eyes.

"Well, if it's garbled, it can still be helpful.

We might get his name, or where he comes from," Dan reminded the doctor as they went into the small room.

"It's not that." Clark paused to raise his hand in greeting to the nurse passing the door on her way to the intensive care station.

"What is it, then. Are you trying to cover your bets in case he is brain-damaged, or what?" Dan did not take the seat Clark indicated.

Clark did not answer at once. He took his chair behind the desk and pulled out a pack of cigarettes. When he had lit one and exhaled, he said, "There's no way to guess about that yet, and that's all we can do—guess. In a case like this, amnesia surrounding the accident itself is not unusual. You know that. After what he's been through, it's likely that there will be some brain damage, but it's anybody's guess as to how much, or what kind."

"Then what is it?" Dan persisted, growing irritated with Clark's procrastination.

"Purely a mechanical problem. He has no lips."

Slowly, Dan sank into the chair.

The man in the intensive care room came awake abruptly, ragged breath gurgling in his chest, pain cutting through him like a saw. The panic did not hit him at first and he had only his pain to contend with. Gradually the questions came, clumsily constructed, as if they were in an ill-remembered foreign language. Where was he? How had he come here? What had happened? His vision was distorted, but he now realized that he was in a hospital room. But why? Two feeble attempts indicated that he could not move, and the sickening agony the effort brought made him glad to lie still, drifting on the edge of consciousness.

There was another person in the room, a figure in white. Gratefully the man looked toward her as she approached. Her nose and cheeks were powdered with freckles and her beautiful red hair was tucked under a starched cap. She did not need to be in her mint green shirtwaist dress for the man to recognize her. To his horror—his terror—she was coming nearer.

"Awake, are we?" she murmured, leaning close to him. "The Adrenalin did it." She put her hand on his bandaged chest. "Lie still. This will only take a moment."

The restraints held him so that he could not move, but they were hardly necessary for he had little strength and no control over his body. A muffled gurgling sound came from his chest, a scream that could not be heard. His heart leaped wildly behind his ribs and the television screen above him dutifully showed this.

"You surprised us," the redhead in the nurse's uniform went on. "We were certain that you died in the car. You were supposed to be dead. All this trouble for you. I didn't think we'd be able to get to you so quickly, but there are enough of us now that we can arrange things in Potter's Bluff. You'd think a small town like this would make it hard, but it's actually quite easy." She touched the bandages on his head lightly. "You don't want to live now, you know. Not after the burns. You wouldn't like how you'd have to live. We're not doing anything you wouldn't want us to do, if you had the time to think about it." Her hands moved again, coming to rest near the top of his hips.

It wasn't real, the man on the bed thought. This was all a nightmare or an experiment or a crazy game or some nutty fantasy to tell to a shrink. He had a vague memory of a woman in a housecoat and a woman in a cocktail dress and a man in overalls. His mind flinched at that, and would not bring back the rest of it. He could not be in this bed. He refused to accept it. Those people drifting through his mind could not have been real.

"Now, this won't take long, and then we'll all have what we want." Her hands had reached the bandage that held the needle in place, carrying saline, drugs, glucose and water into his vein. She pulled the adhesive tape back inexpertly, and withdrew the five-inch-long fine steel needle.

He did not believe that this could happen to him until he felt the first prick of the instrument.

An instant later the cardiac display looked like paths of forked lightning and the lung tracing nearly went off the page. Outside the room a light went on, and three seconds later an alarm began to blare.

The redheaded woman came out of the room and almost ran into Dr. Ed Thurston. "Oh!" she cried weakly. "It's terrible. I can't!" She pulled away from him and ran off down the hall in the direction of the women's rest room.

Ed Thurston did not hesitate. He rushed into the intensive care room, ready to administer cardiac massage. The sight that met his eyes made him stop still, gagging.

Four nurses, Dr. Clark Vanderbury, Sheriff Dan Gillis and an orderly arrived on the run within five seconds, and all of them stood aghast at the sight of the man lying on the bed.

"Lord Jesus!" Doctor Vanderbury whispered, looking from the figure to the flat line on the cardiac television monitor and then to the inactive stylus on the lung tracing.

"Oh, God." Dan had seen a few things that had been too grisly to remember, but nothing had been as wholly callous as this.

The man lay in his soft restraints on the water-filled mattress, the electrodes of the heart and lung monitors still fixed in place. The stand that held his various drips had overturned, the bottles broken now and spilling their colors and scents on the vinyl tile floor. From the stand there ran a tube, which ended in a five-inch-long steel needle—which was buried in the man's unbandaged left eye.

• • •

"Who could have got in there?" Dan demanded of the seven people crowded into Vanderbury's office. The four nurses shook their heads and said nothing, the orderly scowled at the sheriff. Ed Thurston exchanged a hopeless look with Clark Vanderbury.

"Look, she was in uniform—" the orderly started, surliness replacing his earlier subservience.

"There are only twelve nurses in this entire town," Dan said caustically. "You know all of them. You let an unknown woman into that man's room!"

Ed Thurston cleared his throat. "I let her get away, Dan. She came out of the room in a state, and I . . . I was confused. I hope I was worried for the patient, too worried to ask who the nurse was."

"You hope?" Dan repeated.

"That's the best I can do. I wasn't thinking. It happened very fast." The young resident looked miserable now. "I can't explain it, Dan."

"What about Maggie at the front desk? Has anyone spoken to her?" Clark Vanderbury suggested. His weariness was more pronounced than it had been.

"I'll go," one of the nurses volunteered, grateful for the excuse to leave the room, if only for a moment.

"Bring her back here," Dan said. "And don't make me come looking for you."

The nurse nodded and fled.

"Well," Dan said after a short silence, "I'm going to have to get a statement from each one of you. I'll have to find out how she got in here. Are you all sure that none of you knew her?"

"She had red hair, I think. Maybe blond," the orderly said.

"Young? Old? Tall? Short?" Dan rapped out the questions and was answered by a shrug.

"Mid-twenties, I suppose," Ed Thurston muttered. "Medium height, probably a pretty good build, but you can't tell much in those uniforms. That's the trouble. Put a woman in a white uniform and she stops having a face."

Dan had taken his notebook from his breast pocket and started to write. The description, such as it was, might apply to any one of a dozen women in town.

"She reminded me a little of Doris Haskins," the orderly said, and looked around at the others in the sudden, hostile silence. "Not the way she was at the end, of course, but when she first came here."

Clark Vanderbury shuffled awkwardly, his face darkening. "That's not remotely funny, Gary."

"It wasn't meant to be," the orderly snapped. "The sheriff wanted to know what she looked like, and I think she might have looked something like Doris Haskins. Can't I mention her name? Crap on all of you."

Ed nodded reluctantly. "I think I know what he means. There was a resemblance. This woman was more attractive, but, it's like Gary said, the way Doris looked toward the end . . ." He stopped. "Has anyone told Tolliver about this?"

"Not yet," Clark answered. "I thought we'd have him in here with us, but he might not want to hear a word. It'd put him off his golf game."

One of the nurses began to cry, and gave a pleading look to the others. "I'm sorry. I don't know why I'm doing this. I've seen people die before . . ."

"Not from a needle in the brain, I'll bet," Gary said viciously.

"Cut it out!" Ed muttered, and took a couple of steps away from the orderly.

The door opened and the nurse returned with the day receptionist, Maggie Land. "I'm back," the nurse said timorously. "Maggie said—"

Maggie interrupted. "Look, Sheriff, I was getting a cup of coffee to go with my sandwich. I heard the door open on the emergency side, and I thought it was Ed. Virginia told me that someone in a nurse's uniform got in. If she did, I didn't see who it was." There was a defiant angle to her chin. Maggie Land, at forty-one, had survived a disastrous marriage and raised three sons on her own. She was a tough, vulnerable, thoroughly pragmatic women. "Besides, I don't think I'd pay any attention to a nurse. And I know most of the people who come to visit folks in the hospital. I'm not making excuses for myself, Sheriff. I want you to know that. But how was I to know what was going to happen?"

"Nobody knew," Dan admitted. He sat down in Clark's chair and began to toy with the pen in his hand. "I'm not blaming anyone. This whole thing is . . . crazy. But I have to get answers. No one can ignore a murder in the hospital. Whatever is going on, whatever's behind it, it's got to be stopped." He read solemn agreement in the faces of the others. "There aren't that many strangers in Potter's Bluff. Someone must know who was here. Well, think about it. Who looks like Doris Haskins?" Dan had been a friend of Doris and Lee Haskins and those last dreadful months before Doris died had been a terrible time for him. Janet had come to the hospital every day after school to read to Doris after she had become too weak to hold a book.

"Maybe Amy Andrews?" Ed ventured without a great deal of conviction. "Her hair is kind of red."

"And she's got a figure like a sack of walnuts," Gary said, closing the matter.

The door opened again and Dr. Tolliver stepped into the room, portentous as a thundercloud. "Why wasn't I notified at once?" He quivered with indignation.

"I didn't allow it, Tolliver," Dan said. He did not rise for the hospital administrator. "I wanted to speak to all those who saw the woman while their impressions were clear."

Dr. Tolliver was the sort of weak man who indulged in bouts of petty tyranny when he suspected his position was threatened. "You gave orders without consulting me, Sheriff? I remind you that I am administrator of this hospital, and nothing takes place here that is not under my jurisdiction!"

"Are you confessing to putting a needle into that patient's eye?" Dan asked amiably. "If you are, good, because it will make my work much easier."

Tolliver did not precisely turn pale but some of his arrogance slipped. "That's not the least amusing, Sheriff."

"It wasn't intended to be," Dan said. He braced his elbows on the desk and stared at the pen he held. "How do I account for this? In this hospital? In this town? We all know each other. And yet an unrecognized woman gets into an intensive care room and kills an unknown man. What's going on?" He looked up at the man beside him. "You have any ideas, Clark? Ed? Any of you?"

The oldest nurse started to say something, then was as silent as the rest.

• • •

When Dan came through the doors of the Potter's Bluff Cafe, what little conversation there had been stopped. He stood a moment, his hat in one hand, as his eyes moved over the various men gathered around the two central tables. After a moment he raised his hand in cautious greeting. Then he saw the strangers in the booth near the back, and strolled over toward them as soon as he had hung his hat up. "Afternoon, folks. I don't believe I know you."

The man looked up from his hamburger. He had the wary look most people wore when talking to cops. "I'm Ron Cousins. This is my wife Linda and our boy Jamie. Your name, Officer?"

"I'm Dan Gillis." He tried to be more friendly with these people. "We don't see many tourists in Potter's Bluff, especially not in the fall. If you have trouble finding places, give me or my office a call. Trouble with people around here is that they all know each other so well that they assume everyone is as familiar with the place as they are."

Ron Cousins' face relaxed. "That's good of you, Officer."

"Sheriff," Dan corrected with a smile.

"Sheriff," Ron said, nodding.

For the benefit of the others in the room, Dan spoke a little louder. "If some of the folks seem a bit unfriendly, you'll have to excuse them. We've had a bad fire at the boatyard and a man was killed. Lots of people are jumpy as a result."

"Oh, dear," Linda said. A look passed between her and her husband, a subtle acknowledgment.

"You visiting or passing through, or what?" Dan asked, trying not to make it seem like an interrogation.

Ron's half-smile remained fixed but under it there was resentment. "Actually, we're looking for a place to buy. Not necessarily in Potter's Bluff, but away from the city. The pace, and the conditions, and with Jamie . . ." He didn't say any more.

"I know what you mean," Dan said. "I lived in a city long enough to get my master's, and then came back here. Well, if you decide to look around here, there're a couple nice places you might like. Tubby Bass is the man to talk to about real estate. He owns the Bowie Street Hotel."

"We're staying there," Linda put in. She was an attractive young woman, dressed with a fashionable gloss that was foreign to Potter's Bluff. Her clothes, though sporty, were quite new, expensively cut. Compared to her, every woman in town was out-of-date.

"Then talk to Tubby. He'll fill you in on what's around and price ranges." Dan nodded and strolled away toward the center tables.

Ron scowled after him. "Why'd he do that?" he whispered to his wife.

"It's a small town," Linda said with a fleeting smile, as if that explained it.

Penny Strickland came out of the kitchen carrying a tall glass. "Hey, I'm sorry," she said to the Cousins as she came to their booth. "I forgot about the shake for the boy. I should've brought it earlier." She put it down on the table and made an apologetic gesture. "Sorry."

"It's okay," Ron said with a trace of irritation, and then he noticed that Linda had that questioning look she wore on rare occasions. "Honey?"

Linda had been staring at Penny, a faint line between her brows. "Hum?" She tossed her head. "Thank you, Miss. I—"

"Penny, I need a refill!" Herman Ewing called from the center table.

"Sure, Herman," she said, and turned away from the strangers in the booth. "Coffee for you, Sheriff?"

"Love some." Dan had taken the chair that was offered to him, and he sank down slowly. He was grateful for this little ritual, for the ordinariness of it all. He thought briefly of Betty, now at the hospital taking statements. "Thanks, Penny," he murmured as she put a cup of creamed coffee in front of him.

"So what's new and exciting, Sheriff?" Herman asked easily. "Any more fires?"

Dan took a moment to answer. "No. Not today. The guy who was burned in the car?"—he saw the nods from the others—"he didn't make it."

"Poor bastard," Phil Preston said with a shake of his head.

Sam Evans, who was at the other end of the table, looked up. "Dead?"

"Yes," Dan said without elaboration.

"Shit. Still, it's a wonder he was alive at all. Him and Nils. What's this town coming to?" He pushed back his chair and rose.

His departing question echoed in Dan's mind. What *was* Potter's Bluff coming to? He stared at his coffee without tasting it, and only when Phil had raised his voice and called his name twice did he look up. "Sorry, Phil. I guess I've got that guy . . ."

"Understandable." He gestured to the old man in the cardigan sweater at his side. "Aaron here was telling me he's been selling extinguishers like mad. You know, those red kind, like they have in the hotel?"

Aaron nodded his confirmation. "Locks've been selling real good, too." He had a childish voice, as sometimes happens in old age, and his heavy glasses magnified his eyes to that they were like undersea creatures. "Strange goings on."

The others at the table agreed, and Gus Dickerson, who set type for Horace Andrews at the *Potter's Bluff Sentinel,* piped up, "What're you gonna do about it, Dan'l?"

It was better, Dan knew, to give Gus a casual answer now than to have to contend with Horace later. He tried to be lighthearted in his reply "Well, the first thing is to find out who that man was. We have a lead on him, but the identification hasn't been confirmed. Then we'll proceed with the investigation. Tony Chapman's boatyard is another question. I've sent samples to the county lab of various bits of ash, to see where and how the fire started. So far, it looks like it could be accidental, but I haven't made up my mind about that yet."

"You're talking a lot, Dan'l, but you're not saying much of anything," Gus observed with an eyebrow raised.

"Because there isn't a lot to say yet," Dan retorted. "What do you want me to do? Make a lot of accusations that have no basis in fact and would cause any case that comes up—*if* there are cases—to be thrown out of court? You know I can't do that, Gus."

"Sheriff's got a point there, Gus," Aaron said, and being the oldest man at the table, his intervention ended the matter.

Herman cleared his throat. "I heard some of the kids was plannin' to have a bonfire out at the point this weekend. Got anything against that, Sheriff?"

"Not if it's supervised. You know that." Dan frowned.

"I was just thinkin' that with two guys dead from burning, you might not want another fire, even for fun, is all." Herman's face was sly, and he waited for Dan's reaction.

Just as Dan started to speak, the door to the Potter's Bluff Cafe banged open and Harry Clemens swaggered in. "Hey, there, Sheriff—I just heard the news. That guy we pulled out of the car got offed!" His news did not create quite the sensation he had hoped, but he had the satisfaction of hearing Herman say, "He died. What do you mean, got offed?"

"Harry, not here!" Dan said sharply.

But Harry ignored him. "Yeah. I just heard that someone snuck into his room and stuck an ice pick in his eye!" He took the chair Sam Evans had vacated. "Nobody knows how it was done, or who did it."

The men at the table muttered, and Herman gave Dan a reproachful stare. "You didn't say nothing about the ice pick."

"It wasn't an ice pick," Dan muttered. "Harry, you don't help when you go spreading stories like that."

"But the guy was killed?" Herman persisted.

"Yeah, it looks like it," Dan answered.

Penny Strickland had been returning to the table for refills on the coffee cups when she saw the horrified expressions on the faces of the strangers in the booth. She came over to them and said quietly, "Don't pay Harry any attention. He's always like that, a real blowhard."

Ron looked at her nervously. "But he said—"

"A guy had a bad accident, and they took him to the hospital," she said gently, as if to someone who did not understand her language too well. "He was burned all over and nobody thought he would make it."

"You mean, aside from the man the sheriff told us about?" Linda said, staring at Penny intently.

Penny nodded vigorously. "It's terrible, what's been happening. But the sheriff is working hard on it. Mr. Bass told Mr. Andrews this morning that he thought the fire at the boatyard was an accident. It was just too bad that an old drunk like Nils didn't know enough to get out of it." With a blithe smile she turned away from them, leaving the check.

Linda leaned forward and said in an urgent undervoice, "This is the *safe* country you want to live in?"

"What's happening, Mom?" Jamie asked.

Ron's face hardened. "Two accidental deaths here is news. In the city it's business as usual. It's so common that no one talks about it, that's all." He looked away from Linda. "Finish your milkshake, Jamie."

"Maybe we got us some weirdos at work," Harry said loudly. "What'd you think of that, Sheriff?"

"It's possible. But if that's what's going on, how come no one's noticed anything unusual?" Dan got up from the table. "There should be word from the county by now. We'll find out for sure who that man was. And Harry," he added as he started toward the cash register, "if there are any more wild rumors in town, I'm coming straight to you. It's bad enough having those two deaths, but if you spook the town badly enough, other people are going to get hurt. Understand me?"

"Sure, Sheriff." He laughed. "If it wasn't an ice pick, what was it?"

Dan paid the bill and said nothing.

Chapter 5

"I wish you wouldn't do this, Ron," Linda said to her husband as they sat in their room at the Bowie Street Hotel. "I know it's silly, but I think we'd better try Smiths Landing. After all that stuff in the cafe, I feel . . . creepy." She cast an anxious look at Jamie, but he was occupied with his comic books.

"That's foolish," Ron told her. "You're the one who suggested the move in the first place. You want to live in a small town. You said you want to have the feeling of being part of a community again instead of a number by a doorbell." He paused, and took a more reasonable tone. "Look, we don't have to do anything. If this Bass guy doesn't give us any useful leads, then we can forget Potter's Bluff. But if he does, we might as well check them out. Maybe we can get a lead on jobs, too. I have a feeling that towns like Potter's Bluff don't have much use for a computer programmer."

Linda sighed. "It's such a strange place."

"Honey," Ron said carefully, "I think it's more you than the place. You've been on edge since we went into the cafe." He watched her closely, uncertain of her reaction.

"The cafe." She shook her head. "That waitress. It was so odd. She looked a lot like Midge Hawthorn. You remember her, don't you?"

"The one who disappeared?" Ron asked, and saw her nod. "You think so?"

"An awful lot like her. The same blond hair, and that baby face . . ."

Ron reached over and put his arm around Linda's shoulder. "That was four years ago. Midge would have changed. She'd be . . . what? Twenty-two or twenty-three now, wouldn't she? That girl in the cafe isn't a day over nineteen. You can bet on it."

"Midge looked young. She could look nineteen." Linda leaned her head on Ron's shoulder. "You're right. It's silly. I don't know what got to me. All this driving, and having a headache . . ."

Ron tightened his hold. "We can always change our minds."

"And get robbed again? I keep thinking of what would have happened if we'd got home while they were still in the apartment." She shivered.

"Shh, shh," Ron whispered, rubbing the back of her neck with his free hand. "It's okay, Linda. It didn't happen."

She put her arms around his waist. "I know. But I can't stop worrying. It's silly—"

"Then let me call this Mr. Bass."

Linda sniffed. "I'm sorry. You're good to put up with my collywobbles." She got off the bed and went to the bathroom door. "I'm going to do something about my face while you call."

"Great." Ron reached over and touched Jamie's shoulder affectionately. Then he picked up the phone and waited for the desk to answer. "This is Mr. Cousins in room 317. I'd like to talk to a Mr. Bass. He was recommended to us as a man knowing real estate in this town."

Ben Collier was manning the front desk and the phones, and he said to Ron, "Why, yes. Mr. Bass is the best man to talk to. I'll put you through to his office." He dialed the number automatically, and put Ron on hold as he heard Tubby answer the phone. "It's Ben. There's a young couple here at the hotel who's interested in buying a place in Potter's Bluff. Nice folks. Name of Cousins. He has a wife and a young boy. They seem to have a bit of money."

"Thanks, Ben. Put me through."

"Mr. Bass?" Ron said as he was taken off hold.

"Yes, Mr. Cousins." He had that plummy, self-satisfied tone that only men who are very big fish in very small ponds ever seem to achieve. "Ben tells me you're asking about real estate in Potter's Bluff. What can I do to help you?"

"My wife and I are in town looking for a place to buy, perhaps. Sheriff—is it Gillis?—said that we should talk to you."

"Dan Gillis is a good man. I'm grateful for his recommendation. Perhaps you'd like to come by the office in, say, half an hour, and we can talk about the kind of place you're interested in. I'm on Clipper Street, just off Main

Street, around the corner from the bank. Turn just after the mortuary—that's the frame building with the statue on top."

This was going much faster than Ron was prepared for. "Well—"

"Bring your wife and son with you. We like to deal with the whole family in this town." He gave a round chuckle.

"All right," Ron said. "Half an hour. We'll be there."

"I'm looking forward to it, Mr. Cousins."

Linda came back into the bedroom as Ron put the receiver back in its cradle. "Well?"

"We've got an appointment at his office in half an hour," Ron said.

"Good." Linda gave him her best determined smile.

Ron became enthusiastic. "Why don't we get ready now and we'll walk over to Bass' office? That'll give us a chance to look at the town up close."

Linda was openly grateful for his suggestion. "Wonderful," she said eagerly. "Give me ten minutes."

In fifteen minutes, the three Cousins were on the corner of Bowie and Main Streets, bundled against the incoming fog. Ron looked about, then pointed out the mortuary. "That's the direction."

They crossed the street heading north, Linda putting a scarf around her hair. She glanced at the statue, a ghostly presence above them in the thickening fog. "What do you suppose it is?"

Ron shrugged. "Theme and variation on

American Gothic, probably." He looked down to be sure that Jamie was staying close to them. "Ma and Pa."

They were almost in front of the mortuary now, and Linda looked up again. "No," she said after a moment. "It's not that. There's a girl with a spinning wheel or a churn or something, and the man behind her . . . he's holding her hair. He's got a scythe." She shuddered.

"Charming," Ron said, but did not look at the statue again. "You know what these little towns can be like, sometimes." He looked down the street. "That's where we turn."

They came to the corner and were about to cross the street when two cars barreled by. Linda stared after them as they stepped off the curb. "It's strange. I haven't seen a single new car since we got here," she remarked.

"We haven't been here very long," Ron reminded her.

"But still . . ." She frowned, then dismissed it from her mind as they neared Tubby Bass' office. A slightly dusty four-year-old Cadillac was parked in front of the door. "See?" she said.

"It's a Caddy," Ron said with a shrug, and opened the door, holding it for Linda and Jamie.

Tubby Bass waved to them from his desk. He was on the phone, and indicated that it would not be a long conversation. "That's fine, Janet," he was saying. "I'll let you know as soon as I can." He listened a moment, his round, fleshy face growing serious. "No, of course there won't be any trouble. I can assure you of it . . . All right, fine. . . . I will, right. . . . Regards to Dan. Bye." He hung up with a show of relief. "Sorry, folks. We're sponsoring a little competition at the high school and I had to straighten a few things out. Now, you're obviously the Cousins. I'm Tubby Bass." He held out a plump, well-cared-for hand.

Ron shook it, saying, "Yes. I'm Ron Cousins, and this is my wife Linda and our son Jamie."

Tubby Bass was beaming. "Linda. Jamie. Oh, I can see that you'll do fine here. Real, real fine."

• • •

Potter's Bluff Cemetery was conveniently located behind the mortuary, and it was there that Dan found Dobbs, late that afternoon.

"Ah, Sheriff, I see you've caught up with me," Dobbs said as he stood beside a half-dug grave.

"I've got to be sure that the arrangements have been made . . ."

" . . . for the burial." He pointed out a wooden board leaning against the fence. "Otis delivered it half an hour ago. Not much of a job, but it's such short notice, and since there's no family to express their wishes in the matter . . ." He walked through the damp grass to the board.

It was about four-feet high, rounded on the top, and deeply carved in simple letters. The pencil guidelines were still visible on the surface.

GEORGE LEMOIR
ITINERANT
APPROXIMATELY AGED 30 YEARS
"IN THE MIDST OF LIFE WE ARE IN THE MIDST
OF DEATH"

Dobbs looked down at the grave marker and shook his head. "Oh, Daniel, my boy, you're a great disappointment to me."

"Oh? Why's that?" Dan asked in a guarded tone.

"It's truly lamentable." Dobbs touched the grave marker. "You haven't been able to find out that unfortunate man's true identity. We're stuck with a John Doe grave, or George LeMoir. I was so hoping that those dental impressions would bear fruit, but Betty called me an hour ago and said that they haven't been able to get a positive identification."

"It takes time, Dobbs. You know that. In a month or so . . ." Dan spoke with a patience he did not actually feel.

"But in a month it won't matter to me. Then we'll change the marker or exhume the casket and ship it off, if that's required, but I'll have lost my opportunity."

"Your opportunity?" He felt a return of annoyance with Dobbs. "What're you talking about?"

Dobbs stepped back from the grave marker, his gnomish face somber in the fading light. "There'll be a sealed casket. A sealed casket! That's what we'll put in the ground tomorrow after Reverend Gower finishes the obsequies. A sealed casket! Had you been able to find that poor man's family, they might have allowed me to perform some of my magic. I told you when we took the man out of the wreck that he would have been a wonderful challenge, but somehow he seems to elude me. I wanted to work on that face, to restore it . . ."

Dan made no effort to conceal his distaste. "You know, Dobbs, sometimes you make me sick."

"*I* make *you* sick? Why, Sheriff, how do you imagine I feel at a time like this? You present me with a body with such a stimulating difficulty and then you ask me to keep it, untouched, until it's rotten, on the off chance that there will be an identification. That's not possible, thank goodness. If Andrews had required that the body not be interred, I would have insisted that it be sent to the county morgue. What do you want me to do? Stick it in someone's deep-freeze, like a Christmas turkey, until we get a positive identification? Do you know what that body will be like in a day or two, let alone in a week? And still you want me to keep it on hand!" Dobbs's sallow cheeks had two bright spots in them now. "You asked that of me, and you have the colossal nerve to tell me that *I* make *you* sick!"

Dan heard him out in silence, admitting to himself that the objections were just. When Dobbs was through, he said mildly, "Yeah, you're right."

"Well, well, well," Dobbs murmured, giving Dan an appraising look.

The frustration that had been building in Dan at last got the better of him. "I know I handled this badly. When they found that guy this morning, you can't imagine all the questions I wanted to ask, and all the dead ends I've found. God damn it, Dobbs! Nothing adds up. And the more I search, the less sense it all makes. Look, first Janet says she knows him, then she says she doesn't know his last name or where he's from. Then she remembers the last name, but no one ever heard of him. Yet he gets killed in the hospital by some woman right under the nose of half the staff. Then Nils Uhri gets burned to death. I don't buy it. No, sir. Not accidental death by fire, not after what happened to LeMoir. I can't prove Uhri's death was anything but death by misadventure. But I know in my guts, Dobbs, I *know* he was murdered. Two murders. A stranger and an old drunk with no family. Pretty handy in a town this size, don't you think? Safe to kill them. I wish to God I could find out what's going on here." He looked back across the graveyard to the half-completed hole that was being dug for George LeMoir.

• • •

Before driving home, Dan stopped at Winslow's Service Station to get his tank refilled. His talk with Dobbs still occupied his mind, and as he pulled up to the gas pumps, he hardly noticed the new attendant.

A car pulled up beside him, and the force of habit brought Dan out of his reverie. When he recognized the driver of the '72 Buick, he got out of his squad car and walked over to the other man. "Hello, Mr. Haskell," he said as he came up to the Buick's open window.

Paul Haskell looked up. There was a faint air of pedantry about him, a stiffness in his face, a tucking in of his hands, that labeled him as surely as the plaque on his office door. He was the principal of Potter's Bluff High School. "Oh. Hello, Dan."

Dan took his notebook out of his pocket, and then a pen. "I was wondering if you'd object to answering a couple questions for me?"

"Why . . . no." The principal's eyes flickered nervously. "What is this about?"

"I want to get some information from you," Dan said, not answering Haskell's question. "That guy who died in the hospital, the one who was so badly burned—"

"Oh, gracious yes. A terrible thing, terrible." Haskell's face was prim and he spoke with measured gravity.

"Yes, it was. I have reason to believe that he might have been George LeMoir, and—"

"Who?" Haskell asked, puzzled.

"George LeMoir. The school bought photographic equipment from him, I understand. But Janet said she couldn't remember what company he was with." Dan was rather startled to see Paul Haskell become more confused.

"I beg your pardon, Sheriff, but I don't know who or what you are talking about."

Dan's pen hovered over the blank page of his notebook. "You *don't* buy photographic equipment from George LeMoir?"

Haskell sat more stiffly behind the wheel.

"Not only do we not buy it from him, we don't buy such equipment at all. This is a small district. We don't have a budget for such extravagances."

After a second or two, Dan asked, "Is it possible this is a transaction you don't know about, or a special project?"

"I know *everything* that goes on at the school."

Dan put the notebook away. "Yeah. Well, I'm sorry to have troubled you. Thanks, Mr. Haskell."

Slightly mollified, Haskell said, "Think nothing of it, Sheriff. I'm only sorry I couldn't have been of more help."

With a nod, Dan turned and went back to his squad car, more baffled than before. He waited while the new attendant finished wiping his windshield, then reached for the door. He glanced at the attendant with a touch of curiosity: most of the guys who worked for Cal Winslow were high school students, but this man was clearly older than that, perhaps as old as thirty. He was of medium height and build, and his features were regular, pleasant without being striking or handsome. Only a small, crescent-shaped scar just below his left eye made his face memorable.

The attendant gave a self-effacing smile. "You're Sheriff Gillis."

Dan handed the attendant a couple of bills and waited for the man to get change from the cashbox set between the two pumps. He opened the door of the squad car, and prepared to get in.

While the attendant made change, he said to Dan, "My name is Freddie, Freddie Murdoch. I figured since I'm new in town, I'd better introduce myself to the law." He came back with two singles and a handful of change.

"Thanks." Dan pocketed the money without looking at it He looked once at Haskell's Buick, but decided not to press the principal yet. As he got into the car and started it up, he heard the new attendant—what had he said his name was? Freddie?—call out "Adios, Sheriff."

Belatedly, as he drove away Dan looked into the rearview mirror at the attendant, and wondered idly if that pleasant stranger would be the next burned body he found. Then as he swerved around a rabbit in the road, he told himself to pay attention to his driving.

• • •

To Dan's surprise, Janet was not home when he got there. The driveway was empty and the house dark. He parked his squad car and let himself in by the kitchen door. The house felt odd without her. The kitchen was cold and strange, as if it belonged to someone else. To banish this disquieting sensation, Dan busied himself with making a cup of coffee, taking a great deal of care with the preparation.

He was sitting at the kitchen table, the coffee in front of him cold, when Janet at last pulled into the driveway, a good half hour after he had arrived. Dan heard the car door slam, then open and slam again. There were hasty steps up the walk, along the breezeway, and then the back door was flung open.

"Hi!" Janet called out as she came into the kitchen. Her arms were full of packages and her hair was in disarray. She dropped the packages on the drainboard, then turned to give her husband a quick, perfunctory kiss. "God, what a day!"

Dan moved his coffee cup away. "Where have you been?"

"Everywhere," she said with a sigh. "The hardware store, the drug store, the bank. I haven't stopped moving since school let out." She was starting to sort out the packages she had brought in, putting two of them on the table and the rest in her utility cabinet. "I've had a million errands to run. And tonight's the big PTA meeting. I don't know why all these arrangements get left to the last minute, but they do."

"Yeah." Dan watched her as she hurried about. Her frenetic activity was unusual and left Dan disquieted.

While she went on with her chores, Janet said, "The whole day's been like this. On top of everything, we had another locker check today. Can you imagine! I think what Paul Haskell likes most about being principal is being able to have locker checks. I can't think of any other reason for it. That's three times in the last two weeks. This time, Barbara Ann Ellison said that somebody stole her transistor radio. So right in the middle of fourth period, we had a locker check. Naturally, the radio didn't turn up. Students aren't supposed to have radios at school anyway, so she had a lot of nerve asking for the locker check. If I had caught her with it, *I'd* have stolen it." She paused a moment and put her hand on Dan's face. "Are you feeling okay, Danny? You're awfully quiet." Without waiting for an answer, she was off down the hall. "I've got to change and do something with my hair. It looks like I combed it with an eggbeater."

Dan got up from the table and went to stand in the doorway to the hall. There were questions he knew he had to ask her, but he did not want to make her lie to him.

Janet stuck her head out of the bedroom door. She was running a brush through her hair and was wearing only her bra and a skirt. "There are days like this, but what a pain. You're sure you don't want to go to PTA tonight? It's at the Bowie Street Hotel, in the Tudor Room. If it gets too much for you, you can go down to the cafe and I'll meet you there later. It'd do you good to get out for a night. You know how much fun I have at these things. Why deny yourself a little pleasure?" She ducked back into the bedroom, but her voice continued, occasionally muffled as she dressed. "If you're worried about people making comments, don't be. Everyone's being very low-key at school. We decided that it would be best for the kids if we kept speculation to a minimum. It's tragic about George and Nils, but there isn't much to be done, is there?" She came out of the bedroom, her hair neat, a shirt and blazer over her skirt. In one hand she carried a purse and in the other a stack of mimeographed sheets. She smiled up at Dan. "You coming?"

He looked down at her, not quite frowning. "No . . . I can't."

"I really didn't think you'd want to go," she said a little sadly as she came up to him and kissed him lightly. "Danny, I was just giving you a hard time. I don't know how else to cheer you up. What's the matter?"

"Nothing." He turned away and went back into the kitchen.

She followed him. "Something is the matter."

He sat down, his elbows on the table, his chin propped on his linked hands. He wished he did not have to say this. "Janet, I was talking to . . ." He stopped. He was letting the case get to him and was taking it out on her. "Look, really, nothing's the matter, not that way. It's the . . . deaths, you know."

Janet put her hands on his shoulders. "My God, yes. The deaths. I keep forgetting how terrible it is for you. We make a policy decision about it at school, and that's that, but you have to live with it all day long. Poor love." She bent down and kissed his hair. "I wish I could help you, Danny."

He did not know how to respond to her, and did not trust himself to talk.

When he had been silent a bit, she stood back from him. "Well, I've got to go." She opened her purse and pulled a small paper bag out and dropped it on the table. "Oh, will you do me a favor? I forgot to take care of this earlier, and the drug store is closed now. Can you drop this off at Ernie's for me tomorrow morning on your way in?"

Dan picked up the bag and held it a moment. "Why? What is it?"

"Some film that my students shot. They're making a film, a class project. In this wonderful age of movies and TV, I figured it would be a good way to teach them about narrative. Pictures arranged in sequence. Maybe some of them will make the connection. Ernie said he'd develop them for me—for free, thank goodness."

"Yeah," Dan said in a voice that seemed to him to come from another room. "Sure. Tomorrow morning."

"Thanks." Janet started across the room, but stopped to look back at Dan. "You'll find out what's going on, Danny, I know you will." She gave him her most reassuring smile, and it filled him with doubt. "Love you," she said, more warmly. "Love me?"

"Yeah. You know it." It sounded phony even to him and he saw the distress at the back of her eyes. "Don't worry about me. I'll be okay."

She studied his face, then said, "Well, I should be back fairly early. I'll give you a call before I leave the hotel."

"Okay." He rubbed his face and made a gesture that might have been a wave as she pulled the door closed. He listened to her steps going down the breezeway to the driveway. A moment later, her car door opened, then closed. The engine started. Dan got up from the table and walked to the side window. He saw the headlights flash as Janet backed her car down the driveway, then turned and headed toward Main Street. Dan stayed at the window for several minutes, resolutely keeping his thoughts at bay. When he was certain that he had regained control of himself, he went back to the table and sat down again, the cold cup of coffee in front of him. He sat in the dark for more than twenty minutes, aware only of the silence in the house.

• • •

Paul Haskell stood in the entrance to the Bowie Street Hotel talking with PTA members as they left the meeting. It was twenty past ten, about the usual time for the meeting to end.

"A foggy night like this," one of the parents was saying to Haskell, "it shows you who cares."

"Very true," Haskell agreed with a prissy, political smile. "You take Mrs. Robinson here—she's been at every PTA meeting for the last eleven years."

The matron indicated had a righteous expression and was known to be the most difficult parent in the entire district. She marched up to Paul Haskell and said, "Not enough parents take their responsibilities seriously these days. Those who do should set an example."

There were murmurs of cowed assent around her, and three of the teachers took this opportunity to escape. They had made it as far as the curb when Dan Gillis drove up in his squad car and leaned out the window.

Pete Dales, a lanky young man who taught algebra and geometry, raised his hand in greeting. "Hello, Dan. Missed you tonight. What's doing?"

Dan returned the wave. "Hi, Pete. Is Janet still here? I wanted to talk to her. I've got to go out on a call, and you know how much she hates to come home to an empty house."

Joyce Cardiff, the history teacher, blinked in shock. "Janet? But she wasn't here—"

Before Joyce could say anything more that might be overheard and misunderstood, Pete took over. "Dan, I don't believe Janet was here tonight. I looked for her, and there weren't that many people attending—just sixty or so. Joyce, you didn't see Janet Gillis. What about you, Stephanie?"

Stephanie Holt shook her head. "No, I didn't, and I was looking for her, too."

A cold, indigestible lump of dread settled into Dan's stomach. He was glad for the poor lighting here, for otherwise he was certain that the three teachers would read the distress in his eyes. With a considerable effort he made his tone light. "Well, serves her right, then. She said she might not come to PTA. She was thinking of taking in a movie in Smiths Landing instead. And I don't have time to drive over there and tell her I'm going to be out for a while."

"If I see her, I'll give her the message,"

Pete called, and Dan wondered if it was only his imagination, or if there was a note of pity in Pete's voice.

"Okay. Thanks. Good night." He signaled and drew away from the curb, making certain he did the usual things—waved, called out hellos to those people he knew, smiled. He drove the length of Main Street, watching the buildings loom out of the fog like ships at sea. He kept a careful eye on the other cars, looking for those that were familiar. In a town like Potter's Bluff, most cars were as familiar and easily identified as faces, but when the fog was in, as it was tonight, the commonplace became strange, exotic. Twice Dan saw cars that he thought might be Janet's Duster, but after following them a block or so, he noticed the license plates, or saw the color in the glare of a streetlight and knew he had been mistaken.

Where was she? Where had she gone? And worst of all, why had she lied to him? Was she with another man? Perhaps she had simply decided to skip the meeting and spend some time with one of her friends. Or had there been another accident? Only this time it was Janet—his own, lovely, treasured Janet, caught in the middle of a bright, flaming cage that would devour her. This last thought filled him with a fear that bordered on fury. He was so shaken by this vision that he almost did not see the car that turned across the intersection ahead of him. It was a Duster, the same orange shade as Janet's.

Dan shook himself, and drove faster, then

slammed on his brakes as the venerable old De Soto belonging to Gus Dickerson coasted through the stop sign, its engine wheezing.

When the road was clear, Dan rushed on, hoping that he could find the side street where the Duster had disappeared. He took the first street, drove for a block and realized that the car was not ahead of him. Resolutely he turned back for Ocean Drive. The buildings here were close together, tall and narrow, and they seemed to condense the fog. Dan knew that in another block there would be two side streets and an alley where the Duster might be, but he glanced down the occasional driveways to see what cars were parked there. It was not easy to make out the shapes.

Dan was glancing down a narrow cut between two old buildings, when he caught a movement in front of the car out of the corner of his eye. He turned at once, only to see an uncertain shape fall and feel his squad car lurch in impact. Horrified, Dan jammed on the brakes, put the car on idle and got out, dreading what he would see even as he ran the few steps to the front.

There was a figure in an old coat lying facedown, pressed against the grillwork, caught somehow on the front bumper. In the uncertain light and the thickening fog, Dan could not see who it was. He knelt down, pulling his flashlight from his belt. He knew that he should not move the victim in any way, and only played the beam of the flashlight over the fallen man.

With a sigh the man fell a bit further and

Dan reached out automatically to steady him. The sheriff bent over the fallen man, seeing the side of his face now, and leaned close to see how severely hurt he was.

In the next moment Dan stifled a shout, for something brushed the side of his face. He turned sharply toward the front of his squad car, and his eyes widened in horror as he saw a severed arm caught in the grill. The fingers grasped at the air, seeming to want to grab him.

Dan half staggered to his feet, his mind numb. Breathing was an effort; moving was impossible. In some submerged part of his consciousness, he knew he should get into the car and call an ambulance, that he should get his first aid kit out and do something to aid the man whose arm dangled from the grill of his squad car. "No, no," he moaned, turning away from the destruction before him.

A quick, scrambling movement behind him brought Dan back to himself just before a heavy weight slammed into his side.

The flashlight went out as Dan fell, and his head struck a glancing blow on the curb. As his vision wobbled, Dan thought he saw the pedestrian he had struck standing beside him. Then a hand reached down and tugged the severed arm out of the grill. There were scuffling footsteps as the pedestrian ran off carrying the arm clasped to his chest.

Pain lanced along his skull as Dan tottered to his feet. He stared dumbly at the front of his car, where no victim lay. He touched the grill and found it empty. He squinted into the fog and thought he saw the flapping coat of the pedestrian near the corner of the block. Dan started after the man, stumbling once. His temples were throbbing and he feared he was going to be sick. He turned the flashlight back on as he made his way along the narrow street.

At the corner he groped his way toward the cross street. His head was growing more painful, his vision blurring. He could hear footsteps but could not determine the direction the pedestrian had taken. Sound bounced, echoed, bounced again along the old, narrow buildings. The steps filled his head, and Dan stopped, confused. He pointed the beam of the flashlight down the fog-shrouded streets, but there was nothing moving along them. Had it actually happened? He had seen a man lying against the front of his squad car. He was sure he had. Dan gazed into the fog, doubt filling him.

Suddenly a terrific crash rang out, the noise magnified by the closeness of the buildings.

Dan spun around, bringing his flashlight with him, his head singing with pain. A low, involuntary cry escaped him.

A trash can rolled toward him, dribbling papers and moist packages. Its lid lay on the pavement like a discarded shield. A pointed, masked face peered over the side, making that rasping sound which passes for a snarl among raccoons. It blinked in the light, then lumbered into the shadows, oblivious of the terror it had brought Dan.

He took a few, faltering steps toward the trash can, and was dismayed when his knees almost buckled under him. Automatically he reached out, and touched the peeling wall of one of the houses. The sensation of the worn boards began to restore him. They, at least, were solid. Realizing that he had been breathing quickly, shallowly, he forced himself to inhale a huge, slow lungful of air.

It was more than three minutes before Dan trusted himself to return to his squad car. His headache had dulled to a penetrating ache and he walked carefully, but he was no longer possessed by the worst of his doubt. When he reached his squad car, he got in, taking comfort from the ordinary sound of the idling engine.

Ten minutes later he was ready to drive home through the fog.

Chapter 6

Janet turned over in bed and looked up sleepily at Dan. "What?"

"Where were you tonight?" His voice shook and his face was white. He leaned over the bed and stared down at her as if he did not know her.

"There was a PTA meeting, you know that," she murmured, raising one hand to block the light.

"But you weren't there, were you?" he said harshly.

"I stopped at Inez Winslow's house. Norman wasn't home yet, and you know how she's been feeling, what with the baby dying like that, so I stayed with her until Norm got back. It must have been after ten when I left." She was a bit more awake and stared at him. "What's this all about?"

Dan answered in a rush: "I went by the hotel to see you. When I didn't spot your car, I waited around until the meeting was out, oh, about ten minutes later, and there was no sign of you. I talked to Pete and Joyce, and they said you hadn't been there at all. With everything that's been happening, I thought that you'd . . . you'd . . ." He sank down on the side of the bed, his head between his hands.

Janet sat up, her expression sympathetic. "Poor Danny. I should have called you. I didn't think you'd . . . check up on me." She put her hand up to ruffle his hair, which he usually endured stoically. Now he flinched. "Danny?"

"Sorry," he muttered as he moved away from her slightly.

"What is it, Danny?" Janet, fully awake now, could see that her husband's pallor was due to something more than upset. There was a mark over his right brow that looked like a purple smear, as if he had wiped his face with a paint-soaked rag. "What did you do to yourself?"

"Nothing." He got up abruptly and began to pace the room. His hands, when he held them out for emphasis, were not steady. "I—it's nothing. I drove around looking for you. I thought I saw your car. Shit, Janet, there's a maniac loose in this town, and you go blithely off without telling me where or why! I don't want anything to happen to you. You didn't see that man with the needle sticking out of his eye. . . ." As he spoke, he regretted it. There were too many questions about the man, and where Janet fit into his life, if she did at all. Dan stopped at the end of the bed and glared down at her. "And then Nils Uhri. There's no way to tell who will be next. If there is another death. Got to say death, can't say murder. A man with a needle through his eye into his brain has died of misadventure, according to our coroner and Justice of the Peace. They won't convene a jury to hear the evidence; they just sign the papers, and there it is. So no murder has happened, just two unrelated, shocking, accidental deaths. *And that's fucking bullshit!*"

Janet was on her knees on the bed now, reaching toward Dan. "No, no, don't let it get to you, Danny." She reached up to touch his face, ignoring his attempts to brush her hands away. "You're tired and angry and upset. You've let all this get bottled up inside. Danny, Danny, you mustn't do this to yourself." Her hair was loose around her face and tumbled onto her shoulders. Her nightgown was open and her flesh still warm from the blankets. She reached to embrace him.

"Janet?" Dan said, blinking slightly, as if waking from a nightmare. "What's happening here? What's going on?"

"Hush," she whispered as she drew him down beside her. "Your poor head." She kissed the edge of the bruise.

"Janet—"

"Not now." Her fingers worked to unfasten the buttons of his shirt. "Tomorrow, when you're rested, you can think about it. You'll see it all more clearly in the morning. Think about me, Danny." She kissed the corner of his mouth. "Take off your clothes and come to bed, Danny. Come to bed with me."

Obediently he began to tug at his belt. Gratefully he lost himself in her arms. She was probably right. He had gotten too close to the problem and his judgment was suffering.

"Here, Danny." She slipped her hand inside the top of his pants. "Take those off, and your shoes."

He did, as if in a stupor. When he had come home, he had had so much on his mind. He tossed his trousers on the ladder-back chair in the corner, then bent to pull off his shoes. For the first time in years he forgot to put his belt where he could reach the pistol in his belt holster. The sheets and blankets were as engulfing as the sea, and Janet was part of it all. She surrounded his senses. His headache no longer mattered. There was nothing on his mind but the overhelming need for Janet. He let the rest of it go and gave himself up to her.

• • •

The Potter's Bluff Cafe opened for business every morning at 7:00, and by 7:30 the breakfast crowd filled the place. Dan nodded to several of the people at the tables as he came through the door at 7:45.

"Hi, Sheriff," Penny called as she came out of the kitchen. "We don't usually see you this early."

"Janet's sleeping in an extra half hour," Dan said, the indistinct memories of last night softening the firm line of his mouth.

"Lucky lady," Penny sighed, and her meaning was clear. "What can I do for you?"

"I'd like a Danish and two cups of strong coffee with cream to go." He cast a look over his shoulder. Outside the sun made little headway against the gray drizzle of the morning.

Penny was by the cash register now, and could see his face plainly. "Sheriff, what did you do to yourself?"

Dan touched the bruise on his forehead. "Bumped it. A damnfool thing to do." He gave her a gently self-deprecating grimace.

"That's too bad," she said, and went back toward the kitchen. "I'll be with you in a couple minutes, Sheriff."

"Hey, Penny, where's my eggs?" one of the customers shouted to her.

"They aren't ready yet, unless you want 'em runny," she yelled back and, amid general good-humored laughter, went through the kitchen doors.

Aaron came up to the cash register, his eyes, enlarged by his glasses, seeming to precede him by half a step. "Good morning to you, Dan," he said amiably. "I hear the town's been quiet."

"For almost twenty-four hours," Dan agreed. "How's the hardware business, Aaron?"

"As it's always been," Aaron answered as he put fifty-two cents on the glass counter beside the cash register. "That's Potter's Bluff for you." He chuckled, shook his head, and went out into the soggy morning, pulling an aged mackintosh on as he walked.

Penny came bustling back from the kitchen, a brown paper bag in her hand. "There's two cups of coffee in the bottom of the bag, so you carry it careful," she said as she held it out to him.

"Thanks," Dan said, taking the bag and handing Penny a dollar.

"You must be busy," she said as she gave him his change.

"Some. Not as much as you'd expect."

Behind Dan the door opened and Harry Clemens came in with Phil Preston. They were both wrapped in heavy jackets and Phil wore mud-caked rubber boots. "Morning, Sheriff," Phil said.

"Morning, Phil, Harry," Dan responded without giving either man much attention.

"Damn weather," Harry said cheerfully. "I've had to pull two cars out of the mud since sunup." He cuffed Dan on the arm. "You aren't leaving, are you? Where are you going that's so important? If it's another dead body, it'll wait. Sit down and have some breakfast with us."

Dan lifted his paper bag. "Sorry, Harry. No more dead bodies. I've got my breakfast right here. I'm going to have it at the office while I read over the reports from yesterday."

Phil shook his head. "You're getting like those big city cops, Dan, carrying off your meal in a little brown bag. Take some time. Don't be in such a rush."

"I can't. I'll have coffee with you later." He was able to maintain a bantering good humor this morning, more so than he had been able to do for the last three days. These were men he had known most of his life. While his personality clashed with a couple of them, he knew that they were not bad people. It was easy to deal with them.

Phil hesitated near the door while Harry tromped away toward his usual place at the table. "Hey, Sheriff, I've been thinking about that George Le What's it—you know? He was a traveling salesman of some kind, right?"

"Apparently," Dan said.

"Well, you know traveling salesmen. You've heard all the jokes. Did ya ever consider that maybe he went and took up with someone's wife!"

"How do you mean, Phil?" Dan asked carefully.

"Well, they say that no one in town knows him, or will admit it, anyway. That means that maybe somebody's lying. Who'd lie about a guy like that? A person with something to hide—that's who. Who'd have something to hide? A wife having an affair!" Phil was obviously proud of his reasoning.

"Or a man being blackmailed, or someone who doesn't want to be bothered, or someone who's forgetful or has other things on his mind," Dan said patiently. "That's not to say you're wrong, Phil; it just means that it's not the only explanation."

Phil's face sagged. "Yeah, I guess you're right. But I think my idea's the best."

Dan continued out the door, trying to ignore Phil's implications. He started toward his squad car when a cheerful greeting brought him up short.

Herman Ewing was coming along the street wearing a navy pea coat and thick twill trousers. His left arm was in a massive plaster cast supported by a very professional looking sling. "How's it going, Dan?"

"Oh . . . Morning, Herman. What happened to you?"

"Stupid thing to do," he said merrily. "Yesterday evening I decided to fix that leak in my garage roof. Started late in the day, which I should've known better than do. I fell off the side while I was reaching for the sealant. Like to broke my neck instead of my arm."

It was a coincidence, Dan said to himself. Men who lose arms don't appear the next morning with a cast and a sling. But men who lose arms don't pull them out of car grills and run off down the street, either. "Sorry to hear that, Herman. How bad is it?"

"Ed Thurston said it would be about six weeks if we're lucky. I told Reynolds at the lumberyard that I couldn't pull grades for a couple of months. Had me working on the twelve-foot boards last week. I don't mind not doing that for a while. Pulling those long boards is a bitch." Herman's smile was self-congratulatory, and he laughed as he opened the door to the Potter's Bluff Cafe.

Dan stared at Herman's back, and told himself with some severity that he was crazy. Carefully holding the paper bag with his coffee and Danish, he started toward his office.

• • •

Betty Hollister was in her mid-forties, a small, efficient woman who wore neatly tailored suits at work and jeans at home. Her brown hair was knotted at the nape of her neck and she wore sensible shoes. She looked up as Dan came in. "Good morning, Sheriff. The statements from the hospital are finished and on your desk. There was a phone call from a veterinarian in Smiths Landing—he said he would phone back after ten. Tubby Bass would like you to call. There are two letters from the county, one a request for information on a missing teenager and one the notice of extension of crime lab hours."

Most of the time Betty's formidable efficiency amused Dan, but not this morning. It was hard to be polite to her. "I'll go over them, thanks."

Betty gave one crisp nod and put a new sheet of paper into her typewriter.

Their desks were separated by a plywood partition. Dan went back to his desk and looked at the neatly stacked sheets waiting for him. He put the paper bag down on the empty typing extension arm, and opened it. As he drank his coffee, he realized that his earlier euphoria had deserted him. Idly he reached for the top page and began to read as he ate. He would have to do it eventually, he told himself, and it might as well be now.

Half an hour later, when he had tried to reach Tubby Bass without success, Dan made up his mind to call Dobbs.

"Dobbs's Mortuary," Jimmy said in a bored voice.

"This is Sheriff Gillis, Jimmy. Let me talk to Dobbs." As he waited, he restacked the papers on his desk and lined up the pages.

"Good morning, Daniel. I've been anticipating a call from you. What are you going to allow me to have the pleasure of doing for you?"

Dobbs's ebullience, as always, pained Dan. "I have to talk to you about the man you're burying this evening. That LeMoir man, if that's his name."

"Ah, yes," Dobbs said sadly. "Tragic. What about him?"

"Are you still insisting that he died by misadventure, with a needle in his eye?" Dan's glance flicked over the statement of Clark Vanderbury.

"Dan, Dan, my boy, I thought this was all settled."

Dan hesitated, knowing that Dobbs could be a formidable enemy. "I can't accept that, Dobbs, and you know it. If you continue to maintain that the man died by accident, then I'm going to make an official complaint to the county, and ask for a full hearing on the incident, investigating both your conduct and that of Andrews."

Dobbs clicked his tongue. "Dan, you distress me. You most certainly do." There was a pause while Dobbs gathered his thoughts. "I assume you have statements from the hospital staff and you feel they support your position well enough for you to make this... shall we call it a gesture?"

"That's part of it. And you know that there's no one at the county seat who is going to believe that that death was an accident. They may even insist on a more thorough investigation of Nils Uhri's death. If that's what you want, then tell me now and I'll start making phone calls. If you're willing to do your job, then I'll ease off." Dan felt a savage satisfaction. At last he was taking action, useful, real action. "I also want an effort made to find out where LeMoir was actually killed. I mean, where he was attacked." He forced himself to slow down. "I think that whole thing on the road was a cover, and you know that."

Dobbs gave an unfriendly sound that might have been intended as a chuckle. "I see. We cooperate now, or you bring in the big guns, is that it, Dan? You realize that I am not the only citizen of our community who would prefer that you accept things as they are. We do what's best for our people in this town, Dan, my boy, and an investigation of the unaccountable deaths of vagrants does not come high on our list of priorities."

"And now that you've made your speech, and gone on the record, get to work. Do you want to call Andrews, or shall I?" Dan had made up his mind to call Tolliver next so that there would not be time for Andrews or Dobbs to get to the hospital administrator. He pulled a sheet of foolscap from his desk and began to make notes on it as he talked to Dobbs. "I suggest we meet here, at my office, tomorrow morning, so that we can plan how best to proceed."

"Tomorrow morning at what time?" Dobbs did not sound pleased.

"Ten. That will let you and Andrews open your businesses before coming here. Do you think that we ought to bother His Honor, or should we simply handle this ourselves?" Dan waited for an answer.

"Tomorrow at ten. It would be wisest, I believe, if we confine this nonsense to as few people as possible. There will be plenty of time to get the mayor riled up later, if you insist that we play this farce through to the end. I will call Horace Andrews and tell him that upon reconsideration, I feel that LeMoir may have met with some sort of adversity before we took him out of his van, and that you believe that his death in the hospital was an act of premeditated malice."

"And Nils?" Dan had now written seven items on his foolscap and was working on the eighth.

"That is rather more farfetched. On the other hand, I'm not the detective, you are. I'll anticipate a lively time in your office tomorrow morning, Dan. Do keep up the good work. Good-bye." He hung up before Dan had the chance to speak to him again.

Dan returned the receiver to its cradle, then got up from the desk to do the first task on his list.

There was a supply cabinet in the corner, a large steel box with a locked door. Dan opened it with his key and took out a stiff brush, a dental pick, two lengths of gauze, and a small plastic envelope in a container with a sterile seal on it. He relocked the cabinet and came out of his part of the office.

"Sheriff—" Betty began.

"Just a moment, Betty. I won't be long." Dan walked out into the small parking lot on the side of the police station. He went down on one knee in front of his car, thinking that he should have done this last night. He examined the grill meticulously, then commenced to scrape a few miscellaneous bits of material onto the gauze, using the dental pick. When he had done that, he put the gauze into the sterile envelope, then delicately brushed over the grill and bumper, again catching the small amounts of residue on a length of gauze which then joined its fellow in the sterile envelope. Satisfied, Dan returned to his desk. He lifted the receiver and dialed the number of the hospital.

Dr. Tolliver had not yet arrived at the hospital, and Dr. Vanderbury was with a patient. Dr. Thurston, however, could take the call. Dan hesitated a moment, then decided that Ed might be the best person to talk to, after all. "Put him on," he said.

"Ed Thurston here," a tired voice said.

"Ed, this is Dan Gillis—"

"Hi, Sheriff," Ed interrupted in a lighter tone.

"Look, you told me when you heard that Dobbs and Andrews have put the wraps on the LeMoir killing, that you thought it was a disgrace and shouldn't be allowed to happen. Do you still feel that way?" He had checked off number one and his pencil hovered over number two.

"I sure as hell do. That man didn't die by accident. He didn't take the needle and put it in his own eye, you know that as well as I do. We know that a redheaded woman in a nurse's outfit that none of us had ever seen was in his room and probably did it, but we don't know who she was or why she did it, and yes, I still think we should find out." His voice was more stern.

"Are you willing to back me up with the county, if I have to take it to them?" Dan asked, feeling now that Ed's answer would be critical.

"If it comes to that, you know I will. When you work in a hospital, you don't want to think that anything like that can happen. I'll go to the county or the state or the AMA if I have to."

Dan could hear the tight smile in Ed's voice. "I'll hold you to that. I'm warning you that there's a good chance that there's going to be a fair amount of pressure put on you over at the hospital. Tolliver will probably go along with it. I'm out on a limb now, and if you aren't willing to stick to your guns, I might be all by myself, sawing away on the wrong side of the branch. I don't want you to be frightened, I just want you to understand what you and I might be up against."

"You mean the Good Old Boy network? I don't give a shit about that. After seeing that man—" He broke off. "I'll stand by what I said. And I'll talk to the others. I think Clark will support you, but Tolliver will put more pressure on him than on me. I'm not important enough. Same thing for the nurses."

"I'll count on it," Dan said, and then went on cautiously, "There's one more thing, Ed.

I've got some samples that should be tested in a lab and I'd rather not have to send them to the county seat."

"Do they have anything to do with what we've been talking about?"

Dan considered his answer. "Possibly. Not directly."

"What kind of samples?" Ed's tone was slightly less courteous.

"Accident–locale stuff. I need to know if any of the particles contain traces of human skin or blood. I scraped them off the front of a car that—may have been involved in a . . . a hit-and-run accident."

"LeMoir, you think?"

"I doubt it, but I think the two may be connected." That was truthful enough, Dan reassured himself. "I'd appreciate it if you could keep this kind of quiet. With the pressure that's coming, I want to keep as much out of sight as I can."

"I can understand that. Okay. If you like, I'll do the tests myself."

"Thanks." He was genuinely grateful. "I'll drop the samples off at the hospital around noon, if that's convenient."

"I'll be waiting for them. And by then I should know how Tolliver's going to play this round."

"Good. We'll talk later." They exchanged goodbyes and hung up. He checked off the second item and stared at the third. He was about to get up when he heard the outer office door open and hasty steps approach Betty's desk. A voice speaking rapidly and with import, just below the level of hearing, came through the partition to him.

"Sheriff," Betty called out in disapproving accents, "Ben Collier wants to talk to you. He says it's urgent."

"Send him back, Betty." Dan wondered why the manager of the Bowie Street Hotel would seek out the Sheriff. It was a rarity.

Ben looked harried. His tie was askew, his usually neat, dark hair was disarrayed. His eyes had a slick, feverish shine. "Sheriff! Dan. You gotta talk to me." He did not take the chair on the other side of the desk.

"Come in, Ben, sit down. Tell me what this is all about." He had learned over the years how best to soothe people who had become upset.

"You're not gonna believe this," Ben said, his face twisted into a beseeching grin, a travesty of his usual politic smile. "I wouldn't, not if someone else told me. But it's true, Dan, I'm not making it up. I wouldn't do that—honest."

Dan pointed to the other chair, and said gently, "Sit down, Ben. And tell me what's wrong. What won't I believe?"

Ben sat. He was not willing to meet Dan's eyes with his own. "Look . . . that guy . . . the one you came to see me about, the one who left all his things in the room . . . you know?"

"Yes," Dan said encouragingly. "That's the man we assume was in the car that caught fire. Do you have other information—" Ben was shaking his head violently.

"No. It can't be the same guy, Dan, it *can't!* That's what I want to tell you. We must've made a mistake. There's been a mix-up. I . . ."

"How was it a mistake, Ben? What's happened that you think we've made a mistake?"

Ben's eyes moved restlessly about the room. "You gotta understand. I didn't lie to you before. I really thought he was gone, that he'd disappeared."

"You mean he came back to the hotel?"

"No, not to the hotel," Ben said impatiently, his eyes slightly less wild. The worst of his panic was over, and he made an effort to speak clearly. "Dan, you gotta listen. That guy who was at the hotel, the one whose room you checked, the one that Janet visited,"—his forehead grew ruddy as he said this last—"that man. I just saw him."

Dan controlled the urge to yell. "What do you mean, you just saw him? Where did you see him?"

A little of the fright returned. "That's what I'm trying to explain. I saw him over at the service station, pumping gas."

"That's just Freddie, the new help. I talked to him a little while ago. He's new in town, but . . ." Dan was aware he could not have any more wild rumors circulating in Potter's Bluff. He also noted that Betty's typewriter had stopped.

"No, I looked at him. That's the photographer who was saying at the hotel. Really, Dan, he is." Ben's voice rose a few notes.

"Look, Ben, I can understand why you're upset. That man's death was shocking, and we're all aware that it was more than an accident. You want to protect the reputation of the hotel, and that's fine. It's good that you want to do that. But that man—"

Ben cut in more loudly, "You go over and take a look at him—see if it isn't the same guy."

"I never saw his face," Dan reminded Ben, and they were both quiet a moment. "Not until after he was burned. I haven't any idea what he looked like except for the description you gave Betty. Obviously this Freddie looks a lot like him, and that's hard enough to deal with—"

"It's the same guy," Ben insisted mulishly. "Remember what I said about the scar under his eye? This guy has a scar there. It's not a strong resemblance, it's the *same guy*. I'm not crazy. I know that strangers often look alike. Hell, we joke about it sometimes, Tubby and me. Tubby claims he can tell where the people come from by the way they dress, but says that it's almost impossible to remember their faces. That's true enough. But a thing like a scar, that's something else. This guy at Winslow's has a scar under his left eye. I was standing right next to him, and that's the man!" Ben leaned forward and pounded one meaty fist on the desk.

"Is something wrong, Sheriff?" Betty called out sharply.

"Everything's fine, Betty," Dan answered

quickly. "Ben's worried, that's all. Go back to work." He gave Ben a warning look from under his brows, and said in a low voice. "Keep it down, or the next thing you know, Betty will be telling everyone that you're seeing ghosts."

Shamefaced and baffled, Ben glared at Dan. "Sure. Okay. Right. I'll keep quiet. Bet your left ball, I will." He made a nervous, resigned gesture as he stepped back. "But it's the same damn guy, no matter who he says he is. That's the man, and you can't change it. If you don't believe me," he added with a glint of malice in his small eyes, "ask your wife. She knows him, right enough."

"Ben—" Dan had half risen.

"I'm going, I'm going," Ben said, edging around the partition.

By the time Dan had come around the end of the desk, Ben was slamming the main door to the office. Dan heard that final sound and his face set into hard lines.

"Sheriff?" Betty asked uncertainly. Her expression was curiously satisfied as well as sympathetic.

"It's nothing," Dan snapped, and turned away. "I'm going out. If you need me, use the radio to call me."

• • •

Ed Thurston took the sterile envelope and held it up to the light. "Two gauzes, are there?"

"Two. One's scrapings, the other is material brushed off the . . . suspect vehicle." Dan was sitting in the small emergency room with Ed.

"All right. Suspected of being involved in a hit-and-run, you said? You want the usual tissue checks, am I right?" He was already filling out a card.

Dan touched his shoulder. "Uh, Ed, do you mind if this isn't official just yet?"

Ed frowned, giving Dan a sharp look. "That's a bit irregular, Sheriff. Do you mind telling me why?" His pen was poised over the card, but he had stopped writing on it.

"Yeah, I know it's irregular," he said with a smile that didn't quite make it. "But I don't want to take action unless I know I'm on firm ground." It was waffling. He knew it; so did Ed Thurston.

The young doctor folded his arms, friendly annoyance in his features. "I'm going to make a guess, and you don't have to say a damn thing to me, Sheriff, but since I can't make any sense of that load of crap you just handed me, I've got a few assumptions I think you might like to hear. First, I think it's just possible that there are a few of our highly placed citizens who might, upon occasion, stretch the law for their own convenience. You'll concede the possibility, won't you?"

"For the moment, I will," Dan said.

"Good, good. Further, I will opine that it is just possible that on one or two occasions some of these excellent citizens have exceeded any tolerable limit of law stretching. However, since Potter's Bluff is, in every sense of the word, a small town, it is difficult to approach these august men over so potentially embarrassing an episode as the sort I might postulate, given what you've brought me." He paused, mustering his thoughts.

"You sound just like Dobbs," Dan interjected.

Ed shrugged. "Maybe pussyfooting does it to you, I don't know. Anyway, I figure you want to keep your ass covered while you investigate. And I must reluctantly admit that if any breath of this came to Dr. Tolliver's ears, he might take steps to squelch it, or make a few phone calls."

"It's possible," Dan said, thinking that it was close enough to the truth.

"And I don't mind going along with you," Ed said, grinning, "because I want my ass covered, too."

Dan chuckled. "Thanks for cooperating with me. I'll let you know what I turn up after I have your report."

"Maybe then you can tell me what it's all about." Ed let his wishes be known.

"Maybe I can," Dan agreed as he started toward the door. Then he added, as an afterthought, "How bad is Herman Ewing's arm?"

"What?"

"Herman Ewing's broken arm. I saw him this morning, and—"

Ed got off the desk. "Herman broke his arm? When did it happen?"

Dan looked at Ed, his brows lowering. "He said it happened yesterday. He said you took care of it." The sense of unreality, which had retreated somewhat during the last half hour, returned full force. Dan tried to recall exactly what Herman had told him outside the cafe.

"I haven't seen him. Maybe Vanderbury did it." Ed looked confused. "I never treated a broken arm yesterday. You can check the records if you like."

"I believe you," Dan said, nonetheless thinking that if Ed were willing to delay one report he would be willing to delay another. "But he said that you'd done it."

"I told you, I didn't." Ed's face had darkened. "This is the first I've heard of it, no matter what Herman says. How did he say it happened?"

"He was fixing the garage roof and fell," Dan answered distantly. "He didn't say anything more than that. I don't know if he called Dobbs for the ambulance or had someone drive him over. He's got a full, professional-looking cast on, so somebody must've done it for him."

"Well, Herman couldn't do it for himself, not one-handed. No one could," Ed said with an attempt at lightness.

"Still, who fixed it?" Dan asked. He and Ed exchanged a long look.

Ed shook his head. "Good luck in figuring it out. I'll ask the nurses about it, if you like. Maybe they know something."

"If you want. There's no rush," Dan said, without conviction. "Well, thanks, Ed, and I'll look forward to your call."

"Sure," Ed said, tapping the envelope. "This is easy. Herman is apt to be more difficult. I don't want to change jobs."

Chapter 7

Winslow's Service Station had just turned on their lights when Dan and Janet drove up in her Duster. Janet, in the passenger seat, gave Dan a quick, impatient look. "I just put some in this morning, on my way to work."

"I think it needs oil. You know you don't always have it checked." He pulled up beside the tanks and tapped the horn once.

"Well, that's possible," she said. "You usually remember for me." With a warm laugh she moved closer to him. "We don't have very many dates, you and I. There are times I think I saw more of you before we got married than I do now."

"It's work. You've got the school, and I have—"

"The crooks?" she suggested as she put her hand on his thigh. "We need time for ourselves, together, Danny."

A face appeared at the window and a hand tapped. "Folks? What can I do for you?" asked Freddie.

Dan rolled the window down. He was not looking at the attendant, but at Janet. "Yeah," he said as he studied his wife's face. "Put in a quart of thirty weight."

"He's new?" Janet asked as the young man walked away toward the display rack of oil cans.

"Yeah," Dan said, his eyes on her face. There was not the least flicker of recognition in her eyes as she glanced over at the attendant.

"He's a little old for this kind of job, isn't he?" she asked idly.

"I don't know. How old is he?" He saw her shrug. "Does he remind you of anyone? Someone from school, maybe?" Dan felt terrible, asking these leading questions and scrutinizing her answers as if she were a suspect. It was demeaning. If Freddie had not been at work under the hood, Dan might have started the car and driven off, putting an end to this inquiry.

"Not really. But you know how much kids change after high school. He could have gone there before I started teaching there. He looks old enough for that. Why not ask Paul Haskell about him? I think Paul remembers every student who's passed through those doors for the last twenty years." She looked up as the hood slammed down. "What's he done? Why are you interested in him?"

"Oh," Dan said uncomfortably, "he's a stranger, and strangers don't seem to be having very good luck in Potter's Bluff these days."

"Have you talked to him?" She smiled to take the sting out of the question.

"A little," Dan answered evasively.

"That'll be a dollar ten, Sheriff," Freddie said as he came back to the window.

Dan reached into his pocket and pulled out the correct change. "Here you are. See you later."

"Sure thing, Sheriff." He stood back as the Duster's engine roared into life.

At the corner, Dan passed a battered old pickup truck with POTTER'S BLUFF BOAT WORKS, ANTHONY CHAPMAN, PROPRIETOR, painted on the side. Although it was too dark to see the driver, Dan tapped his horn in greeting and it was returned by a squawk from the pickup's horn.

"Where's Tony going?" Janet wondered aloud. "I thought this was his poker night."

"He's probably going to Tom Barnet's place. It's out Weaver Road." Dan watched the pickup as it was swallowed up by the dusk. He was worried about Janet. She had not recognized Freddie, he was sure of that, but he was bothered by what Ben Collier had implied earlier.

"A penny for your thoughts, Danny," Janet murmured as he turned up their street. "Maybe a nickle, because of inflation."

He gave her a quick look out of the corner of his eye. After what had happened to him the night before, he was afraid to take his eyes off the road even for a moment. He noticed that she was smiling. "Nothing. This case."

"Dan," she said seriously, "you're letting this thing get to you. You mustn't do that, darling. There's no reason for it. You'll find out what happened and you'll handle it well. Don't let it take you over. Okay?"

"Okay," he said, turning into their driveway. It was a lie and he knew it.

• • •

At a crossroad there was a roadsign:

POTTER'S BLUFF 12
SMITHS LANDING 19
PORT HERON 87

And beside the sign, leaning against its support post, was a young woman hitchhiking. She wore the uniform of the rebellious young—faded levis and an army fatigue jacket over a plaid flannel shirt and well-worn hiking boots. There was a rucksack at her feet. She brushed her tangled hair out of her eyes and looked up hopefully as she heard the sound of an approaching automobile. The hitchhiker straightened up and took the traditional stance, arm extended, thumb out. She hated to admit it, but she was growing desperate. This stretch of road was not busy and she had seen only four cars in the last hour. She fixed a smile on her face.

The pickup rounded the bend at a good clip and very nearly passed her by. Then it skidded to a halt a couple hundred feet down the road and the door opened. A weathered hand poked out the window and a raspy voice called out, "Well, come on, if you want a ride."

The girl did not need a second invitation. She hoisted her rucksack and ran for the battered old truck.

"Climb in the other side," the voice told her. "It's unlocked."

She did as she was told, relieved that she would not have to camp out on a night that promised to be cold and dank. "Thanks, Mister," she said as she got into the cab.

The driver was old, his face seamed and weathered. He wore a shapeless seaman's sweater with the cuffs turned back and rolled to the elbows. There was a tattoo on one arm. He grinned at her. "You sure you wanna ride with me, young lady? How do you know I'm not a dirty old man?"

"I'll chance it," she told him with unruffled calm. "Men who ask that question don't hassle me. It's the ones who try to make bargains that give me the trouble."

The driver put the truck in gear. "How far are you goin'?"

"How far are *you* going?" she countered.

"I'm going into Potter's Bluff. On my way back from a job upriver. Some damn fool rammed his speedboat into a pier near Twin Trees Resort."

"I'll go into Potter's Bluff. Is there a place I can stay? Not too expensive?" She had a couple hundred dollars with her, along with her driver's license and passport, but thought it best not to mention such things.

"There's the Bowie Street Hotel in town, and the Hide-Away Motel a couple miles out, but I don't think it's your style. Better stay at the hotel." He drove fast but with confidence.

"Tell me where it is." It was off-season and in these little coastal towns most of the hotels were fairly inexpensive.

"I'll do better than that, I'll take you there. But first, I got to stop at the boatyard and leave off a couple of things. Don't worry about Potter's Bluff," he added in a kindly way. "It's a real nice place. You ever been there?"

"No. I never heard of it before," she said.

"It's nice," he repeated. "You headin' any place in particular?"

"No place in particular," she answered, and turned to look out at the fleeting shapes of the trees in the twilight.

"Maybe you ought to think 'bout stayin' here a spell. Damn sure rather live in a nice little town like this than a big city full of robbers and dope fiends and lyin' politicians on the take. Don't think I haven't been around, though. See that tattoo?" He pointed to the crossed anchors on his forearm. "I got those while I was in the navy. I been to France and Tangiers and Australia and Japan. I'm not just a hick who don't know beans about what it's like outside."

"Um-hum," she murmured to show she was listening.

"But I came back to Potter's Bluff. You can ask anyone in town and they'll tell you the same thing; they wouldn't live anywhere else." He pointed to a break in the trees ahead. "See it? We're almost there. That fence there—I don't know if you can see it—is the boatworks. We had a fire there a while back."

They were out of the trees now and heading along the gently sloping bluff toward the town which showed faintly against the last afterglow.

The driver turned down a side road. He had not yet flipped his lights on, but since he knew the way so well, the girl thought it best not to comment. She was tired and wanted a ride to the Bowie Street Hotel. The truck drove through leaning, blackened gates toward a shape like a warehouse or large workshop. The truck braked unevenly.

"I won't be more'n a minute or two. I gotta leave off a couple of things, like I said . . ." After opening the door and getting out, he paused. "I meant what I said about living here. You can ask anyone—they'll tell you the same thing." He slammed the door and stepped back.

The place smelled of burning and gasoline. The hitchhiker wrinkled her nose and tried to ignore the oppressive odor. She looked out the side window and dimly saw a burly man in mechanic's overalls. This ordinary sight reassured her. For a moment she had thought the place was deserted. Then a movement to her left caught her eye, and she turned to see a middle-aged woman in what appeared to be a pink flowered housecoat staring in at her from the driver's side.

Just then, the passenger door was pulled open and the driver grinned at her. "You ask anyone," he insisted. "They all know that Nils Uhri wouldn't live anyplace but Potter's Bluff."

The hitchhiker stared at him, uncomprehending but suddenly, horribly afraid. Beyond the driver she could make out a woman in a business suit and a tall man in a Coast Guard uniform. There was something strange about his head. And there was a girl, quite pretty, in a halter top, with a camera thrust in the top of her cutoff jeans. She felt strong hands pull her from the cab. As the hitchhiker stared at her, the girl took the camera out of her jeans, lifted it, and called out "Smile."

White, dazzling glare flooded the dark place, and the smell of gasoline was overpowering. The hitchhiker looked down in disbelief at her soaked clothing.

Then she heard the match.

• • •

Dan was halfway through his second lamb chop when the phone rang. He gave Janet an apologetic look as he rose to answer it.

"Betty, Sheriff," said the efficient voice.

"What is it, Betty?" Dan felt his meal coagulate in his stomach.

"Probably nothing, but I thought you'd better know about it. Phil Preston just called in from his place. He said that he saw something at the side of the road near the Narrow Point turnoff. He thought it might be a hit-and-run. It's most likely a dog or a deer, but I told him I'd let you know about it." She gave him the report with the air of one imparting spurious information.

"That's fine, Betty. I'd better check it out. With what's been going on here this last week . . ." He looked toward Janet and made an apologetic gesture. "I'll be on my way in five minutes."

"Danny!" Janet protested, getting up from the table.

"I'll wait for you to call in, Sheriff," Betty said. It was plain that she had overheard Janet.

"Thanks, Betty," Dan said coolly as he hung up. "Now, Janet—"

"Don't you 'now Janet' me, Daniel Stephen Gillis: I don't want to hear it. This is the first night we've had time to ourselves in over a week, and you're going to ruin it." Her face was flushed and there was a shine in her eyes that might be tears.

"There's something lying by the road out by the Narrow Point turn off. I'd better have a look at it, just in case." He tried to sound reasonable, but could hear the pleading sound in his voice.

"And what if it's a dog?" she demanded. "You're going out there now just to look at a dead dog!"

Dan sighed. "Let's not argue about it, Janet. I have to do it, and you know it. Every deputy I have is a volunteer, and if there is anything wrong out there, they have to call me about it, and I have to go. If I check it out now, it'll be over with and we can still have time together tonight." He had been looking forward to being alone with Janet. "I don't want to go, Janet, but you know I have to. Don't make it any harder for me than it is already."

She shrugged elaborately. "Well, there's a movie on television I wanted to watch."

"Janet, I'm sorry . . ."

She turned on him, rueful and piqued at once. "Oh, go on, damn you. Go drag that dog or whatever it is off the road. If you don't, it'll haunt you all night!" With a toss of her head, she went past him into the darkened living room.

• • •

Dan pulled to the shoulder. His headlights poked into the darkness, but he could not see very much. The turnoff for Narrow Point was fifty yards ahead. He left the motor running and the lights on as he got out of his squad car. He had brought along his wide-beam, high-power flashlight, and as he switched it on, the blue-tinged glare was reassuringly bright. He went to the right side of the car and looked along the side of the road, the flashlight revealing the ground in stark colors.

When he had gone as far as the turnoff, he crossed to the other side of the road. On this side there was a shallow ditch that ran parallel to the highway.

Seen briefly, the object resembled the tumbled body of an animal. But it wasn't.

The clothes were black and the features

obliterated. Dan stopped still and fought the revulsion and nausea that swept through him. Another one! Burned, abandoned, unrecognizable. He stumbled back across the road to his squad car and reached for the radio microphone. Once he had it in his hand, however, he sat, his lips pressed together, his face the color of chalk, as he tried to block the sight from his mind. Finally he pressed the button.

"Betty?" he said in a thick whisper.

"Unit one ready, Sheriff."

"Damn it, Betty, cut the crap! I need help out here. We've got another body on our hands! Now, patch me through to Dobbs." He had not meant to shout at her. He would apologize later, he told himself. Right now, he needed the coroner and his ambulance out here.

"I'm trying to reach Dobbs," Betty said in a wounded tone.

"Don't try; get him!" Dan found to his disgust that his hands were shaking. He blinked against the wetness in his eyes. Christ, what was happening to him? To Potter's Bluff? He clamped his teeth together and hoped that Dobbs wouldn't answer at once.

"I'm calling the mortuary now, Sheriff—the after-hours number," Betty informed him icily. "The line is ringing." There was a pause and then Betty said, "Mr. Dobbs, Sheriff Gillis would like to speak with you."

"Oh, would he?" Dobbs voice crackled down the line. "I'm not sure I want to talk to him. He's given me no end of trouble these last few days. He's not the most opportune man in this town. Tell him I'll call him back—"

Dan shouted into the microphone, "Dobbs, there's another one out by the turnoff to Narrow Point. Burned. Dead. Get out here!" He thumbed the button and almost flung the microphone across the front seat. A few moments later he heard Betty signal him, but he had already gotten up and was going, with leaden steps, back across the road to the charred heap lying in the ditch.

• • •

"Dear, dear me," Dobbs said mildly as he bent over the corpse. "How distressing. Judging by the condition of that one hand that is more or less untouched, she was quite young. I can see why you were disturbed, Sheriff. Gracious, she can't have been here very long, can she?" He stood up and rubbed his hands, either as an indication of fastidiousness or delight—it was impossible to tell which.

"That's not my concern, Dobbs, it's yours," Dan said shortly.

"True, very true. And I will do all that I can, I assure you. You say that Phil Preston alerted you to this latest . . . misfortune. How very surprising. Phil is a most estimable man in his way—please don't mistake my meaning—but one would hardly cast him in the role of Good Samaritan. Yet he tells you of this. There are always surprises to be had in life, aren't there, Sheriff?" Dobbs started toward his ambulance at a brisk pace. "I'm afraid you'll have to help me. My worthy apprentice is deep in the toils of chemical formulae and could not be spared for this errand."

Dan did not want to handle the body, but he forced himself to keep his voice calm. "Right. Two man job."

"Oh, yes, certainly." He opened the back door of the ambulance and pulled out the stretcher. "You may have noticed that rigor is setting in, and that always makes moving the body difficult. The extensive damage to the skin is distressing. Do you still subscribe to your theory of malicious intent, Sheriff?" He was carrying the stretcher across the road as he talked, turning back over his shoulder to talk to Dan as he went.

"Don't you?" Dan asked, incredulous.

"It seems likely. There may be a new fad in suicide. That *doesn't* seem likely. But if this is the work of a maniac"—he paused to set the stretcher down beside the body—"then where is he? Jack the Ripper might be able to vanish into the teeming slums of Whitechapel, but this is Potter's Bluff. We all know each other. It could be that the neighbors are in on it, but that would indicate a conspiracy, and that strikes me as most unlikely. Who would head it? Tubby Bass? What about Clark Vanderbury? Penny Strickland? You see how unconvincing that possibility is. So you are left with two equally unacceptable alternatives. Or three, if you seriously entertain the possibility of a suicide epidemic. Unbeknownst to us, Potter's Bluff has become the place to die. Lends a certain glamour to the town, don't you think?" His gnomish face wrinkled up with his smile and he patted Dan on the arm. "We'll get this unsavory task behind us, and by then you may have come up with a more plausible explanation for the perturbing events of the last week."

• • •

"It wasn't a dog," Dan said quietly as he came into the living room where Janet was still watching television.

She looked up at him. "What?"

"It wasn't a dog." He dropped into his chair and stared at nothing in particular. "It was a woman, pretty young. She was burned, like the others. Someone had poured gasoline over her and set fire to her." He spoke in a monotone, his eyes open so that he did not have to see her in his mind again.

"Oh, Danny." Janet got up and turned off the television. "How awful."

"Dobbs has taken her back to the mortuary. He's taken a few samples of skin—I dropped them off at the hospital on the way home—so the cause of death can be confirmed. Gasoline leaves traces on the skin when it burns, and for the record, he wants it verified." He spoke as if reading words he did not know.

Janet was standing by his chair now, her hand touching his face. "You'll handle it, Danny. Right now, you should rest."

He could not laugh, not even sarcastically.

"You know better than that. How can I rest, after that? I can't get the sight of her out of my mind now, and I'm awake. If I go to sleep . . ."

She bent and kissed his ear. "Leave that to me. I'll make you forget her."

He was glad to open his arms to her, to be lost in her. And though the sight of that burned woman came back to him toward morning, for most of the night Janet's body kept that hellish vision away.

• • •

Ed Thurston's office was the smallest one at the hospital, and his desk was the oldest. Instead of a couch for his visitors, he had two ladder-back chairs. His bookcases were cheap metal.

"You had quite a night last night." He was fresh from home, his face shiny and newly shaved and his hair not quite dry. He lit a cigarette and pointed to one of the two chairs. "Sit down."

Dan sat. In comparison to Ed, he was haggard. His eyes were dark-rimmed, his khaki uniform a little less easily worn. "Yeah, it was that."

"The tissue samples show residues indicating that the body had been in contact with burning gasoline. That's not exactly surprising. Dobbs is sending over dental impressions later today. I said I'd process them for him. We don't have anything much to go on. The poor kid was one of those wandering ones, from the look of it." He studied Dan. "You look shitty,

Sheriff. No insult intended. You're letting this wear you down."

"Wouldn't you, in my place? I don't have any help in town, and I've tacitly agreed not to call in the county for the time being. That was before this last death. I had a call from Tubby before I left the house, reminding me that I'd agreed to be circumspect. If I want his continued cooperation, then no county."

"But the sheriff's office is a county office," Ed reminded him reasonably. "Won't someone over there start asking questions?"

"Not so long as I continue to work on the case. That's why the whole Undersheriff system was developed. Me, Brad Taylor in Westbend, Pat Sontag in Brenton, Eric Watson in Hollis, and Randy Sims in Farleyville—we're all pretty much on our own. A county this size, and rural, can't depend entirely on deputies, you know. They tried that and it didn't work. And let's face it, George Widdowes would rather stay at the county seat as much as he can. So long as the five of us do our jobs, Widdowes leaves us alone. And right now, that suits me fine. If George Widdowes knew about these killings, he'd make political hay with them, and nothing would get done." Dan was startled by this outburst almost as much as Ed was.

"Well," Ed said slowly, "if that's the way you want to do it."

"I don't know," Dan said wearily. "I just know that I don't want the county messing in this, and not simply as a favor to Horace Andrews and Tubby Bass."

"Okay, we'll do it that way." Ed finished

his cigarette and stubbed it out in his olive plastic ashtray. "And the samples you left off yesterday?"

"Have you got a report on them?"

"Yep. I did the tests last night. I've got the report right here"—he lifted a few yellow, legal-sized sheets with crabbed writing on them—"just as I did them. I haven't handed them over to the secretary yet because I haven't done an entry form on them. Have you made up your mind yet whether you want this to be official?"

"I'd rather it was confidential, but if you feel you'd better log it in, go ahead." Dan sat a little straighter in his chair, his hands in his lap locked together.

"Let me tell you about them. Maybe you'll change your mind." Ed had picked up a pencil and he tapped it on the yellow sheets of paper. "When did this hit-and-run take place, do you have any idea?"

"A couple nights ago, I think," Dan said cautiously.

Ed sighed and shook his head. "Then this can't be right. There's no way the material you gave me could be involved."

"What? But that's not possible!"

"It's got to be," Ed told him. "Look, with everything that's been going on, you couldn't have mixed it up with another piece of evidence, from an earlier accident, could you?"

"An earlier accident? No way." He saw the frown deepen in Ed's face. "What is it? What's wrong?"

Ed propped the pencil behind his ear.

"Well, if that's the case, this is weirder than I thought. Look, I checked my results three times, and they came out the same each time. I know that the equipment is good, and I used a different chemical batch the second time I did the tests. So that kind of error doesn't account for it. Are you sure you checked the right car?"

"Absolutely. That's one thing I'm sure of."

"It can't have been the car. You've made a wrong identification. Could that have happened?" Ed was growing more uneasy.

"It's impossible."

"Well, you might want to send this to the county seat or to the crime lab upstate at the capital, but they'll tell you the same thing. These bits of flesh are from a body that has been dead for at least three or four months."

Dan felt himself go white. "You're sure?"

"That's what I just told you. So, you see, whenever that car hit someone, it wasn't a couple days ago. It had to have been last summer sometime. There's another thing that bothers me. In one of the samples there was a substance that might have been embalming fluid. Now before you start yelling at me about it, let me tell you that it was just a trace, hardly enough to get a reading from, and that might not be right. Is there someone in town who ran over a disinterred corpse recently? Because that's the only way this tissue could be involved in a recent hit-and-run." Ed tipped his chair back, balancing on the two rear legs. "You can see why this one bothers me, Dan."

Dan's face was ghastly. "And you can see why it bothers me." He stood up, pleasantly surprised that his knees did not buckle. "I think you better keep that report under your hat, don't you?"

"Damn right."

• • •

In the Potter's Bluff Cafe the conversation was subdued but far from dull. Only Harry Clemens seemed to find any amusement in the latest death.

"Hey, a girl this time—that's different. Wonder what happened to her before the gasoline? Could'a been anything." He rolled his eyes upward and put his hand on his paunch, rubbing suggestively.

"If you'd seen her," Phil Preston said with a shudder, "you wouldn't find that funny. I only had a quick look at her, and that was more'n enough. It was like someone left the roast in the oven too long. No hair, most of the features gone, the bits of clothes falling off like soot . . . It was really horrible. When I saw her, I didn't think it could be a person. And when I found out that it was—"

"Still, the fire might have covered up something," Harry said, his grin widening. "I don't think they checked out Nils or the guy we took out of the van, but it's possible that they'd had . . . things done to them. You know what it can be like. There's some pretty strange people who live around here, and sure as hell, somebody's getting his jollies doing in these guys. Maybe they've been doin' more than fryin'. That's what I think, anyway." He held up his coffee cup and called out for Penny Strickland.

Aaron was very quiet and still. "I've been thinking it over, and I wouldn't be surprised if it was devil worshipers. Stands to reason, all that burning. It's not like those Manson murders in Hollywood. This is different. Three people all burned, people without families, no one to raise a ruckus." His eyes, seen through the lenses, were large and watery, much too large for his head.

"Devil worshipers!" Harry laughed. "This ain't the Dark Ages. People don't do that here. You read about people like that in the cities, and that's different. But out here? If anything like that was going on, we'd know about it. Hell, it might be kinda fun to give it a try."

Penny came to the table and poured coffee for Harry and then the others. "I think you're all being terrible. That poor girl! And you, Harry, you think it's a joke that somebody burned her. How'd you like it if it was Inez or Stephanie or Janet or Helen or Betty? Or me? Would you think it's funny then?"

"But that's just my point," Harry said, giving Penny's flank a pat before she could get out of range. "Nobody here gives a damn about the victims. It's real neat that way. The sheriff can go around asking questions from now till doomsday and never has to lock anybody up, and everyone in town knows they're safe. Me, I wouldn't want to stay arround here if I was a stranger. No, sir. No way."

Phil got up from the table. "I can't listen to this any longer. Sorry, Harry." He was on his way before Harry could protest, and as he reached the door, it opened and Sam Evans came in. Phil nodded to him quickly, like a suspect in the presence of an investigator, put money on the counter by the cash register, and left.

"What's eating him?" Sam Evans asked.

"Didn't you hear about the new one?" Harry called out delightedly. "Well, Phil found her. Shook him up some. He'll get over it."

Sam's eyes flickered. "I heard. Talked to the sheriff this morning." He came over to the table, to the chair Phil had just vacated. "Harry, if I were you, I wouldn't be noisy about this. There's too much going on. Keep a lid on it?"

"Why? You scared too, Sam?" Harry leaned back in his chair and laughed. "You're all a bunch of old ladies. I'm telling you, none of us have to worry about it. We *live* here. Whoever's doing the killing ain't gonna touch any of us!"

• • •

Horace Andrews had eyebrows that made him appear to be hiding in a bush; his small, bright eyes peeked out at the world from their protection. He was a portly man of medium height and strained cordiality. He was used to the idea of being an important person in Potter's Bluff and as such expected to be deferred to by most of its citizens. He frowned at Dan as the sheriff closed the door to Andrews' private office.

"Now, Sheriff, I didn't ask you to stop by to see me for no reason. I wouldn't waste your time when you have so much on your mind. You're handling this crisis most discreetly, and I assure you that the mayor and I appreciate it. But I do think that it's time you and I discussed the matter."

Dan stood, waiting for Andrews to make himself clear. He had just come from seeing Dobbs and had had one more look at the gruesome body of the young woman.

"I have said very little in the *Sentinel* about these deaths. I don't feel that it is in the community interest to dwell on such occurrences," Andrews announced as he turned his leather chair forward. "It would be best to continue in this way until you have some encouraging news, I believe. There are those who use the press irresponsibly, but I am not one of them, and trust I will never be one of them."

Dan made his gambit: "I'd prefer it if you'd print a bit of information about the killings. There may be people in town with information that could help me, and it might put a stop to some of the more dangerous rumors that have been circulating the last couple of days. If someone has any lead on the identity of the unknown victims, I want to know about it. The *Sentinel* can be a great deal of help there. A simple request for information, no matter how minor or insignificant, could provide my office with valuable leads."

"I hadn't considered that," Andrews said. His tone implied he was not pleased to do so now.

"There are also a few precautions that people may want to take, for their own safety, and the paper is the best place to run such material. Three deaths from burning—"

Horace Andrews interrupted him. "You're probably right, and if there are any more such deaths in this area, then I'll devote most of an issue to the problem. But I don't think it would be appropriate to do such a story now."

"You mean that because the victims so far have been either strangers or Nils Uhri, that it's not necessary to warn the people of Potter's Bluff that there is a murderer on the loose? What would it take to convince you otherwise?" Dan hooked his thumbs in the sides of his belt and waited.

"Sheriff, you admit that you don't know what is actually happening here, yet you are willing to throw the town into panic." Horace waited, an unctuous smile on his thin-lipped, cupid's-bow mouth.

"It's true that I don't know much, except that there are three dead bodies that weren't here last week. There isn't a great deal to go on with these killings. I can't tell you if they have anything in common other than being outsiders in one way or another. That's why identifying them is so important. I have that much of a pattern to go on, but only after the fact, and that's not a very useful time for it." Dan paused, wishing desperately that he had even a bit more information to present to the justice of the peace. "Dobbs is making a full report on the woman we found last night, and the hospital has records on the man who was killed there. You'll have to wait for the formal insurance statement to Tony Chapman about Nils Uhri, but I think it's safe to assume he's part of this outrage."

Andrews heard Dan out, pulling his lower lip thoughtfully as the sheriff talked. At the end he was silent for a moment. "The reports are helpful, I can see that. You're over a barrel without more community assistance, that's obvious. You'll have to speak to a fair number of our citizens, won't you?"

"It's likely."

"And the more current the information, the more useful it can be," Andrews said, as if this were news to Dan. "I begin to see why you want me to run a report. Very well, Sheriff. I'll revise my editorial and encourage our people to contact you if they have any information that might have a bearing on these tragic occurrences."

Briefly, Dan wondered if Andrews and Bass talked that way at home, over drinks. "Thanks. It would be of help."

"Glad to do it. A pleasure, Dan." He held out his hand, indicating that he regarded their conversation as over.

"Oh, that request goes for you, too, of course," Dan remarked casually. "A man in your position hears a lot. I know you'll bear that in mind."

"Naturally," Andrews said, but it seemed to Dan that his tone was a shade less hearty and the hidden eyes glistened with fear.

Chapter 8

Janet arrived home a little after four to find Dan already there. He was in the living room, rummaging through the drawers of the hideous antique desk in the alcove under the attic stairs.

"This is a pleasant surprise," she said, a tinge of sarcasm in her voice when Dan did not look up as she came in.

"I don't have time right now, honey," he told her as he pulled out yet another drawer and pawed through the contents. "Cleaners receipts for the last five years. Don't you ever throw them away?"

"I doubt it." She came a few steps nearer and stood watching him. "What're you looking for? Maybe I can help you."

He closed that drawer and went on to the next. "I had some shells in one of these drawers. Did you see them?" He could not keep the anxiety out of his voice now, and he could feel tension in his shoulders and neck.

"Shells? When were you at the beach?"

He cut her laughter short. "Bullets! Bullets, Janet."

She shrugged, though a fine line rose between her brows. "God knows. I don't use them. Why would I want them? Why do *you* want them?"

Dan had no answer for her. He slammed the last drawer shut and went across the room to the coffee table. There were three drawers under its glossy top, and he pulled one open. A stack of old Christmas cards met his eye. He pushed that drawer closed and reached for the next. "What's this?"

The book was oversized, elegantly bound in stamped leather: WITCHCRAFT AND VOODOOISM, *Shamanism and Animism in Traditional Pagan Religion.*

Dan took the volume from the drawer and held it out to Janet. For an instant her eyes avoided his, shiny with anger, and then she looked back at him. "You know I had that. You've seen it before."

"I don't remember it." There was a ribbon in the book, and he opened it to the page it marked: "which ancient folklore has, they can only be made from persons dying by sudden and violent means so that the death . . ."

"I've found your bullets for you." Janet had opened the third drawer and held up a small box.

Dan regarded her evenly. "You used to do a lot of reading about occultism, didn't you? Witchcraft, the supernatural, shamanism, all that sort of thing?"

"Sure. You know I did. I still do. My master's thesis was on the treatment of sixteenth-century suspected witches, remember? You read it before I submitted it. You said it was a lot of nonsense. That was one of my texts; you called it mumbo jumbo." She offered him the box of bullets, her other hand open to take the book.

"Why are you reading this now? You finished your thesis years ago." He refused to look at the box in her hand.

"I'm brushing up on it. I've been giving lectures at school on anthropology and social development. Kids love creepy things, and they learn better if they're entertained. Material like this keeps them from getting bored in class."

Dan put the book down on the coffee table.

Janet continued, "The kids were fascinated when I introduced the subject, so I've been doing more of it. Roberta Andrews is doing a report on the pre-Christian Hawaiians and Chris Winslow is making a model of Stonehenge. That kind of interest is rare in schoolkids these days." She abandoned her defensive posture. "I don't like this, Danny. You know I am a good teacher. Why do I have to explain myself like this?"

"I'm sorry." It was inadequate. Janet had every right to be insulted by the way he was behaving. "You know how much pressure I've been under. I get worried—"

"Oh, Danny, I know you do." She picked up the book and put it back in the drawer. "It's been terrible. If snapping at me makes it easier, I suppose you ought to go ahead and do it, but it makes me feel pretty rotten. What did you think I was doing? Sacrificing virgins at the autumnal equinox?"

That sounded so ludicrous that Dan gave a tight laugh. "I'm beginning to think that somebody is."

"That's not funny," Janet said after a second's pause.

"I didn't mean it to be." They stood for a moment, their eyes locked, and said nothing. "I'm keyed up, Janet. You haven't seen the bodies."

Janet came closer so that she could put her hands on his shoulders. "I'm glad I haven't. I doubt I could stand it. I don't know how you're able to take it. There are times I think this job demands too much of you. George Widdowes demands more than he should from you."

"Don't blame George," Dan said. "He doesn't know what's going on in Potter's Bluff, and for the time being, we want to keep it that way. If word of these deaths gets out, then the town could turn into a circus, and you know how little people would like that." He took one of Janet's hands and led her to the couch. "Imagine it. Potter's Bluff on the news as the new murder capital of the good old USA. John Chancellor reciting per capita incidents of murder in, oh, Chicago, as compared to Potter's Bluff. Horace Andrews would have a stroke. Think of Dan Rather interviewing Harry Clemens. Wouldn't that do this town a world of good? We'd have people all over the place for a month or so, and then we'd be shunned. You know that's true. You've seen it happen before.

Tubby Bass wouldn't sell another house in his life and you and I would be out of jobs, because most of the town would move away. We'd be like Narrow Point in less than a year."

"I don't know about that," she said slowly. "People here might surprise you. They're pretty loyal to their town." She rested her head on his shoulder. "I know what you mean though. It might be a good idea not to put it to the test."

Dan kissed her gently, her forehead, the arch of her brow, her upper lip. "I know I'm being impossible, but bear with me, will you, Janet? This case is the thing that's doing it to me. When it's solved—look, I promise you we'll have a vacation, you and me. You tell me where you want to go, and I'll get us there if I have to hock everything we own. Okay?"

She chuckled. "Fine, so long as it isn't during the school year. And speaking of the school year," she went on more briskly, "did you give that film to Ernie to develop?"

"Film?" Dan asked.

"Oh, Danny, I told you it was a project." She tried to look annoyed, but Dan thought she was adorable.

"No. Honey, I'm sorry. I forgot."

"You've got a lot on your mind, I know, I know. But the kids . . . You didn't lose it, did you?"

"No, I've got it. It's in the trunk of the car, I think." He could vaguely remember putting it there. He'd check it out soon. "I'll make sure it gets done, Janet. I promise you."

"The kids worked so hard on this project."

The soft touch she gave his hand did not entirely eliminate the reproach from her manner. "It means a lot to them."

Dan gave her a brusque, guilty answer. "I'll take care of it."

• • •

Dan was about to leave the next morning when he got a call from Ed Thurston at the hospital. "Nothing really important. I was running the tests on those tissue samples you gave me, the ones from the hit-and-run?"

"The ones from a corpse," Dan said with irritation.

"That's the guy. I've got one bit of additional information. It probably doesn't mean anything, but there might be something in your records that would give you a clue, and since you have so little to go on—"

"Get to the point!" Dan snapped.

"There were traces, really minute traces, of what's probably insulin in the tissue. Not as you'd expect to find it. I wish I had a little more material to work with, but there's no help for that, is there?" He chuckled without humor.

"What does that indicate?" Playing twenty questions with Ed did not amuse Dan.

"It *may* mean—and understand, it's not positive, since I'm not absolutely certain that this is insulin at all—that the corpse was diabetic. If you check over records at the hospital here and send out the information, you might turn up something worthwhile. You want someone who died two to three months ago who may have had diabetes." He paused. "Well, that's it. I told you it might not be worth a great deal, but you might think about it."

"Sure. Thanks." He started to hang up, but asked, on impulse, "Ed, if the guy had been dead for that long, why would the insulin show up at all? Doesn't that stuff change or deteriorate, along with the body?"

"Sure. Everything does. That's why I said I'm not sure it's insulin. And that's another thing," he added with increased curiosity. "If it *is* insulin, then I don't know how to interpret it."

"Why's that?"

"Well," Ed said uneasily, "as near as I can figure, to have insulin in that state on this skin, somebody had to pour it over him when he'd been dead a couple of months. I don't know what to make of it."

Dan thought for a moment. "Suppose the guy was diabetic and kept a spare on him, and some was in the suit he was buried in, and after a while it leaked . . . ?" It sounded completely unbelievable to him, and saying it out loud made it seem even more absurd.

"The stuff was fairly recent. And you've got to keep in mind that I'm not wholly satisfied that the stuff is insulin at all. I'm just saying that I found minute traces of something that resembles insulin. Give me more of it and I'll be more positive." Ed coughed. "Look, forget this. It's probably nothing. Could be that

Josie didn't clean off her equipment the way she should have and this is an overlap from something else."

"Do you believe that it's an overlap?" Dan asked in a tone that demanded an answer.

Ed paused. "No. As impossible as it sounds, I think that the guy had insulin, or something like insulin, applied to his skin after—*long* after—his death." After this admission, Ed almost held his breath.

"Thanks," Dan said, meaning it this time. "I'll talk to you later. Keep me posted, Ed." He heard the few words Ed muttered as he hung up, then put the receiver on its cradle. For the better part of two minutes he stared thoughtfully at the kitchen sink, then went out to his squad car.

• • •

Dan had found the film where he had left it, in the trunk. He was more relieved than he would willingly admit to Janet that he had not lost the film. He drove into town and stopped at Ernie Sutton's store. There were magazines, paperbacks, lotions, greeting cards, and fishing tackle in the front, then a few shelves of shampoo, cosmetics and cold remedies, and last, the pharmacy counter and photo-processing stand. Ernie Sutton sat on a tall stool by the counter. Like his older cousin Jake, he was aging without any grace whatsoever. But while Jake was lean, bushy-browed and sardonic, Ernie was nearly hairless and softly pear-shaped. Both men had the large Sutton nose and long, narrow jaw, but beyond that the resemblance ceased.

"Dan, Dan, how good to see you!" Ernie caroled in his fluty voice. "You haven't been in here often enough. I've just got in a new line of pipes, if you'd like to have a look at them."

"I don't smoke," Dan reminded him as he came up to the counter.

"No, of course you don't. But you might like the pipes. About the only person in town who appreciates them is Dobbs." When disappointed, Ernie had something of the lugubrious look of a Basset hound.

"We don't have very many sophisticates in Potter's Bluff," Dan said, hoping that Ernie would regard that as commiseration.

"All they buy is cigarettes. Except for old Mrs. Whitney. She buys snuff." He said this last in a delighted whisper, as if imparting a secret, though everyone knew about Edna Whitney's snuff-taking.

"Ernie," Dan said after a moment, "I've got some film here I want you to develop for me, okay?"

"Sure, Dan. Glad to do it. What is it?" His eyes turned bright and he waited for an answer.

"You . . . might call it evidence," he answered hesitantly.

"Has something to do with all these terrible burnings?" Ernie lifted his baby-fine brows toward his shiny pink pate.

"It might," Dan said carefully, thinking

that it was as honest an answer as any he could give.

"Oh, Dan, you don't need to be so cagey with me," Ernie said. "Why, I remember you when you and your brother used to come in to steal penny candy after baseball practice." Ernie's round face glowed with his good nature.

"Brother?" Dan repeated, taken aback. "I don't have a brother, Ernie. I never did." For a second he felt distressed, as though he had once had a brother and had unforgivably forgotten him.

"Eh? Not have—" Ernie swallowed guiltily. "I've been here too long, that's what it is, Dan. I've run this place forty-two years and sometimes they all run together. Still, I thought for sure . . ." His voice trailed off.

Dan forced a smile. "Hell, Ernie, it's easy enough to do. I have to stop myself every now and then with people. If I'm this bad in Potter's Bluff, then what would I be like in a big city? No wonder city cops feel alienated."

"Sure. Stands to reason." Ernie grinned ingratiatingly, then adroitly changed the subject. "This film—anything special about it?"

"How do you mean, special?"

"Is it overexposed, underexposed, taken with floodlights, anything of that nature?"

Dan shook his head. "I don't know, Ernie. I don't know what's on it. And that's another thing," he went on more quietly. "Whatever there is on that film, will you keep it to yourself? I'd rather you don't even mention you have it. Not to anyone." What had come over him, Dan wondered. This was only Janet's class project and he was behaving as if there were something incriminating on the roll. Yet he could not tell Ernie that it was a joke he was playing, because he did not believe it was. "Don't even say anything to Janet if she comes in. I don't . . . want to upset her."

Ernie gave Dan a wide, conspiratorial wink. "Yes, Sheriff. Yes, siree!"

"When do you think the film'll be ready?" he asked, not willing to go along with Ernie's clowning.

"Oh, a day or two. Pick it around noon, day after tomorrow. I'll have it for you then."

"Okay. I'll see you then." He stepped back from the counter. "And Ernie, I mean it. Don't mention this to anyone. It's important that you don't."

Ernie waved. "Whatever you say, Sheriff."

• • •

Tubby Bass shook hands with Ron Cousins. "Well, it's been a pleasure dealing with you folks. Wish we had more people like you coming to Potter's Bluff. We need a few more like you."

"Well, we'll probably be back. We're going to stop by that place you mentioned on Cove Road." He meant this to sound encouraging and was pleased to see Bass smile.

"That's a good house. New roof put on four years ago. Termite inspection in August said that it's sound. It was rewired in '62. It even has its own generator for when we have storms. A place that far out, the power can go off for half a day in very bad weather."

"I still like the Victorian on the bluff," Linda said wistfully.

Tubby switched leads without missing a beat. "That's a grand place. Get the right people in there, fix it up right, and that would be a real showplace. Those old Victorians are good investments, if you restore them properly. Five years from now, you could double its value."

"Yeah," Ron said, trying to break away. "Well, we'll think about it. I'll call you in a day or two."

"Excellent. Excellent." Tubby rubbed his hands together and stepped back, then said, as if it had just occurred to him, "Say, if you're going over to Cove Road, you don't want to come all the way back into town and then double back on the highway, do you? You'll lose more'n ninety minutes that way. Tell you what: when you've seen the house, come back to Miller Street and turn left. I know, I know,"—Bass raised his hands to forestall Ron's objections—"that's away from the town and the highway, but if you go out Miller Street past the McDermott place, you can pick up the back road to the Farleyville highway. It's a narrow road, but the scenery is pretty and you'll knock a lot of miles off your trip. Remember, turn left on Miller, go out past the McDermott place, and take the first fork to the north. Got that?"

"Sure," Ron said, repeating the instructions to himself. "Thanks, Mr. Bass. That's kind of you." He took Linda's arm and beckoned to Jamie.

Tubby closed the door and watched as the Cousins got into their car. He waved once, smiling a smile that did not reach his eyes.

• • •

G. William Dobbs, B.S., M.S., M.D., etc., etc., was whistling as he came into the workroom of his mortuary. He had a stack of baroque trumpet records on the stereo and at the moment the shrill, optimistic sounds of Vivaldi ricocheted merrily off the tile walls. Dobbs liked Vivaldi, taking real pleasure in the joyous rapidity of it. He could never understand morticians who insisted on playing soft, somber music to work by. It was all very well to have hymns and gentle, inoffensive tunes played in the reposing room, but when it came to work, then, by God, he wanted something invigorating.

Dobbs stopped by the only occupied table and stared down at the shape under the sheet. His face was serious now, and his eyes bright. He reached down with care and drew the cloth back. The corpse of the hitchhiker waited for him.

The skin was crusted and black, but it had been washed. There were no broken bones to give the limbs harsh, unnatural angles, and no peeling away of the tissue, as the sea so often treated its victims. One of the ears was burned away, but the other was intact, though charred.

Dobbs touched this knowledgeably. "Yes," he said to himself between whistles, "yes, there's enough left to work with. Pity about the nose, but there's a bit of the cartilege left. Something can be arranged."

The Vivaldi ended and was replaced by the first of six Purcell Voluntaries. Dobbs did not like Purcell nearly as much as Vivaldi.

Dobbs folded the sheet and then, using it as a pillow, carefully put it under the body's head. "That's better. Yes, indeed. It's much better. My dear, you have been subjected to the most disgraceful ill use. That is an insult I will avenge for you. You're so lovely, so frail, so young. You've been cheated of your greatest beauty. Life betrayed you, but you have not lost. How could anyone mar such a face, such splendid youth? You must not worry. This—this is only temporary. You are not doomed to be so . . . besmirched. You have my word on it. You will not remain this blackened travesty of yourself. My dear, I will make you beautiful . . . again." He turned and selected one of his tool carts and rolled it near the table.

"First," he explained as he picked up one of the scalpels, "I must get rid of the ragged edges. Nothing uneven to mar you. Just a very minor procedure, my dear. A nick there, a snip here, and there will be less difficulty, don't you know?" As he spoke, he trimmed away the ragged, charred part of her remaining ear, then cut away the hard, crusted skin of her neck, exposing some of the smooth muscles beneath. He loosened the burned and ruptured skin on her face, taking care to keep as much of the lips as he could. "Mouths are tricksy things, my dear," he explained as he bent close over her. "One little slip with the knife and a sweet smile becomes a sneer. That would never do. If you were an aged banker who had lived your life saying no to everything but greed, then I would perhaps not be so careful, or perhaps nature would already have carved that curl in the lip without my assistance. But you were so young, and life had not yet put much of a stamp on you, had it?" He stood back to give his handiwork critical inspection. "Not too bad, if I say so myself. With a degree of care on my part, I think you will be quite satisfied with the outcome of my treatment." He reached over and picked up a cotton swab. "There are a few preparations, my dear. First I'll have to put on some of my special compound." He began to smear a translucent amber gel across her face. "This is my very own trade secret, my dear, developed after years of study and modification. It's astounding how much the beginning of life can affect the end of it. Had you noticed? And how much the tools of veterinarians can have very human applications. Take this substance. Part of it is veterinary tissue cement. It will keep your damaged muscles from giving way entirely. Remarkable stuff. Truly remarkable. A molecular binder of the very highest order. I've improved it a bit, as well." Now he was smoothing the gel on her neck and shoulders. "Over the years, embryology has contributed a great deal to my area of expertise. I use a modified form of twin polypeptide chains that were identified more than thirty years ago as nerve growth factors. You may consider it a stimulant, if you wish. It has some of that function. You may find it . . . refreshing."

Dobbs had finished with his secret compound and he stood back once again. "I'll give you about ten minutes alone. There is a special attachment to your table that will conduct a low-grade current through it which will have a beneficial effect on my compound. I've been trying to think of a name for it. How does *Dobbs's Wonder Cream* strike you? Or *Dobbs's Miracle Gelée?* I'm a recognized expert in the morticians' world, and this is my crowning achievement. You'll discover what I mean in a short while." There was a toggle switch at the head of the table and Dobbs turned it on. "I'll return shortly, my dear. I must ask that you be patient a little longer."

With victorious Purcell trumpets ringing in his ears, Dobbs left the workroom and strolled out toward the reception desk where Jimmy had just started to work on his history assignment.

• • •

The Potter's Bluff Cafe was half empty. The last of the lunch crowd was just finishing up and the majority of the afternoon crowd had not yet arrived. Penny Strickland sat behind the counter, a tuna sandwich on the plate in front of her. She had that harried look which indicated a busy lunch crowd. As Herman Ewing came in the door, she sighed without apology. "Coffee, Herman?"

"O' course," he said as he pulled out the head chair at the center table. "I tell you, this cast is a nuisance." He was not wearing his sling today, and his arm thunked as he put it down on the table. "You seen Phil yet, or Aaron?"

"Not yet," Penny said as she came around the counter with a tray. "I'm gonna leave the pot with you, Herman. Otherwise I'll spend the next half hour running back and forth between here and the kitchen. We're shorthanded, and I've gotta help get ready for the dinner crowd."

Herman was stirring another cup of coffee when the door opened and Phil Preston came into the Potter's Bluff Cafe. "Hi there, Herman," he said as he hung up his jacket by the door. "How's the arm?"

"Gettin' better." He shoved one of the chairs out with his foot.

The door opened again and Sam Evans came over to the table. "You fellas heard anything about something going on out at the old Hollister place tonight?" He took a seat and reached for a mug. "I had a call ten, fifteen minutes ago."

"The Hollister place?" Phil asked. "Nothing yet. But I haven't been home since ten this morning."

"Yeah, old Jake Sutton told me about it," Herman said. "He called me a while ago. Said he had a couple more calls to make."

"Who's gonna be there?" Phil said to Sam.

"Most of the town, I guess. One of those special occasions." He sugared his coffee and leaned back from the table. "If either of you need a ride, let me know."

"That's generous of you, Sam," Herman said, knowing that the offer was being made to him. "I might take you up on it."

"Good. You be over at Aaron's store after work and I'll give both of you a lift. Sorry I can't stay around, but I got a couple errands to run. I'll see you tonight." He got up, tossing two quarters onto the table as he did. "I got to drop some stuff off at Dobbs's place and run a stack of paper over to the *Sentinel*. Then back to work."

"No rest for the wicked," Phil chuckled as Sam hastened toward the door of the Potter's Bluff Cafe.

"Ain't it the truth?" Sam said as he opened the door.

• • •

G. William Dobbs smiled down at the body of the hitchhiker when he returned to his workroom. He had his makeup case in one hand, and he laid it down on the rolling cart beside the table. "Ah, that's much better," he said.

On the table, the girl's flesh was more complete, more genuine. Her neck was no longer a mass of exposed muscles, her face had a soft translucency suggesting lips and cheeks and nose. Her hands, which had been blackened sticks, now had the tapering beauty of young hands. There were faint crescents of nails at the ends of her fingers and in a few more hours the first delicate whorls would begin to appear.

"Much better," Dobbs said as he switched off the current. "Amazing substance, isn't it, my dear? It could revolutionize the entire mortuary industry, if I ever chose to exploit it. Your nose has turned out particularly well. I think it is most attractive. A pity that I can't show you off. Now, if you had family coming here, they would be so impressed with you. They would never know how hideous you were when you died. They would see you as I see you now, beautiful and serene, as if death had lured you in a moment of pleasant slumber. There is nothing clumsy now, no hidden burns, no peeling flesh. You're beautiful again. I promised you that you would be. How could I disappoint you?" He touched her eyelids. "You'll appreciate how well this is done. You're a girl—a woman—of great discernment. You'll approve. Nothing garish or inappropriate. Your face will be the color of the palest of fresh apricots, mixed with a little amber, and lightened, lightened, so that your lovely face will shine in the dark, so pale and fine it is." He had reached for his makeup kit as he spoke and now he opened the top of the case. "Nothing so gross as pancake makeup will do. I have, I assure you, the finest of greasepaint, with blendable tints that are truly remarkable. Most of it is Factor and Stein, but I also import my colors from Europe." He had picked up a tube and squeezed out a small amount of its beige-colored contents onto the heel of his palm. He put the tube back in its place and selected another. "You will find that this will be beautiful. A perfect shade for you. I'll use one of those muted rose shades for your cheeks, and a peach for highlights. Then a taupe on your eyelids, and a hint of—blue? green?—and a mascara that is not too dark. Nothing severe or overdone. Restraint is what's needed, my dear."

Dobbs had begun to smear the two greasepaints together in his left palm. He held the resulting color up to the light and frowned. "Not quite right." Bending down, he took another tube from the makeup kit and added this new shade to what he had mixed, and began to work in the color. "Better," he said when he had given the result his critical inspection. Swiftly and expertly he began to apply the greasepaint to the dead girl's face, neck and shoulders.

"I have quite a variety of wigs," he informed her as he smoothed the makeup so that the color was flawless. "I have one that is fairly long, a wonderful shade of light brown with a subtle touch of blond. It will be best, I think. Much darker and the hair would overwhelm your complexion, and that simply will not do. I won't do anything so unesthetic." He straightened up as he realized there was no music in the room. With an impatient clicking of his tongue, he went over to his turntable and looked at the stack on it. "Baroque trumpet music is perhaps not entirely right." He turned to the shelves and the albums there, grinning as he pulled out the complete Swan Lake. "Three disks," he said happily as he went back to the turntable.

Four of the six sides had played when Dobbs stood back from the table and stared down at the girl. Except for her hairless head, there was nothing about her that suggested that she had died violently. Her face was tinted to a lifelike perfection. There was a faint flush in her cheeks, her brow was clear and untroubled, her mouth rose up at the corners as if in anticipation of a smile.

"Remarkable, my dear," Dobbs said to her in a hushed voice. "You're quite the most successful example of my art I have created in very many days. How fortunate that you've turned out so well. What perspicacity caused me to take such extra care with you, I wonder? Was it my happy anticipation of this moment? There is only the matter of your wig and your eyes, and the work is finished." He went across the room, humming along with the passionate strings. "What color were your eyes, my dear? Perhaps they were green with flecks of gold. I've seen that a few times. A reddish brown? That is striking, but not, I think, compatible with your coloring and your hair. We must find eyes that will be suitable with the rest. You may object that you will not have to see them, that no one will see them, but I won't be sloppy now." He opened a cabinet and began to pull out a number of small drawers, not unlike the kind in which buttons are kept.

Eyes of every shade, color and variety looked up at him. There were pale blue eyes with intense rings around the outside of the iris. There were eyes of a brown so intense that they were almost black, like melting fudge. There were eyes of glowing green, of steely gray, turquoise and cerulean blue. There were eyes of tan, burnt sienna, fulvous and stone brown. Dobbs pawed through them until he came to a pair of lustrous hazel eyes flecked with gold. He lifted the pair and smiled.

When the eyes were in place and the lids closed over them, Dobbs went to another cabinet and opened it. There was a large assortment of wig blocks, each with its topping of carefully combed hair. Dobbs moved the first two—a short, black, man's toupee and a splendidly styled flip of salt-and-pepper brown—and pulled out the long wig he had described. He took it carefully from the wig block and carried it to the table. "It's simply perfect, my dear. You'll be as beautiful as you were the night of your senior prom. I'll have to ask Mrs. Turner if she has the right kind of dress for you. Something very simple, I should think, with a touch of lace at the neck." He fitted the wig over her head with the deceptive ease of long practice. "Ah," he said as he looked down at her. "No father could be more proud of his daughter, my dear. If your own father could see you, he would be so delighted that he could not say everything he felt. You must accept me as his substitute." Very gently he bent and kissed her cold, beautiful forehead. "Something with lace, simple, perfectly made." He touched her hair, adjusting the fall of a wave by her cheek. "You will have to excuse me, my dear. I really must go talk to Mrs. Turner at once."

He walked away from the table to his workroom door and opened it onto the dark hall beyond. Then, realizing that the ballet would finish before his return, he turned off the turntable, the speakers and the overhead light.

Only a tensor lamp lit her face now, and Dobbs smiled with deep pleasure. All of his subjects looked good, but here was a work of art. "What shame is there in death, if one can look so fair?" he asked the darkness, and went out the open door, closing it behind him.

The shadows in the room seemed denser with Dobbs gone, filled with a physical presence that the little pool of intense light made more potent. One shadow detached itself from the others, and fell across the body of the girl.

The shadowy figure seemed to perform certain rituals.

For more than a minute, nothing happened, and then there was a stirring in the supine figure. Slowly, gracefully, the girl sat up, turning so that her legs fell over the side of the table. Her posture was perfect, as if she were waiting to recite in class. Her hands were folded primly in her lap.

The shadow flickered before her; her gold-flecked hazel eyes opened.

Chapter 9

Pallid, narrow clouds like keloid scars seamed the pink belly of the sky as the light faded. The winding road seemed to disappear into the towering bulk of the trees as if being devoured by darkness. Ron Cousins turned on the headlights and discovered that the stark, white illumination did little to dispell the massive darkness growing around them.

Linda rather nervously poured a bit more of the orange juice in the thermos into one of the two remaining dixie cups. For the last few miles she had said nothing; her face was set into an uneasy half-smile and she had pulled at the loose strand of hair by her ear from time to time.

"I could use some of that," Ron said, surprised to hear how exhausted his voice sounded.

"Okay," Linda responded with more concern than he thought was warranted. "I just want another sip and you can have the rest of this. There's not much left and I think we ought to save some of it for Jamie."

"Good idea. He'll be thirsty when he

wakes up," he agreed. His hands were aching on the steering wheel.

Linda glanced into the backseat as she had done at about ten minute intervals for the last hour. "He's not awake yet. I'm glad he's still sleeping. This road . . ." They had gone such a long way, she thought.

"Um." Ron guided the car down a long, slowly tightening curve. "You want to doze awhile yourself?"

She shook her head. "I don't think so. We might . . ." The frown deepened on her brow. "Ron, don't you . . . isn't it a little strange that . . ."

"What?" He rapped the word out.

"Are you *sure* it was the McDermott place we saw? This doesn't seem like the right road, does it? Isn't there supposed to be a highway intersection here?" She passed the orange juice to him as if offering him an apology.

Only when he had finished the juice in the paper cup did he speak to her, and what he said was not truly an answer. "You saw the sign, didn't you?"

"But that bush . . . it might have been another name. I said I wasn't sure—"

"Look, we saw DER. We both agreed that it had to be McDermott. Do you want to go back and look at it again, to be sure?" He was half hoping that she would want to do just that, giving him an excuse to return to Potter's Bluff so that they could take what Tubby Bass had insisted was the long way around. "If Bass had just told us that the road was like this!"

"I'll drive for a while, if you like," she offered tentatively.

"No, that's okay." He gave her a brief, genuine smile but turned back to the road almost at once. He had the oddest feeling that it would change if he did not watch it closely. There must be a river nearby, he thought, for a low, wraithlike mist was rising, spreading out along the road, insinuating itself through the trees, making eerie figures of shadows that loomed out at the car, only to vanish as the headlights touched them. Night was taking over the sky.

She poured more juice for him.

"Keep your eye out for lights," he said grimly. "Maybe we can find a farmhouse and ask for directions. Maybe we missed a turning back there somewhere . . ."

"I will," she said, grateful for something to do. After a few more seconds of silence she turned to look again at her sleeping son.

Ron had lifted the cup to his lips when he saw a shape loom out of the fog at him. It moved in the glare of the headlights, a darting, black shadow that grew and twisted in the pallid mists.

An instant later, he swore as he slammed on the brakes. Orange juice splashed over his hand and jacket and spattered the arm and shoulder of Linda's sweater.

With an alarmed cry, she flung out her arms to keep from being thrown forward, and in the backseat there was a thud. Jamie moaned.

The car was stopped almost in the middle of the road. Its idling engine sounded too loud now. The night hovered just out of range of the narrow line of the headlights. It was several moments before either Ron or Linda could gather their senses enough to realize what had happened.

"That man . . . Christ! It must have been a man," Ron said to himself. He turned toward Linda. "You okay?"

"Why'd you brake like that?" Her voice had a shrill edge to it.

"Something . . . a man . . . I swear, Linda, something ran in front of the car!" Saying it made it at once more real but even less comprehensible.

"Mom!" Jamie cried out.

Linda turned to him at once, delayed fear making her giddy. "Jamie? Honey?"

"I hit my head," he yelled. "What happened?"

"Hold still, Jamie," Linda said, hoping to soothe Jamie while she found out if her son was hurt. She knelt awkwardly on the seat and leaned forward on the head rest, reaching out to touch the boy.

"My *head hurts!*" His voice was louder. "MOM!"

Linda put her hand gingerly on Jamie's forehead and felt a ridged lump rising over his right eyebrow. "Ron," she said tensely, "will you turn on the overhead?"

Ron moved sluggishly as the might-have-happeneds jostled his thoughts. Finally he managed to get the light on. They saw on Jamie's head an angry purplish welt.

"He's hurt, Ron," Linda said before she

could stop herself. "We need to get a cold compress on that."

The fog parted as the wind came up and for a moment the headlights picked out the great bulk of a house which until then they had seen only faintly through the fog. It was a short way off the road, and seemed to be enormous. "Look!" Linda shouted, pointing at the place. "There!"

"Yes, there's a house," Ron said as if he did not entirely believe it. He was sure that he had seen light from one of the windows, but could not now tell which one. "It's not too late," he heard himself say, "and we need to get directions, anyway. They'll probably let us have some ice for a cold compress. Maybe we can phone a doctor." He went on, trying to convince himself as well as persuade Linda. "People living along roads like this, they get used to having strangers stop for help. They know that accidents happen, and people get lost. Maybe they'll have a map they can show us."

"Maybe." Linda got out of her side of the car and moved the seat forward for Jamie to get out. "Is there a road up to that house? I don't see it."

"I think so, but I don't know what condition it's in. I think I'd better park on the shoulder. If the road up to the house is rutted, we might damage something." He motioned her to stand clear of the car, and drove a dozen yards farther on, coming to a stop on the graveled shoulder.

Linda took Jamie by the hand and tried

not to shiver. She could no longer see a light on in the house.

"My stomach feels funny," Jamie said as he walked beside her. "My head hurts."

"I know, Jamie," she said, hoping that he was not badly injured. "Ron," she said as she came up to him, "I'm worried. That's a bad bump Jamie's got on his forehead. I think he might have a—" She hesitated and then resorted to the old parental strategy: "A C-O-N-C-U-S-S-I-O-N," she spelled.

"What's that?" Jamie asked.

"A kind of hurt," Ron said brusquely, adding more quietly to Linda, "Do you think so? He seems okay."

"He's got a terrible lump," she repeated.

They had started down the rutted driveway, Jamie walking between his parents, his lagging footsteps forcing them to make their way slowly.

"I could go on ahead and knock, tell them what the trouble is," Ron suggested, then changed his mind. "But Jamie might need . . ." He did not finish.

"It's cold," Jamie said.

Though it was quite dark now, Ron's and Linda's eyes met for an instant, then Linda bent down to talk to the child. "You knocked your head, Jamie. You have to be careful. You don't want to make it any worse, okay? So if you start to get dizzy or sleepy, you tell Dad or me, okay?" She did not sound as calm and reassuring as she wished.

"Just a bit farther, Jamie. We're almost at the house." Ron had been looking at the huge building as they got nearer, and was beginning to be concerned again. There were no lights in any of the windows; what they had mistaken for illumination must have been the reflection of the headlights off the window glass.

Jamie stumbled and moaned.

"I hope to hell they're home," Ron muttered as they came up the least, steepest part of the driveway.

The house was certainly quite large, about a hundred years old, but lacking all the exuberance usually associated with carpenter gothic. There were no balustrades, widow's walks, cupolas, curlicues or gingerbread. This was an oppressively simple three-story frame house with a wide porch running across the front and around one side of the building. Two pillars framing the recessed front door were the only architectural excesses on the entire structure.

Ron knocked—and the front door opened under his knock, as if by magic.

Only darkness from inside stared back at them.

"That's funny," Ron said.

"It's spooky." Jamie hung back at the open door.

"All old houses are spooky to you," Ron said, recalling how delighted his son had been with the Victorian they had seen in Potter's Bluff.

Linda took Jamie's hand firmly in her own. "The sooner we get this done, the sooner we can leave."

"Awright," the boy said quietly, and allowed himself to be led into the old house.

"Anybody home?" Ron shouted.

"Please, we had a car accident. Our son . . . may be hurt," Linda called out.

No response.

Walking carefully, they made their way a little further into the darkened house. Reaching another room, Ron groped on the walls until he found a light switch, and tried it. Nothing happened.

"Linda, I'm afraid this house is just deserted. There's no electricity, and with the door just left opened like that . . ."

Linda held up her hand abruptly, "Wait! Quiet! I heard a noise downstairs."

"That's probably just rats—in the basement. I'm telling you, the house is deserted. I'm sorry honey, but there is nothing we can do."

"No! I told you I saw a light—I know! The fuse probably blew out, and they're in the basement replacing it. That's why the switch doesn't work now. The electricity *just* blew out on them."

Ron sighed in exasperation. "All right, I'll go down there and take a look. You two wait here."

Ron made his way through the house carefully, his hands held out in front of him as if he were blind. Once he barked his shins on a tumbled chair. Finally he found the basement stairs, and started down. Linda and Jamie remained.

"Mom, I'm scared," Jamie whispered.

"There's nothing to be scared of, Jamie," she said.

"Where's Dad?" he said in a voice so low that she could hardly hear him.

"He's looking for the people who live here, sweetheart."

As she looked around the dark old house, a nameless chill sent a shiver up Linda's back. "I tell you what. I'll try to open some of those drapes, so it won't look so scary in here."

"When will Dad be back?"

"In a minute," she said as she started across the room to the window. When she reached it, she managed to open one of the drapes and, just stood there, peering out. She thought she saw a shadow moving out there—or was it just an over-active imagination?

She walked back over to Jamie, and hugged him—as much for her own comfort as his. "Mom, I have to go the bathroom."

"Daddy's trying to turn the lights on now. Then we will find one."

• • •

The basement stairs swayed when Ron stepped onto them. He went down them carefully, one hand on the rickety banister, the other on a grimy wall. The stairwell smelled musty and unused, as if there were mold growing in the corners and vermin nesting in the crannies. He steadied himself, and when he drew his hand back, it brushed an unfamiliar shape, an unseen thing that slithered away.

At the foot of the stairs he almost tripped over a stool in front of a carpenter's bench. He felt over the old tools, recognizing only the shape of a hammer and a rasp, and it was purely by accident that his fingers closed around a small box which rattled when he picked it up. He had found matches.

Ron opened the box and fingered the contents. The box was half full. When he tried to light a match, the end flew off the stick and was lost. More careful the next time, he was rewarded with a spurt of light. Holding his fingers in a bowl around the flame, Ron sighed with relief. He raised his hand and looked around the underground room. . . .

• • •

Linda was huddled on the floor, Jamie half in her lap and half curled beside her. She was talking quietly, telling him an aimless story about the adventures of a rodeo cowboy to keep him from falling asleep. She stopped abruptly as she heard a match scrape on the far side of the room.

"What?" Jamie said.

"Hush, Jamie," she whispered as she got to her feet, her pulse sounding in her ears like a tom-tom. Her legs seemed to be made of jelly.

A face swam in the light of the match, distorted by the shadows that rose above the lips and nose and brows. Ron looked at them out of the eerie light.

"Oh, God, you terrified me!" Linda said after she had mastered herself. "Why didn't you say something?"

"Who else were you expecting?"

"What about the lights?"

"I found the fuse box and tried it. No luck, as you can tell. It was a long shot, anyway. I'm sorry, honey." He lit another match as the one he held burned down.

"Where did you find those?"

"In the basement. They're pretty old—must've been there for some time. I don't know how long they'll last. I looked around for candles, but there weren't any down there." He had to light another match. "They burn pretty fast, some of them. They won't give us light for too long."

"Did you come across a kitchen or bathroom?" She looked over at Jamie, worried by his stillness. "Ron, I think we really ought to find a doctor. He's sleepy and his head is no better. He told me that his eyes feel squeezed. Maybe he should have an X ray or something. He's got a very bad bruise and he's chilly. It isn't just that this house is cold, either. I've been holding him to keep him warm."

"You're probably right," Ron said, and held the match higher so that he could see more of the room. "What a place this must have been, sixty years ago."

"Ron! We've got to do something about Jamie! Now!" The room seemed to rustle in sympathy with her words.

"Mom," Jamie said thickly, "I think I see somebody."

Linda turned to him at once. "It's okay, Jamie, it's okay. We're going to get help for you real soon. Just take it easy. We'll get out of here in a couple of minutes."

"That's right," Ron said quickly, and lit another match. "As soon as we find the bathroom."

He would be glad to get out of the house. Those minutes in the basement had felt like years, and he wanted to be gone from the place altogether.

"Mom," Jamie said, more loudly and fearfully, "there's someone here. I can see 'em. Look!"

"Christ!" Linda said in a smothered voice. "Ron, we've *got* to get him to a doctor."

"Yeah." He started another match and handed it to Linda. "Hold this. I'll carry him. Never mind the water; we'll leave now."

She took the match and held it protectively as Ron bent to lift Jamie into his arms.

The room was filled with a white glare that was gone as abruptly as it came, and a voice they had never heard before said, "Welcome to Potter's Bluff, Mr. Cousins."

Linda turned so quickly she almost extinguished the match she held. The afterimage of the flashbulb danced in her eyes. "What? Is— Who are you?"

A frumpy middle-aged woman in a flowered pink housecoat and pom-pom slippers came toward them. There was no animation in her doughy, plain face.

Ron had picked up Jamie and held him tightly now, protecting him from danger. "We tried the door," he said to the woman.

"Yes," Linda went on. "We had a near accident outside on the highway, and we just wanted some help and directions. The door was open. We *did* knock. Jamie's had a bad knock on the head. We didn't think you'd mind." She noticed that the woman in the housecoat did not appear to be listening. "We didn't mean any harm, we only wanted to take care of our son."

Someone laughed. It was not the woman, or Ron, or Linda, or Jamie. A young woman in cutoff jeans and a halter top came into the dining room through the French doors. She walked with a long, easy stride and her bare feet padded like the paws of an animal. There was a camera stuck in the top of her jeans, lens resting on the brass snap. She laughed again as the match Linda held went out.

Beyond the French doors shapes could be seen in the watery moonlight. There was an elderly man with what might be a monkey wrench in his hand. Beside him was a kid, not more than seventeen, in track clothes. He had a claw-headed hammer in one hand and a carpenter's awl in the other. An attractive young woman in a nurse's uniform, whose hair might have been red, carried a scalpel. Freddie from the service station had a small welding torch with an oxygen canister attached to it. A rugged-faced old man in a shapeless black sweater with rolled up sleeves revealing crossed-anchor tattoos, had wickedly curved boat hooks in each hand. A man in a minister's collar took a home movie camera out of his pocket and started to operate it. No one pointed out that there was no light to film by. No one seemed aware of it.

"God, dear God," Linda moaned, trying to keep from being overwhelmed by the terror that flooded through her. "Ron . . ."

"We can't go out the French doors. Use the front door, Linda. Move very carefully. They don't look . . ." He did not know what to say.

"Real," she finished for him.

More people were crowding in the door, but the dim light made it hard for Ron and Linda to see them plainly. The only thing that they were sure of was that every person who had come through the French doors carried something in his hands.

Ron nudged Linda and they began to edge toward the hall door, watching the strange figures come slowly after them, neither chasing them nor leaving them alone. Linda fumbled for the doorknob, and almost cried out in desperation when she could not get the door to open.

"Don't rush it," Ron cautioned her in tension-stretched tones.

Linda twisted the knob more firmly and almost fell into the hall as the door swung wide.

"Keep going," Ron whispered to her, and she nodded. "Right down the hall." He felt clumsy with Jamie in his arms, and now that the boy was half awake, he clung to his father with a determined grip that made it more difficult for Ron to move easily. "Son, take it easy," he said quietly, but Jamie's only response was a soft, howling sigh.

Linda was almost to the front door. She turned back toward Ron. "Hurry, Ron, honey. *Please!*" She reached out for her husband and son as the first sinister figures emerged from the dining room door.

Ron stumbled and Jamie shrieked, but they did not fall. Near the door, Linda waited for them, motioning them to hurry. "They're coming," she called, not caring if the silent, blank-faced crowd heard her. "Hurry!"

"I am." Ron felt the air choke in his throat. He came up to Linda, reaching out to steady himself on the newel post at the foot of the stairs. "Okay." He was panting a little and was absolutely certain that it would take all the strength he had to get to the car while he carried Jamie. "Open the door."

"Okay," Linda said, grabbing the door-knob.

There were three people on the porch. One was a woman in a sensible business suit, the second a young man in a Coast Guard uniform whose head was terribly deformed, the third was a stout man in mechanic's overalls.

"*No!*" Linda shouted as she slammed the door.

The figures in the hall were closer now.

"The stairs. Up the stairs," Ron said, shoving Linda ahead of him. The old carpet skidded underfoot, but they were given strength by their desperation.

"Who are they? What are they?" Linda asked breathlessly as she climbed.

Chapter 10

"Can you hear them?" Linda whispered, afraid to make any sound at all.

Ron was pressed against the door. "No," he muttered after a moment. He came back across the dressing room toward her. "I don't know if they'll think to look here. I opened that window in the bedroom across the hall. I hope they'll think we're going down that tree." He was less than a foot away from her but she had to strain to hear him.

"I hope they believe that," Linda said quietly, fervently.

"Why shouldn't they?" He did not expect her to give him an answer.

Linda sat with Jamie close beside her. They were in the corner of the dressing room, looking as if they wanted to be very small. As the first shambling footstep was heard on the stairs, Linda said in a soft, fierce voice, "Shouldn't we move the dresser against the door, in case they come this way. They might think it's stuck."

"Can we do it quietly?" Ron asked. "If they hear us—"

"If it's empty we can carry it. Oh, Ron,

let's do it. I can't stand the thought of them." She pinched the bridge of her nose to keep the tears back. "Please."

"If you think it will help." He was dubious.

The dresser was quite heavy and Ron and Linda were able to move it only a few feet at a time. They concentrated on the task, trying not to listen for foot steps in the hallway.

Jamie huddled in the corner, his knuckles pressed against his teeth as he watched his parents struggle in the darkness with the huge, unwieldly piece of furniture.

"What's behind the other door?" Linda whispered as they at last got the dresser pushed tightly against the door into the hall.

"Probably a bedroom," Ron answered, trying to pant silently.

"We'd better check." She went over very cautiously and opened the door slowly. A narrow passage led to another closed door, and off to the side there was a third door. Linda stepped into the small passage and stared at the third door, which was ajar, letting in a sliver of moonlight. With great care she eased the door open and found a bathroom. The fixtures were old-fashioned, but there was a sink and a toilet, and under a square sash window, a claw-footed tub. The desire to laugh nearly engulfed her, but she bit the insides of her cheeks and closed her hands into fists until the impulse passed.

"Linda!" The sharp whisper came from the door to the dressing room. Ron was peering out of the door, his face worn and anxious.

She came out of the bathroom. "I found

it," she told him, and resisted the giggles that welled in her.

"What?" he asked sharply. He knew she was verging on hysteria again.

"The bathroom." Her mouth trembled and her eyes welled. "Oh, Ron, what's going to happen to us?"

"We'll be okay," he insisted without much conviction. He took her in his arms and held her. They both heard the sounds of lumbering steps coming down the hall. They clung to each other, too terrified to do more than breathe, and that quietly.

The door in the bedroom rattled, opened, then shut. Across the hall, they could hear the same thing was being done. The door to each of the rooms was opened in turn, there was a pause, and then the slow, plodding steps moved on.

Then the knob of the dressing room was tried. It turned easily. They held their breaths but it did not open. The person on the other side of the door pushed at it once again, with more force, but the large dresser did not budge. The steps moved away.

A guttural exclamation brought a number of the inhabitants of the house hurrying to the room across the hall.

"They've found the open window," Ron murmured in Linda's ear.

"Good."

There was a shuffling and a babbling from the mysterious figures. Neither Ron nor Linda could make sense of it through the door and the chest.

"What now?" Linda whispered as the steps milled around in the bedroom and hall just outside the dressing room door.

"I don't know. We wait." Ron leaned against the dresser as if that would barricade them even more effectively. "If only we'd gone back to Potter's Bluff and taken the long way around."

Linda rested her head on his shoulder. "You did what seemed best." She was silent, then asked, "How long do you think we'll have to wait here until it's safe to leave? We've got to get Jamie to the hospital."

Ron nodded, sickened by the thoughts of what might be wrong with Jamie. "I don't know. As soon as they're gone, we'll leave."

"Fine." Linda left him and went back to where Jamie lay.

The footsteps in the hall were moving more purposefully now, heading away from the door to the bedroom where Ron had pulled the window open. There was the distinct sound of one or two persons at the top of the stairs.

As he listened, Ron allowed himself the luxury of sighing. It was going to work after all. He put his hand to his brow and found that in spite of the chill of the house he had been sweating. He took a couple steps back from the dresser.

"They're leaving?" Linda asked.

"I think so. We'd better wait a bit to be sure, but I think so."

"Thank God." Linda sank to the floor beside her son and reached out to hold him. Accidentally she touched his bruised forehead, and Jamie, half asleep, screamed.

"Shit!" Ron muttered and rushed to quiet his boy, though he knew it was already too late. In the hall the footsteps had stopped, and then began to rush toward the dressing room door.

"No, oh, no," Linda said, horrified, as she tried to wake her boy. "No, Jamie, hush. Oh, honey, don't."

"Come on." Ron reached down and grabbed her arm. Heavy blows began to pound the door. "We're leaving."

"But how?" Linda demanded. She shrunk back as a new, metallic noise joined the bludgeoning racket.

"The bedroom overlooks the porch roof. It's only a short drop." Ron knew that this was not entirely true; the old house had high ceilings and even hanging from the windowsill by one's hands would still mean a three-foot fall. "It's our only chance. Once they break that door down . . ."

"Or the bedroom door." Linda's hands began to shake. "Is it closed?"

"Yes," Ron said, as he pulled her to her feet.

"Locked?"

"I don't know. The passage door locks, probably. We can go out the bathroom window." The plan was ridiculous, but the only other alternative was to take their chances with the emotionless, inexorable people in the hall.

"Oh, Dad," Jamie wailed, starting to retch.

"*Jamie!*" Linda shouted, reaching for the

boy. She was crying now, though she did not seem to be aware of it.

"Not now, Jamie," Ron insisted.

"Ron, he's not doing it because he wants to!" Linda turned on him, holding her son tightly.

"Linda, I don't care if he's bleeding or has broken legs. We have to get out of here. Those ... *things* out there in the hall are going to catch us." He was already going into the passageway between the dressing room and the bedroom. He checked the doors and discovered to his relief that all had locks, the kind that turned. Realistically, he knew these would not slow their attackers for long, but it bought them at least a little necessary time.

"Jamie," Linda said unsteadily, "you've got to help us, honey, you have to. Come on, Jamie."

The boy gagged and trembled, but managed to stand up straight. "I'm okay, Mom," he said faintly.

There was a splintering crash and the head of a hammer came through the top of the hall door and embedded itself in the top of the dresser.

"This way!" Ron yelled, holding out his nand to his wife and son.

Apparently encouraged, the people in the hall took to battering the door with renewed impartial fury, and the wood began to split open. As Linda thrust Jamie into the passageway, she saw a number of arms poking through the ruined door, reaching for the top of the dresser.

Ron closed the door and turned the lock, then shoved Jamie and Linda into the bathroom. Behind them there was a single loud bang—the dresser had overturned.

"Out the window! There's a little trellis you can reach, and then you can get down to the porch roof. We can go down the front pillars." Ron closed the bathroom door and leaned an old wicker laundry hamper against it. "The door's locked. We can make it."

Linda was standing in the tub, struggling with the window. "I can't make it move. It's stuck." She turned to Ron.

The trample of feet in the dressing room told them that the people had broken through.

Ron climbed into the tub beside her and fumbled with the window. It was stiff, but he felt it give. He knew they could smash the window to get out, but he did not relish squeezing between shards of glass.

"What if we fall reaching for the trellis?" She did not remind him that Jamie was in no condition to make a perilous climb.

"There are the pipes. They're on the outside. They're right beside the window, I'll bet. We won't fall! It's just a short reach." The window shuddered upward, then moved easily.

"Jamie will never be able to climb," Linda said, the brittle sound back in her voice.

"I'll carry him piggyback if I have to. He can hang on, can't he?"

A series of loud thumps on the dressing room door ended in a grating of metal and wood.

"The lock's gone," Ron said to Linda.

"What if the trellis breaks? It isn't safe," Linda was hugging Jamie. The boy sobbed thinly.

"We've got to chance it." He shared every one of her fears, but the sound of the hinges creaking on the dressing room door overrode every other consideration. "You go first, then Jamie, and then I'll come out. You get on the porch roof, and I can hand Jamie down to you."

There was a thud just outside the bathroom door.

"*Hurry!*" Ron shouted, and boosted Linda toward the window.

Linda pulled on the sides of the sill, her hands scraping on the blistered, ancient paint. She wriggled half out of the window, closing her eyes so that she would not have to look down. Then she turned so that she was sitting on the sill. She felt with her left hand for the drain pipe, and then the right for the trellis. The trellis was wreathed with dead climbing roses which left thorns in her palm. The pipe was more stable, and she held onto this. "Hand Jamie up to me," she said to Ron, making herself think and speak calmly.

"Here." He lifted the boy, feeling how weak he was. "Grab hold of Mom, Jamie. She'll help you."

Jamie nodded and reached for his mother's legs, then hauled himself up to her waist.

The bathroom door began to crack as arms and wrenches and table legs drummed on it.

Linda pulled Jamie into her lap, then

reached out for the drainpipe. "Hang onto my waist, Jamie. Hang on tight. When I get out of the window, we're going to swing, and . . . I don't want,"—a momentary vision of Jamie, fallen, broken, flickered before her eyes—"I don't want anything to go wrong."

"Okay," he said, tightening his hold on her.

"Hurry," Ron said, getting his footing on the side of the tub. The window was high and would be difficult to reach without help. He steadied himself as he heard the wood behind him start to shatter.

Linda grabbed hold of the drainpipe and let herself out of the window. Jamie's legs were still on the sill, and she said softly to him, "You've got to lift your feet, Jamie." The sudden drag of his weight as he swung free astounded her, and she slipped almost a foot on the pipe. Her knuckles were skinned by the rough wood as she fought to stop their fall.

In the window, Ron was tugging himself through, one hand already extended to the drainpipe. With a tremendous effort, he propelled himself forward so that he was almost entirely out of the window, his hands holding on to the drainpipe while he waited to see his wife and son stand clear of it. He kicked out once, as a hand groped for his ankle.

There were four people in the bathroom, only the cramped quarters keeping them from pulling Ron back into the house. In the minute or so while they sorted themselves out, Ron swung out of the window and clung, monkey-fashion, to the drainpipe.

Linda touched the porch roof. It was deep in dead leaves, and there were scurrying sounds, the rustling of insects and animals as she pried Jamie's hands from around her waist. "Dad's coming down," she whispered, then looked up to see Ron descending as the face of a bespectacled old man appeared in the window. "Ron!"

"Get going!" He shouted the order. Though he did not see the danger threatening him, he knew it was there. He could not let himself become confused now, not when they had gotten this far.

The leaves made the footing slippery, so Linda did not run, much as she wanted to. She kept a tight grip on Jamie's shoulder, half carrying him as she made her way along the roof, around the corner of the house. She knew that Ron was behind her, and once she heard him shout a few heartening words.

The face was gone from the bathroom window. Shortly after that, the people in the bathroom and passageway and dressing room were once again in the hall, going toward the stairs. They did not run, but moved with great purpose. Their faces remained expressionless.

As Linda reached the front pillars under the porch, she faltered and looked back to see Ron coming along the slightly sloping porch roof. Moonlight touched them now, giving them a little of the light they had so desperately wanted earlier. However, this moonlight seemed to turn the world to a dead, blasted landscape, and make their faces look like the hollowed, sunken visages of corpses.

"Climb over and get down. You can do it," Ron said as he came up. There was a cut on the back of his right hand. It bled freely.

"What did you do?" Linda demanded as she saw the wound.

"Later!" He pushed her toward the edge of the roof. "Hurry. Get down and start running for the car."

Linda nodded, and this time did not argue. She let herself over the edge of the porch roof and locked her legs around the pillar. The paint was scaled and cracked, so that she felt splinters driven into her calves and thighs through her slacks. Idiotically she imagined how she would explain them to a doctor. Her feet reached the porch railing, and she swung around the pillar and dropped onto the steps.

"Get ready!" Ron called down from above. He held Jamie by the arms and was lowering him over the side of the roof. His hand was hurting now, a steady, acidic ache that seemed to eat its way up his arm. The blood made his hand slippery. "Hang on, Jamie. We're almost there." He was on his knees, and dared not lie on the roof for fear that the slant and the drag of the boy would pull them both over.

Linda planted her feet firmly and reached up for Jamie. With her arms over her head at full extension, she was able to grab his knees. It was the best they could do. "Okay, let him go." She staggered and grunted as Jamie collapsed onto her. Only the ominous beat of steps in the hall beyond the front door gave her the strength to hold herself upright. By the time she had lowered Jamie to the steps beside her, Ron was coming down the pillar.

"Run!" he shouted as he launched himself off the porch railing onto the ground. He flailed his arms to keep from falling.

"Jamie can't!" Linda yelled.

In three long strides Ron was beside her. "You take one arm, I'll take the other. Jamie!" he said in a voice that was new to all of them. "I know you feel rotten, but you've got to help us." He did not wait for the boy to answer, but started away from the house at a fast walk. Linda kept pace with him. As soon as he was sure that Jamie was able, he broke into a fast trot, and then to a run.

Linda was silent, there being no breath to spare for anything but running. She heard, more than felt, Jamie miss two or three steps, and she slowed only enough to get a stronger grasp on her son's shoulder. Once she very nearly tripped in the deep ruts of the driveway, and she cried out. Ron's sharp, obscene retort helped her.

Behind them the door to the house was open and the first of the figures were coming down the steps. The moonlight glistened on the objects in their hands.

As they reached the road, Ron was almost overcome by sudden dizziness. His thighs were sore, the pain in his hand was nearly unbearable and he was becoming disoriented.

"This way!" Linda shouted, pulling Jamie and Ron toward the wide shoulder where their car was parked.

Jamie cried out as he stumbled, his arms

going out in front of him. He shrieked in fear and pain, holding up his bleeding palms.

"Get the door open!" Linda screamed at her husband. "I've got to get Jamie!"

Ron nodded dumbly and rushed on to their car. He found the keys in his pocket and opened the lock, flinging the door wide. He braced himself against the cold metal, then turned back to help Linda.

She had Jamie in her arms and was trying to hurry, but Jamie was whimpering in a steady, determined way, and rocking against her shoulder, and it was all she could do to hold him and walk slowly. She had not dared to look back.

"How is he?" Ron asked as he came up to them.

"Hurt," she said shortly.

"The door's open on the driver's side." He put his arm around Linda to give her extra support as Jamie lurched in her grasp. "Don't do that, son. It makes it harder." His head was starting to throb and his skin felt two sizes too small for his bones.

Jamie cried out in rage as his hands brushed against Ron's shoulder, and Linda nearly fell. Ron reached out to help her and the keys he'd been holding loosely fell from his fingers.

"Shit!" he said under his breath, and started to bend down for them.

"Don't stop!" Linda said.

"We need the keys!" he yelled, and felt in the gravel for them, swearing in quiet determination until he touched the cold, reassuring metal. "Got them." He tucked them into his pocket and came after Linda, who was still struggling with Jamie.

They nearly collapsed against the car as they reached it, and Linda struggled to get Jamie out of her arms and onto the seat. "Ron, get in the other side. You're in no shape to drive!"

He nodded, staggered once, and went around the back of the car for the passenger door. "I'm coming," he said, as much to reassure himself as Linda.

"Hurry! Get in! Get in! Oh, God, Ron! *Hurry!*" She was kneeling on the driver's seat, Jamie in front of her, trying to hold the passenger door open for him. As Ron dropped onto the seat, she turned and reached to close her door. Without turning, she said, "Lock it. Make sure it's locked. They're getting close." She felt in her pockets and then reached for her purse.

"What is it?" Ron asked as he reached for the seat belt.

"The key. The *key!*" As she glanced out the window, she could see six of the figures come out onto the deserted highway.

Ron patted his pocket, then fished his key ring out of his trousers. "Here. I wish we had a flask."

She snatched the key and forced it into the ignition, twisting it viciously. Her foot rammed on the accelerator.

"You're flooding it," Ron warned, and reached over to steady Jamie between them. He was frightened by the listlessness of the child. He wished there were a seat belt for the boy, because in the state he was in . . .

A bony arm with flesh scaled as old paint snaked over the backseat and wrapped itself around Jamie's throat and shoulder. The boy opened his mouth, but no sound escaped, and in the next moment, he had been dragged into the backseat.

Linda put her hands to her face and screamed, and tried to reach back for her child.

Ron's seat belt held him securely and it was several precious seconds before he could turn and attempt to wrest Jamie away from the creature that crouched over him in the backseat. At last he secured a hold on the woman's hair and pulled. To his horror, a section of scalp pulled away and the lank hair dangled in his nerveless fingers. The impossibility of it brought him dangerously near laughter.

Now Linda had turned, kneeling on the seat, and was battering at the woman's head with the thermos bottle, screaming with each blow as if she were the one being struck.

Belatedly, Ron freed himself from the seat belt, and reached into the back of the car, seizing the woman's leg in his aching hands. "Grab Jamie!" he shouted, and began to drag the woman from the car. He held the door open with his leg, and used the last of his strength to tug at the repulsive flesh of the woman. Oh, God, was that hideous thing actually a woman? He felt the skin crack under his fingers as he secured his grip at her knee and pulled.

Linda had reached Jamie and was clinging

to him in desperation. She was crying as she struggled to hold him, and knew that his strange passiveness was almost more sinister than the ghastly thing in the backseat.

A leg, a hip, a shoulder was out of the door, and Ron renewed his efforts. He sank his hand into soft, spongy flesh and at last thrust the woman from the car. As he slammed the door, he shouted, "Get going!"

Linda put Jamie on the seat, one hand on his shoulder as if reassuring herself that he was actually there. She forced herself to be calm and deliberate as she turned the key again. Be cautious, she told herself. Don't flood the engine. That will only make it worse.

The engine sputtered, coughed, sputtered again, and groaned. Then Linda became aware that the light inside the car was still on. "Oh, God," she said. "We left the roof light on. The battery's run down."

"It hasn't been long enough," Ron said tensely.

One of the figures, the youth in the track outfit, was less than ten feet from the car. Linda turned the key again, her right foot pressing the accelerator to the floor.

The old man carrying the wrench came up next to the car and slowly swung his weapon up, then down, with shattering force, on the back window. The sound erupted through the car and dense, spiderweb cracks spread over the glass. Beside him, the girl with the camera took another picture.

"Christ! Sweet Christ Almighty!" Linda's hands shook so badly that it was all she could do to turn the key again. She knew she was behaving stupidly, that she might have flooded the engine by now, and was running the battery down needlessly, but there was nothing she could do to stop herself. "Who are they? *What* are they?" The engine coughed again, and miraculously, growled to life. Linda, giddy now, jerked the car first into reverse, and then into drive. The car leaped backward, then forward lurching onto the road as Linda turned on the lights and accelerated dangerously.

• • •

It was after three in the morning when the phone rang and got Dan Gillis out of bed. He sat up and rubbed his eyes as he picked up the receiver. "Gillis here."

"Dan, this is Eric Watson in Hollis," said a gravelly voice he had not heard for a while.

"Eric." Why was his fellow-undersheriff calling him at this hour? "Is there an emergency?"

"Sort of," Watson said. "I was just over at Doc Grady's place. He called me about an hour ago. Seems there was this young couple and their kid—pretty beat up, and scared shitless. Said they'd been in Potter's Bluff for a couple of days and were going over to Farleyville."

"There was a couple staying at the Bowie Street Hotel," Dan said, frowning. "I saw them at the cafe once or twice. Early thirties, the woman kind of pretty, and a boy fairly young?"

"Sounds like them. Glad you remembered."

"Well, we aren't exactly up to our asses in out-of-towners here," Dan said with a slight chuckle. "What's happened? An accident?"

Janet turned over in bed and looked up at Dan. "Who?" She mouthed the word.

"Eric Watson," he whispered, and motioned her to be silent. "Yeah, go on. I'm listening."

"Well, these two drove into town about ninety minutes ago. Went to Stan's Service Station, the one that's open late, and found Stan just closing up. Well, he took a look at them and their car, and he put in a call to Doc Grady, who sent his son over to pick them up. Anyway, the woman keeps insisting that they want to get to the freeway and make Ashton tonight. Well, Doc's boy told them there's no way they can do that, and that the Highway Patrol would stop them because of the rear window—"

"Wait a minute," Dan cut in. "The rear window?"

"That's what I can't figure out," Eric said. "Now I looked at the thing, and its been shattered. The glass is still hanging together, but the thing looks like lace, I tell you! Well, they say that they got hit with a wrench, but unless it was one of them Olympic strong men who swung it, I can't see how a wrench could make that much damage, and they told us that it was an old man who did it."

Dan was still trying to clear his thoughts. "Back up a bit, Eric. Where were these people, when this happened?"

"I can't rightly figure that one out, but I

think they were on the Narrow Point loop, out your way. They told us how they started and how they came out, and that's what it sounds like to me."

"Narrow Point? But that's hardly more than a ghost town. There's only six families out there now. What were they doing out there?" Dan reached over and opened the drawer of the nightstand and picked up the notebook and two pencils that lay there. He opened the notebook at random to an empty page.

"They told me that Tubby Bass said that was a shortcut to the freeway," Eric said in exasperation.

"Narrow Point Loop a shortcut to . . ." Dan's voice rose in disbelief. "Tubby's not the greatest guide in the world, but he sure as hell knows better than that."

"Yeah, well, that's what they told me," Eric sighed. "Anyway, however it happened, I gather that's where they were. They said they stopped at an old, three-story frame house to ask for directions. They said it was back from the road on a wide curve."

"Sounds like the Hollister place. It's been empty for years," Dan said, still feeling puzzled.

"Well, according to these folks, it isn't empty now. They said that these people were there, all carrying things like wrenches and knives, and took after them."

"What?" Dan was sitting up straight now, and he knew that sleep was lost to him for the rest of the night.

"Yeah. I know how it sounds, but I don't

think these folks are lying, Dan. I really don't. They're too beat up and too scared to lie. They might exaggerate, but nobody makes up a story like this one."

"No," Dan said slowly. "What did these people say to them?"

"Mr. and Mrs. Cousins say they didn't talk at all, didn't make any sounds. Just kept coming after them. The Cousinses got out through an upstairs window when the door was blocked. The kid's got a nasty crack on the skull, and Mr. Cousins has a gash in his hand. All three of them have odd abrasions and contusions, and a whole heap of splinters. They're going to need a new back window for the car and probably a new lid for the trunk. Whatever took out after them wasn't kidding, I'll say that."

"Doesn't sound like it." He swung his legs over the side of the bed. "I'll drive over to the Hollister place and have a look at it—see if I can find anything."

"Better do that," Eric agreed.

"And give the Cousins my apologies for this, will you? We don't like visitors to get such a bad impression of Potter's Bluff."

"Will do," Eric promised. "You be sure and call me if anything turns up."

"I will." Dan was about to hang up, but he added, "What about George Widdowes? You going to tell him about this?"

Eric paused. "I gotta report it, of course. So do you. But I'm not going to point it out to him special, if that's what you mean, unless there's something mighty unsavory behind it all. All Widdowes wants is a way to keep the

Board of Supervisors impressed enough so that he won't have to do anything more difficult than attending political rallies and drinking three martinis with lunch. So long." Eric hung up.

Dan got out of bed and began methodically to dress.

"What is it, Danny?" Janet murmured.

"I've got to go out. There was some . . . unpleasantness out at the Hollister place tonight and I told Eric I'd check it out." He was into his pants and starting to button his shirt.

"Do you have to go? Won't it keep until morning?" The covers had rolled back, exposing her breasts.

"I don't think so, Jan." Desire for her seized him suddenly, as it so often did. "Sorry. I'd rather stay here with you."

"Then wait half an hour. That won't make any difference, will it?" She touched one hardening nipple. "It would be fun, Danny. What's half an hour?"

"I'll be back before long. Then I won't have to run off." He turned and bent over her. "Janet, I'm not doing this to amuse myself. Eric says that three people had serious trouble out at the Hollister place tonight. You know I can't let that alone, or George Widdowes will be on my back about it."

"Then I guess you'd better go," she said remotely. "But it sounds like a tempest in a teapot to me. They're city people. Probably got spooked, being all by themselves in the country." She pulled the covers up to her chin.

"Could be," he allowed as he finished

dressing. He took his leather flight jacket and pulled it on over his uniform. "That fog's getting thick," he said as he looked out the window.

"Drive carefully," was all Janet said to him as he went out of the bedroom and down the hall.

• • •

Wreathed in fog, the Hollister place had something of the look of a medieval fortress. The plain walls were leprous in the filtered moonlight, and the blank windows were hard as stone. Dan had left the squad car back on the road, and as he walked up the rutted driveway, he shone his powerful flashlight over the front of the building. His hands were cold, and mist clung to his skin.

The beam of the flashlight picked out a smear of blood on the right pillar beside the door, and above it, as his light traveled upward, Dan saw where several shingles had been recently dislodged. He frowned. That was not an easy climb. If the Cousins had left the house that way, they must certainly have been desperate.

Dan aimed the beam of the flashlight at the ground. What he saw there disturbed him. Grasses and weeds were flattened and the path was freshly scuffed. In one or two places, small branches were broken, turning back against their stalks. There were imprints of shoes of several sorts and sizes, all quite recently made. Whatever else the Cousins might have imagined, they were right in saying there had been a good number of people at this house not very long ago. Dan went up to the front door and tried it. To his surprise it opened, yawning back into the darkness of the long hall. Dan stood on the threshold, his light aimed into the darkness. He called out once, his voice echoing through the deserted house. It was foolish to go in, he thought. Whatever had happened there was over and he had little to do but make a last, cautious check on the house to be sure that nothing lingered from the events that had taken place there. He was not able to convince himself that he wanted to delve into the events. If half of what Eric Watson said was true, there had been very cruel people here earlier, and Dan did not like to think that he lived with such people.

On impulse he went into the hall, thinking that the story the Cousins had told could be quickly answered by demonstrating that there had been no disturbance in the house. In the dining room he found overturned chairs, but that, he knew, could have happened years ago, the result of prankish kids. The rest of the lower floor—kitchen, pantry, sitting room, parlor, study—had little to offer him. Eric had told him that the Cousins claimed to have got out through a second-floor window. Dan considered leaving the house without bothering, but now that he was inside, he might as well go through the motions. Then he could call Eric back and do whatever he could to clear up the misunderstanding.

The two front bedrooms were untouched. One smelled of mold. From the looks of it, the putty on the windows was gone and dampness had seeped in. Wallpaper hung in long peels from the front wall confirming this. The other had not been touched yet, but it would not be too long before it too, succumbed to the spread of the decay that would at last claim the old house.

The larger of the back bedrooms was locked, and Dan found that puzzling, for that could only mean that it had been locked from the inside. How could that be possible? he wondered as he frowned at the unyielding door. He swept the beam of his flashlight down the hall, and the battered dressing room door caught his eye. Dan walked toward it with more care than he might have used. The door was completely wrecked. There were great splinters of wood sticking out of it and the upper hinge had been torn out of the twisted wood. Inside the room there was a large overturned dresser and many scraps of wood. The door on the other side of the dressing room was similarly shattered, and the door to the bathroom, a few feet beyond, was deeply gouged and standing open.

The bathroom was a shambles.

It was more than an hour later that he left the house; about five in the morning. Dan doubted he would be back to Potter's Bluff much before dawn, because he wanted to make one more sweep of the grounds prior to leaving. He had the uneasy sensation that by evening much of the damage would be restored and the Hollister place would look much as it had for all the years it had stood empty.

Dan searched carefully but found little. Whoever had wrought such destruction in the house had been very careful to leave no token behind. A very few items were in the bag Dan carried—a few buttons, a scrap of denim, part of a shoelace, a bloody leaf that might as easily have been left by the Cousins as by their tormentors—and he walked slowly toward the roadway where his squad car was parked.

At the last moment, something caught his eye, a bright flash beside the deepest rut of the driveway. Dan paused, letting the flashlight play over the ground, looking for that bright wink that had caught his attention. At first he did not find it, and he had almost decided that he had been mistaken when he saw it again, that shiny sliver. Careful not to deflect the flashlight again, he bent over, prodding the dewy earth gently.

He drew his hand back quickly and thrust his cut finger into his mouth, and when he searched again he was considerably more circumspect. Then he had it. He lifted the fine steel instrument from the rut and turned it over in his fingers. A surgical scalpel gleamed back at him.

Chapter 11

Betty was somewhat startled to see Dan so early in the morning, and she apologized at once for her appearance. "I know I should have taken more time, but after last night, all I wanted to do was sleep for as long as I could. My hair's a mess. I was planning to do it over at coffee break." She patted the bun at the back of her neck nervously.

"Late night?" He had not noticed she was not her usual neatly tailored self until she pointed it out to him.

"Very. One of those things that comes up suddenly, and there wasn't an easy way to refuse. I never know how to turn down those sorts of invitations gracefully, do you?" She seemed on edge as she talked to him; she made neat piles of the papers on her desk and then shifted them. "In a town this size, it isn't possible to make up a polite lie."

"I hadn't thought about it, but you're probably right." He went around the partition to his side of the office and picked up the phone, dialing Eric Watson's office in Hollis. The phone rang a number of times and then there was a quiet voice on the line. "Who is this please?"

"This is Sheriff Gillis in Potter's Bluff. I told Eric I'd call him and give him a report on an incident. When can I reach him?" Dan had put his plastic bag on the desk top and was about to open it and begin sorting the contents.

"Oh, dear," said the woman on the line. "Oh, dear. I should have thought they'd have called you by now—"

"I haven't been in," Dan said, interrupting her. "That was what I called to talk to him about."

"Oh, dear," the woman said again, sniffling.

"What's wrong?" Dan was growing impatient with the woman and it embarrassed him to feel that way about her. "If something has happened, tell me about it, will you?"

"Of course. It's so difficult . . . Sheriff Watson was killed a few hours ago."

"*What?*" Dan almost shouted.

"He was on his way back from the medical center in Bradley and his car was sideswiped," the woman went on as if by rote. "Apparently the driver of the other car was half asleep or drunk. Both cars were wrecked, and the drivers killed. It was a terrible thing to happen. Sheriff Watson was such a good man."

"Yes," Dan said slowly. "And the other car?"

"They're tracing the license now. We should have an identity on the driver before noon. I'm sorry to have to tell you this, Sheriff

Gillis. I was certain that by now someone would have told you."

"Thanks," Dan said woodenly. "As I said, I've been out." But why hadn't Betty called him on her precious radio? Then he remembered that she had come late to the office that morning and probably had not had the news herself yet. "I'll call later."

"It was simply one of those unaccountable accidents, Sheriff Gillis," the woman told him. "I've been working as the sheriff's housekeeper for about six months. He was a very good man, an excellent employer. Never gave me a bit of trouble, always pleasant and never inconsiderate."

"He was a good man," Dan agreed, wishing he could get off the phone now. "Will you call my office when the car and driver . . . are identified?" He had a great dislike of these sorts of conversations. "I'm sure you'll miss him."

"Oh, yes. All of Hollis will." She sighed. "Well, thank you for calling, Sheriff Gillis. I'll tell the deputies that you called."

"Fine, fine." Dan hung up more quickly than was polite, and got up from his desk, going around the partition to face Betty. "Eric Watson was killed this morning, a few hours ago, I understand. His car was sideswiped, both drivers dead."

"Oh, dear. That's dreadful!" Betty's face was ashen as she listened. "The poor man."

"Yeah, the poor man." Dan was already on his way to the door. "I've got to go out. I'll probably go by the high school before I come back. You can reach me by radio if you have to." He pulled open the door.

"But where are you going?" Betty asked.

"First I'm going to pick up some stuff from Ernie. After that, the high school. I may stop for some lunch if I can stomach it." He was out of the door and on his way to the car before Betty could protest.

• • •

The sign on Ernie's door said that he was out on an errand and would be back at 2:30, so Dan drove over to the high school to talk to Janet and explain why he had taken so long on his examination of the Hollister place. There were four parking places for visitors, and Dan took the one closest to the main entrance.

He was walking toward the imposing double doors when he realized he was beneath the windows of Janet's classroom. Two of the windows were open, so he paused to listen. He was proud of Janet's abilities, and more than once had listened, without her being aware of him, to the lectures she gave her advanced classes.

"So," Janet said enthusiastically, "you see that voodoo is basically a religion, not simply a superstition. In voodoo worship, belief and conversion are absolutely necessary for its practice to work. There have been many studies made over the years and all but the most prejudiced of them conclude that there is indeed a force at work in the voodoo religion, and that it has a great deal of potency in the daily lives of those who practice it—a great deal more force than Christianity has. Voodoo influences every aspect of the lives of its followers. Possession by gods is a regular, expected experience, and any worshiper, once initiated, anticipates this possession as a ritual of his faith. There is also a great deal of emphasis placed on the manipulation of friends and enemies, both living and dead. Voodoo, unlike Christianity, does not rigidly define the difference between life and death. For the true practitioner of voodoo, death is simply another aspect of life, and as such, it has certain opportunities that can be taken advantage of if one has sufficient skill and knowledge to do so."

Dan listened, a scowl on his pleasant features. So that was what Janet had been reading those books for. He told himself that his recent cases had made him morbidly—the word 'morbidly' lingered in his thoughts with the same unwelcome intensity as a bad taste at the back of the tongue—sensitive.

He walked on, hearing a bit of an explanation of a geometric theorem from the next classroom and Paul Haskell's unctuous voice telling a parent why a particular student had received a disappointing grade in a current events class. "The evening news is not enough, Mrs. Davies. I know that Dick doesn't understand that yet, but your experience through the years must have shown you how important it is to delve into what . . ."

The main doors swung open and two sunny-faced teenaged girls came out. Both were laughing. One waved to Dan calling out, "Hello, Sheriff Gillis!" and the other blushed a furious shade and turned away from him.

There were a few students in the hall, Dan noticed, as he turned down the corridor toward Janet's classroom. A few of them looked sullen or guilty as the sheriff went past, but most were courteous enough, and one of the boys gave him a thumbs-up signal and a quick, mercurial smile.

As Dan opened the back door of the classroom, he heard Janet say, "Despite what you may have seen on the late show, or at the drive-in—that's assuming you were watching at all—the voodoo walking dead are not like something out of a thirties production of *Frankenstein.* Oh, come on," she said, chiding her class humorously. "I know that most of your parents try to keep you from seeing such movies, and I know that most of you go to them because you want to. Right?"

There was a sheepish chorus of agreement. Janet nodded knowingly. "That's what I thought. And your parents pulled the same thing on their parents, you can be sure of that. Now, I've seen a fair number of zombie films and— Yes, Roberta?"

"Mrs. Gillis, do you really *believe* that dead bodies climb out of their graves and go walking around? Really?" Horace Andrews' daughter was attractive in an overly perfect way. Most of her classmates found her slightly condescending manner as hard to take as her obvious intelligence. The only thing Roberta lacked was humor.

"If you mean, do I think that a mad scientist somewhere is going to manufacture a clumsy creature, no, I don't. You know, if someone could revive the dead, I think he'd take the time to do it right, wouldn't you? That means that they would laugh and talk and smile and run like the rest of us. Why do they have to walk around like this?" Janet brought her hands down to her sides and stiffened her body as if she had been strapped to an ironing board. She began to goose-step around the front of the classroom, evoking nervous titters from her students. Janet did not respond, and after two turns at the front of the room, she began to move ponderously toward Roberta Andrews. Now Janet's face was totally expressionless and her steady, awkward pacing became sinister. She bore down on Roberta as the classroom grew silent.

Roberta jumped out of her seat with a weak scream.

At once Janet was herself again. She reached out and gave Roberta an affectionate pat on the shoulder. "That's what I mean. It's fairly scary to see someone act like that, but the trouble is, you would *notice* them. A figure like that certainly stands out in a crowd."

The students laughed and the tension went out of the room. Dan folded his arms and waited at the door.

Janet was back at the board, pointing out her diagram of the religious hierarchy of the voodoo faith. "You see, the wizards occupy the same position of importance as priests, and often serve that function. It is the work of the wizards to bring the dead back for the purpose of doing the will of the worshipers."

"But Mrs. Gillis," said one of the boys by the window, "if a body is dead, how can it—? I mean, well, you know what I mean."

"Yes, Steve, I do." She grinned at the boy. "You're assuming a few matters we haven't discussed yet. You see, even though the bodies are conventionally dead—by which I mean we're not dealing with those in cataleptic shock, for example, but those who have truly ceased all bodily functions of living—under the influence of the voodoo wizard, the dead are capable of very closely imitating the living. That is, of course, assuming that their master desires this, and intends that they should appear to be alive."

"Mrs. Gillis," a towheaded girl in the back of the room said.

"Yes, Elinor?"

"Well, it seems to me . . . it would be hard to control a dead person. If everything in the body has stopped, how does the wizard get it to *do* anything?"

"That's an excellent question, Elinor," Janet approved. "And, as you might expect, it isn't easy. Only the most advanced wizards have this ability, because it takes a great deal of very special training and discipline to achieve that strength of will to control the walking dead. You see, it's the will of the wizard that supplies the energy to the body. It might be possible to reawaken the will of the dead person, but that is not what the voodoo wizard requires. There are reports—not substantiated but not discredited either—of a village in Central America whose residents include a great number of the walking dead. Oh, yes, the practice of voodoo is not limited to the few islands where it is most well-known. It is said that in this Central American village, the walking dead are wholly subservient to their master's will, and that they function as servants to the inhabitants who are not dead. One of the uses these walking dead have been put to is to search the surrounding area, the mountains and the outlying farms, for strangers who could be murdered and brought back to their master to swell the numbers of the walking dead." Janet looked around the room. "At least, that is what the most persistent rumors say, and no one from the outside has yet succeeded in getting into the village to carry on studies."

Dan had been listening with growing unease. Many people found it somehow more comforting to believe that a malignant wizard was at work, deliberately killing strangers and terrifying the countryside than to believe that someone as mundane as a psychopathic killer was on the loose. He wished that Janet had chosen some other time to talk about this aspect of voodoo. Doubtless there would be phone calls to his office this day, and the day after, and the day after that, insisting that a hitherto unknown sorcerer was at work in Potter's Bluff.

"Now," Janet was saying, turning away from the blackboard where she had made a few more notes in her precise hand, "do you want to hear the really creepy part?"

Her class responded eagerly, though Roberta Andrews looked skeptical.

"They say, in this Central American country, that in order for the master to retain control of so many walking dead that he has to have more than his will. He has to cut out the heart of every one of the zombies he has made. He has to keep the heart hidden so that the owner cannot find it, for if the zombie can find his heart and destroy it, then he will die and the wizard will lose all power over him, not just as walking dead, but for all time."

Some of the students were deliciously disgusted to hear this, one or two had turned pale, and two of the boys were grinning. "That Mrs. Gillis," one whispered to the other, unaware that Dan could overhear them. "She's bitchy, but she's good."

Dan grinned wryly, thinking that although he might not dare express it quite that way, he would agree with them.

"Okay, okay, kids," Janet was saying as she clapped her hands twice. "Settle down, now. I didn't tell you this simply to amuse you." She waited until the class was quiet. "I warned you earlier that I expect a report from each of you about folklore, myth and religion from some region of the world. Voodoo is just one example of this kind of religion, and I want you to find others. They don't have to be current. You can bring me examples from the past, and from anywhere in the world where studies have been made. If there are reports written by people on the scene, so much the better. Roberta, you said that you were interested in the pre-

Christians of Hawaii. Well, here's your chance to study them." She glanced up at the clock. "There's five minutes left to the period, so I'd like you to pass in your assignments." She waited while the obligatory groans were heard. "I know just how you feel. I have to spend my weekend correcting those papers, and though none of you has to do more than one paper, I have to read thirty-three of them. Think of that." She left the front of the room as her two monitors got up, and came back to the rear door.

"Pretty impressive demonstration there, teach," Dan said, smiling in spite of himself. Janet was very pretty this morning, and she was glad to see him.

"You didn't come home last night. I should be jealous." There was more than simple teasing in her eyes, and he did not know how to respond. "Trouble?"

"I think so. Something sure as hell happened at the Hollister place last night, but what it was, who knows? I went through the house. There were torn-up doors and smashed furniture. I'm afraid I'm going to have to spend some time on this one."

"Oh, Danny." She made no attempt to conceal her irritation.

"Well," Dan said, "I was hoping that you might let me bribe you with dinner out tomorrow night. I know it won't make up for everything, but you just said that you've got papers to correct this weekend, so I didn't think you'd mind too much if I . . ."

Janet's smile was not entirely forgiving,

but she shrugged. "Dinner it is, so long as we get out of town. Take me into exotic Smiths Landing at least. Some women get housebound, but I'm feeling town-bound."

"What about glorious downtown Farleyville?" The suggestion was not entirely wise, and both of them knew it. Farleyville was slightly more than an hour away from Potter's Bluff. If anything went wrong while Dan and Janet were having dinner, it would take much too long for Dan to get back.

"Farleyville it is," she said, and turned back to the front of the classroom just as the bell sounded.

• • •

Ernie Sutton was still not back, so Dan returned to his office. Betty handed him a stack of notes as he came through the door. "Most of them are requests for callbacks, three of them about Eric Watson. There's also a stack of mail waiting for you, including a manila envelope from George Widdowes."

Dan took the proffered stack of papers and envelopes. "Anything else?"

"Nothing much. Ed Thurston would like to hear from you before this evening, but he stressed that it isn't urgent." Betty's glasses had slid down her nose and it gave her an old-fashioned look. "I called the florist in Hollis and told them to deliver a wreath of flowers to Eric's funeral in your name."

"Thanks," Dan said, quite sincere this time. "Do they know when it will be?"

"Day after tomorrow. I said that you might not be able to be there but that you would send someone in your place if you were busy here." She cleared her throat, waiting to be ordered to act as Dan's lieutenant.

"Did you get your brakes fixed?" Dan asked.

"Yes, and I had my car tuned up last week. It's nine years old, but it runs fine," she insisted defensively.

"Okay." Dan sighed. "If you want to go, fine. I'm pleased you want to. Make sure that you say the right thing to the mayor and anyone else that's there. But do me a favor, Betty."

"What is it, Sheriff?" Her eyes had brightened. It was not often that the sheriff made specfic requests of her.

"Don't mention what's been happening here, okay? I don't want to have this place filled with officers from all over the state having a busman's holiday searching for the person behind these terrible deaths." Dan did not like to admit this, but it had been increasingly on his mind the last two days, and he had come to the conclusion that he had to maintain privacy a little while longer. If there were another killing—he still shied away from the word *murder*—then it would be time to bring in all the reinforcements he could find.

"I won't." She squared her shoulders. "You can count on me, Sheriff."

"I know that, Betty," Dan said, giving her shoulder a comradely pat as he went around the partition to his desk.

It took him a moment to decide what was

wrong, and then he realized that the plastic bag he had had on his desk was gone. "Betty?"

"Yes?"

"What did you do with the bag on my desk?" He made sure it was a casual inquiry and not an accusation.

"The plastic one? I sent it over to the hospital for the lab there, the way I usually do. Wasn't I supposed to? Did you want that sent over to the county offices?"

"No, that's fine." He did not know why her answer did not reassure him. It *was* the usual procedure in his office; Betty had not been the least out of line to act as she had. Yet he could not bring himself to feel comfortable about it.

An hour later Dan had completed most of the calls and was scribbling answers to his mail on a large yellow pad when he heard the outer door open.

"Is the sheriff in?" the voice of G. William Dobbs asked Betty.

"Yes. I'll tell him you're here," she offered.

"Never mind. I'll do it myself," he said. His manner was less effusive than usual, and when he stuck his head around the partition, he seemed almost bashful.

"What are you doing here?" Dan demanded as he set his yellow pad aside. Long experience had taught him that Dobbs was apt to be long-winded.

Dobbs folded his hands, then drew them apart. His hard, buttonlike eyes flickered unhappily, though their expression was unreadable.

Dan waited, then motioned to the other chair in the office. "What are you doing here, Dobbs? What do you want?"

"Good morning, Dan," Dobbs said as he sat down, in an attempt to start their meeting over again.

"Get on with it," Dan sighed. "I've had insufficient sleep, I could use some lunch, and my caffeine level is critically low."

"Don't get so pushy and policemanlike, Daniel. It doesn't become you. Humility, that's the secret." He stared hard at the desk top. "This is all very embarrassing."

"What is?"

"It's so difficult." Dobbs ran a hand through his thinning hair. "You see . . . I want to report . . . a . . . theft."

"From your place?" Dan asked, startled.

"Well, yes. I don't see why you should expect me to report anyone else's theft."

"Grave robbers, I suppose?" Dan's sarcasm covered his apprehension.

"Well . . . yes, that's one way to put it." Dobbs took a deep breath and let it out slowly. He did not look at Dan.

"You're not serious?" Dan was sitting up straight now, his half-finished letter forgotten.

"I'm afraid I am."

"But who . . . what . . . ?" Dan shook his head.

"You know that sad young waif that you found out on the road? She'd been burned, the way the other one was? Female, about five-four or five-five, probably no more than twenty and not—"

"I remember," Dan said tightly, a brusque gesture shutting off Dobbs's recitation. "Are you telling me that someone dug up the body?"

"No. I hadn't buried her yet. I was waiting for final permission from the county. In cases like hers, that's the best way, you know. I'd thought permission would come this morning so that tomorrow I could lay her to rest. But . . . well, she was . . . gone. I came in this morning, and . . . she simply wasn't there."

"Forced entry?" Dan asked sharply.

"No indication of it that I could find. All the windows are intact, the back door was locked and Jimmy said that the front door was locked, both the dead bolt and the simple lock. I don't know what to make of it, Sheriff." Dobbs's hands dangled in his lap as if they did not belong to his body.

"Anything else missing?"

"No, I checked. And there's one occupant of the reposing rooms, and she is completely . . . undisturbed. Apparently the . . . unknown woman . . . was the only . . . desired object." He made a helpless little sound in his throat.

"I see." Dan rocked his chair back on its hind legs. "I don't believe this. A dead body missing from the mortuary. What next? What kind of maniac is running around out there? Killings, terrorizing, and body snatching! It's like something out of a bad novel. What did they call them?—penny dreadfuls. We'll get rattling chains in the night next, and maybe a ghost or two." He laughed bitterly. "If the ghosts could tell me what the hell is going on here, I'd welcome them." Reluctantly Dan started to rise. "Come on, Dobbs. We'll go back to your place and I'll have a look around."

"No!" Dobbs reached out impulsively.

"Why not?" Dan was perplexed now, and in no mood to argue with the coroner.

"We can't let anyone *know* about this. It's bad enough having all those extra bodies of strangers to dispose of, but if it got around that they were *disappearing*... My reputation. Who would entrust their deceased loved ones to a mortician known to have lost a body? Think of the difficulties it might cause. Questions. Needless exhumations, just to be sure that Uncle Silas was actually in his coffin. Such things can happen, Daniel. And the current temperament of this town would foster such suspicions. Right now, if some one you loved died, would you entrust him or her to me in complete confidence? I doubt it."

"For God's sake, Dobbs, don't be ridiculous."

"Well..." Dobbs shook his head. "Maybe I'm panicking? Do you think so? You think that perhaps Jimmy, in a fit of uncharacteristic zeal just slipped her into a drawer and forgot to tell me about it? Would you like me to go check, in case I managed to overlook her? Would you like me to give you a call if I find her in the freezer?"

"Dobbs, don't—" Dan started, then changed his mind. "I sure hope you find her, Dobbs. Between these killings and—" He had to bite back Janet's name. "I've got problems of my own."

It was unusual when Dobbs offered anything but the most unctuous of professional sympathy, but now he did. "I know. Janet has been a bit strange lately."

Dan looked up at the mortician, startled.

"Oh, I do see a great deal more than I'm given credit for, Daniel. My work is fairly solitary, and it gives me time to think. I have heard things, and seen things . . ."

"What things?" Dan asked, hating himself for admitting, even indirectly, that Dobbs was right.

"I realize that I'm intruding, and this is none of my business, Dan, none at all, but . . ."

"But?" Dan echoed bitterly.

"Dan, you hardly know Janet."

Dan was too amazed to be angry. "Hardly know her? She's my *wife!* What are you talking about?"

Dobbs shook his head again and lowered his voice. "Janet comes to see me all the time. Didn't you know that?"

Dan wondered, fleetingly, if G. William Dobbs, of all people, could actually be his rival. It seemed so impossible that he blurted out, "What do you talk about?"

"Things that interest her, and me. There aren't too many well-educated people in Potter's Bluff. She's lonely. Oh, not for another man, if that's what you're thinking. But for conversation, for friends, Dan. She likes the place, that's not the problem, but she requires more . . . stimulus than she gets here." Dobbs spoke tactfully, without a trace of pity in his face.

"You talk about things," Dan mused. "What things? Do you have anything to do with her sudden renewed interest in witchcraft and voodoo and the rest of that occult junk?"

Dobbs was affronted by this suggestion. "No, I do not! Occult studies, indeed! In fact, since you've brought the matter up, you may tell her for me that I was more than mildly insulted when, just because I am a mortician, she had the audacity to insinuate that I might have included the black arts as a hobby. Her remark about raw materials was in the most appalling taste. Really quite unlike her."

"She wasn't serious," Dan said without conviction.

"I am sorry to have to contradict you, Sheriff, but she most certainly was. At the time I attempted to make light of her unfeeling remark, but she insisted that we pursue the matter further. She wanted to experiment with a few spells, she said, just to see what might happen if she did as the old *grimoires* instructed. I warned her at the time that no one would tolerate such execrable behavior, but that didn't seem to bother her. She was amused by my protestations." Dobbs cleared his throat. "I very nearly called you then, but I couldn't bring myself to do it. I'm not entirely sure why, but I could not do it to her. It would upset you, I knew that. I see that you're upset now."

"Do you think there's any connection between . . . the missing body and . . . Janet?" Dan hated to ask the question and the words came out through a grind of hurt. Why had Janet never spoken to him? Why had she never mentioned Dobbs? How far had she gone in her occult experiments? And why?

"It's possible, but I doubt it, for no other reason than that the unfortunate young woman who was so hideously burned weighed a good ten pounds more than Janet, and I am not convinced that Janet could move a corpse without attracting some comment." Dobbs's smile was touched with irony. "Potter's Bluff isn't quite *that* laconic."

"But the body is missing and Janet . . ." Rather than finish that thought, Dan asked Dobbs, "Tell me: Do you think that there's any possibility that it could happen? That through voodoo or something like it, the dead can come back?"

"I devoutly hope not," Dobbs said. "In my profession, it's rather an unpleasant notion."

"It is in anyone's profession," Dan said moodily.

Dobbs laughed outright. The sound of it reminded Dan of something he had read many years ago, when he was a kid, about a professor having a laugh like turtles being crushed by falling palm trees. Dobbs had exactly that sort of laugh, Dan decided. "Oh, Daniel, you do surprise me!" he said at last. "You don't mean to tell me that you believe the missing corpse got up and ambled out of my workroom, do you? For the moment we will ignore the matter of the locked doors and windows. Suffice it to say, someone in this village would have noticed a nude, young, unknown woman, had she done so. And where would she go? If she did walk away, why has no one found her? I can't subscribe to the idea that she could take refuge in a basement or empty house. It makes no sense."

Dan recalled the ruined doors in the Hollister place, and quickly turned his mind away from that. "I agree it sounds improbable, but so does body snatching. You will give me that much, won't you?"

Dobbs nodded several times. "Most certainly I will give you that, Sheriff. I'd be a fool to say otherwise." He stood up. "The fact remains that the body of the young woman is missing. It stands to reason that somebody has it. I don't mean to tell you how to do your job, particularly in so unusual a situation, but I do think that you might find a way to establish how that corpse left my workroom. If there is evidence to support your conclusions, I will accept sunspots, flying saucers, teleportation, sleight of hand or acts of God, providing your explanation accounts for all the circumstances. In the meantime, I should get back to work, as you doubtless wish to do. You need not admonish me about touching surfaces and tampering with possible clues. I, too, have watched my share of television, and it has made me aware of the rudiments of police work."

"Imagine my relief." Dan's sarcasm had returned. "Just remember that since neither you nor I know how the body got out, there's no way of telling where the clues might be, or even what we're looking for." He half rose and took Dobbs's proffered hand. "Do you really talk with Janet, Dobbs?"

"Yes, Sheriff, I really do," he said gravely. "You have a very demanding job. She understands that. I think one of the reasons she sees me, aside from the fact that I once spent considerable time in a university and have yet to give up the habit of reading, is that no one, not even you, would believe for a moment that our relationship is anything other than platonic. Aside from the fact that I am quite literally old enough to be her father—who, I understand, was seven years my junior—I am not the most prepossessing man in this area, and if I were to indulge myself in an affair, it would not be with Janet, who, aside from the fact that she has no interest in such dalliance, is also the wife of the sheriff, making her a woman to be approached with a great deal of circumspection." He had released Dan's hand, but his bright, flat eyes held the younger man's. "If you imagine that you're dealing with a sexual rival, I fear you very much underestimate the situation." With that he made a stiff little bow and turned away, going around the partition in a furtive way, his head bent forward and his shoulders slightly hunched.

Dan made no move to follow him, but sat still, thinking about all that Dobbs had told him. After twenty minutes, he decided that he believed most of what the mortician had said, but did not share his reservations. Dan had also come to the conclusion that whatever had happened at the mortuary, it had a perfectly logical explanation, one which he would be able to uncover almost at once. Satisfied, he returned to dealing with his mail. There were two routine letters, flyers and a catalogue, and then, to Dan's amazement, there was a letter from St. Louis, with an official seal in the corner. He opened the letter with care and took out the elaborately engraved, watermarked paper. It was from the court, and it requested that the body of George LeMoir be exhumed and sent to St. Louis for final disposal. The Missouri judge whose signature appeared in formidable illegibility at the bottom of the page indicated that he would have the cooperation of the coroner's office in Dan's county and that confirmation would follow within twenty-four hours. The letter closed with a few formal lines of appreciation, and a terse farewell. Dan held the letter in his hands for several minutes, reading it through several times. Dobbs, he knew, would resent the order, but doubtless similar notification had been sent to the mortician. Dan got up slowly as he refolded the letter and thrust it into his pocket. He would attend to the matter, and then he would pick up the film at Ernie's.

Chapter 12

A balding head protruded from the weeds like an exotic hybrid. The eyes were fixed in downward concentration. A spadeful of earth arched through the air to land on the growing pile of damp earth beside the new grave.

"Where's Dobbs?" Dan demanded of the gravedigger.

"He hasn't been out here yet today," was the answer, though the man did not stop his work, or look up.

"Don't leave when you're finished there," Dan admonished him. "We have to dig up that George LeMoir."

"Dig up?" the gravedigger repeated incredulously. "I don't dig 'em up. I don't get paid to do that. I just bury 'em."

"Figure extra charges, whatever you want," Dan said sharply. "You're going to dig the coffin up."

The gravedigger tossed another shovel of earth out of the half-finished grave. "Not without Mr. Dobbs's permission. He's the coroner and he hasn't said anything to me about exhuming anyone. You better check it out with him, Sheriff. Then you come talk to me."

"We'll have a court order here by four this afternoon. I called up to be sure. It's official, and whether Dobbs likes it or not, it has to be done." Dan stood on the edge of the grave and stared down. "If you want to argue with the county, go ahead."

The gravedigger gave a snort.

Dan strode through the cemetery toward the back door of the mortuary. The day was turning blustery. Huge, purple clouds tumbled overhead, and inland, over the trees, the first thin veils of rain were falling. Dan pounded on the back door once, then pushed the door open and started down the hall. From the workroom came the unexpected strains of the Moody Blues. Dan stood for a moment, trying to reconcile the music with what he had always heard here. Cautiously he went to the workroom door and opened it. The music welled up at him, drowning his call.

"Dobbs! Dobbs, you here? It's Sheriff Gillis!" He had come all the way into the room, startled at how dark it was. No lights burned—only the music blared out at him. Dan looked around once more and saw that the door to the largest supply cabinet was standing open. He approached this cautiously, not sure what to expect.

As Dan pulled the cabinet door back, Jimmy turned around to look at him, his face wild with surprise. The boy's left hand was cupped, and on the heel of the hand were several smears of unblended grease paint. On Jimmy's right arm there was a large patch of discolored, livid flesh.

"Jimmy!" Dan said, startled as well as concerned. "What the hell are you doing? What happened to you?"

Jimmy's face colored with shame and anger, and then quickly assumed a calm expression. "Nothing. Nothing, Sheriff. Just . . . practicing." He began to mix the greasepaint on the heel of his hand, as Dobbs had taught him to do.

"If you've got a bruise that bad, you'd better have a doctor take a look at it." He wanted to ask how the boy had been hurt, but knew that this would not be tolerated.

"Dobbs is a doctor. He said it's okay. It'll be all right." Jimmy was slightly rattled; he smeared the greasepaint over the bruise, smoothed the cosmetic and reached for the powder to set it. "What do you want, Sheriff?"

"I'm looking for Dobbs. We've got an order for an exhumation." Dan was fascinated with the skill the boy showed. "You're good at that."

"I'm getting there." Jimmy was finished. He wiped his hands on a large paper towel, which he threw into the trash bin, then rolled down his sleeves and looked about for the stack of books which were on the end of one of the tables. "Sorry I can't help you out there, Sheriff. But I gotta go. I got an exam tomorrow." He picked up his books and left the room.

Dan watched him go, listening when Jimmy left the room for the slam of the front door. It came less than a minute later. He waited a bit longer, oddly captivated by the eerie darkness of the mortuary. On the turntable, the record came to an end and the machine shut itself off. The silence was oppressive, far more so than the music had been.

"Dobbs?" Dan called the name again, though he did not expect an answer. He was about to close the cabinet when, on impulse, he looked in at the supplies. There were Dobbs's makeup chest, a number of wigs on stands, several jars of Dobbs's own cosmetic cream, and two good-sized containers of morticians wax. Dan stared at these supplies, as if the solution to the questions nagging him were there, in those vials and tubes and bottles. What was that special compound of Dobbs's? The one Dobbs had boasted about? Tissue cement with something extra? "You're being nuts," Dan said aloud to himself. Unexplained killings and talk about the walking dead, and now he was imagining . . . terrible things. Dobbs was a peculiar man, no question about it, but it did not follow that he was experimenting with . . . What? And Dobbs had already said he had no use for the occult. Another voice within Dan pointed out that Dobbs could be very sly, and might have been lying in order to throw Dan off the track. Dan slammed the cabinet door closed. "No. It's crazy."

His protest rang around the room, mocking him.

• • •

The Potter's Bluff Cafe was almost empty when Dan stopped for his cup of coffee. Penny smiled as he came in. "We've missed you, stranger," she said archly.

"It's been a busy time," Dan answered as he went across the room to the center table where Harry Clemens and Herman Ewing sat. "Afternoon."

"Howdy there, Sheriff," Harry said nastily. "Found yourself the guy with the gas can yet?"

"What makes you think it's a gas can, Harry?" Dan said pointedly as he took his seat.

Harry stared at Dan blankly. "How'd . . . ?" There was something false in his smile. "Well, it's obvious, isn't it, Sheriff? How else did that lady get toasted?"

"There was no gas on the ground around her, and no burn pattern to indicate that there had been. Even if most of it had evaporated, there would have been traces, but there weren't any. That means she was killed somewhere else." Dan was ticking his points off on his fingers. "So, what makes you say gas can?"

"Well, shit, Dan-boy, you never said nothing about her not being burned there. I just thought . . ." He reached over and punched Herman in the arm. "Hey! What do you think, Herm? Think it was a gas can?"

Herman gave a lethargic shrug. "Don't know, Harry, and that's a fact." He stared down at the coffee in his cup, and did not drink.

"You could be right," Dan said, hoping to encourage Harry to talk.

"Nah," Harry disclaimed at once. "I didn't know about those other things."

Dan had never heard Harry back down

before, and it put him on the alert. "How else do you think it happened, Harry?"

"That ain't my job, Sheriff, it's yours." Harry looked smug but there was fright at the back of his eyes.

"You've pointed out that I'm not doing it very well," Dan said, being careful not to look at Harry directly, and trigger his belligerence.

Harry said nothing. His heavy, large features set into a grimace.

"See, I've been thinking," Dan went on, as if this silence were nothing unusual. "I figure in a town this size, someone must have seen something, but they just don't know it's important. Take Herman here: he might have met up with the girl as he walked home. She could have bought something in town. Herman might not think anything of it, but if I knew about it, I could start to trace her actions. Or Aaron might have sold her something. Maybe Phil passed her on the road when he drove home. There's lots of things people know that I could use. You, Harry. You spend a good deal of time in your truck when you're not here. You might have seen her trying for a ride, or being picked up by somebody. You never know." Dan tasted the coffee and put it down. It was really bad today. Dan poured a generous amount of cream into the cup.

"You talk to Agnes Whitestone? That woman sees everything. Sits in her front room with all them cats, and nothing happens that she don't know about it." Harry fidgeted in his chair.

Dan had not talked to the woman, and

now he castigated himself inwardly. Of *course* Agnes Whitestone should be questioned. He thought of that dowdy, middle-aged woman who seemed to live in flowered housecoats and pom-pom slippers. Harry was right, Dan thought. Agnes Whitestone would have to be talked to. He could call her after he finished up with Dobbs.

"Old Agnes, she'll tell you what and who's been in town every day for the past four years, most likely," Herman agreed. He rubbed his hands together, and Dan noticed that the heavy cast had been replaced with an ace bandage.

"Herman, your arm . . ." Dan said, thinking that perhaps Herman had grown impatient with the cast and taken it off himself. "You sure that's okay?"

"Doctor did it last night. The cast was giving me some trouble, so he said we'll splint it instead." Herman chafed his knuckles against his palm again. "It's a little stiff."

"Well, it's broken, isn't it?" Dan demanded. He had never heard of such treatment. "Was this Ed Thurston's idea?" He wanted to find out if Herman would lie to him again.

"Sort of. Doesn't seem to be doing too bad, though." Herman hunched down in his chair defensively. "If it hurts, they'll put a cast back on it, I guess."

"You mean it doesn't hurt?" Dan was complete baffled now.

"Not much. Nothing I can't handle," Herman boasted petulantly.

"Well, I'm glad to hear that, Herman," Dan said uncertainly as he got up from the table. "Sorry I can't stay, but there are people I've got to see."

"Sure, Sheriff," Harry responded, making no effort to urge him to stay.

Dan left the proper amount on the counter, and called out to Penny, telling her where the money was. As he stepped outside, the cold wind whipped around him.

Overhead the purple clouds were jostling along, harried by the first stormy bluster off the ocean. Dan zipped up his leather flight jacket and went quickly to his squad car, anticipating the welcome blast of hot air from the heater.

• • •

After an hour of aimless conversation with Agnes Whitestone, Dan was glad to leave her and go back to Dobbs's mortuary. By now, Dobbs himself must have seen the order of exhumation and with any luck, had told the gravedigger to go to work. He sat in the car and read over his notes. Doubtless there were valuable bits of information in all that rambling. He would sort it out after the business with LeMoir had been cleared up.

The gravedigger was almost finished with digging up LeMoir's coffin as Dan came up to him. He glanced up at Dan. "Dobbs said to go ahead and do this," he explained as he tossed more of the earth out of the hole.

"It makes it easier for all of us, doesn't it?"

Dan said evenly. "How much longer will it take you to finish?"

"Not much longer. Ten, twenty minutes." He gestured to the heavy rope at the edge of the grave. "I already got that around one end. I'll soon have the other end ready to haul out."

Dan winced as the shovel struck the lid of the coffin. The sound was ominously hollow, muffled and loud at once "Sure you don't need any help?"

"Not just yet, Sheriff. Maybe when I start pulling it up." He swung another load of earth onto the pile beside the grave. "There isn't room enough in here for two unless one of 'em's lying down." His chuckle was rusty.

Dan made no response. He stood waiting while the gravedigger finished his work and the first spatters of rain began to fall.

"Give me a hand out, will you, Sheriff?" he asked, holding up his muddy, gnarled hand.

"Sure." Dan grabbed and pulled. "What do you want me to do?"

"Take that rope, and I'll take this one. The ends are around the handles. Coffin hasn't been in the ground long enough to rot the hardware off. Shouldn't take very long, two of us working together like this." He had already bent to pick up the rope, and he hefted it experimentally. "I'm glad I don't have to do this by myself in the rain. That's not a thing I'd enjoy at *all*."

Dan walked to the other end of the grave and picked up the rope. "When do we begin?"

"Anytime you like, Sheriff."

Dan tugged at the rope. In the grave the boards of the coffin groaned in protest. There was a faint, obscene kissing sound as the coffin rose out of the earth. The gravedigger turned, the rope angling down his back from his shoulder so that the box could swing over the edge of the grave. Dan held his rope steady, and reached out once or twice to guide the coffin to a solid bit of ground.

It was raining harder, and the sound of the drops on the wooden top of the coffin was like the rattle of distant gunfire. Dan let his rope drop and looked about for tools. "Do you have a crowbar?"

"What for?" The gravedigger had bent to pick up his shovel.

"To open the coffin," Dan said bluntly.

"Are you crazy? Here? With the rain?" He took a hasty step backward.

"We've got to open it. Now." Dan was soaked and his heavy twill trousers stuck to his legs. "Come on. Give me the shovel."

"I don't like seeing corpses, not when they've had a little time to rot. No, thanks, Sheriff. You want that open, you do it on your own."

Dan frowned at the gravedigger. "This coffin doesn't weigh enough to have a corpse in it. That's why I want it opened, right now." He saw the gravedigger hesitate, and reached out to pull the shovel out of his hands.

"Sheriff, what the hell are you—"

Dan brought the shovel up over his head in a powerful arc, then brought it down with all the force of his swing on the lid of the coffin. The long box jumped under the blow, and gave another muted thud.

"You're gonna smash that body to bits, and . . . Sheriff, those things smell bad enough without you opening them up. That lid—you'll want to be able to close it up." The gravedigger was backing away from Dan.

A second and third blow struck the coffin, and then one of the boards buckled and the upper and lower ends of it pulled away from the nails. Dan stopped pounding and stuck the blade of the shovel under the spring board and leaned on the handle. The nails shrieked as Dan levered them out of the wood.

"Hey, Sheriff, don't—" the gravedigger began.

Two of the boards came away and Dan tossed them aside. "Have a look for yourself," he said, feeling vindicated and disgusted at once.

The coffin was simple and quite inexpensive. On the quilted cotton lining where the body of George LeMoir should have been there was only a tightly wrapped package about the size of a grapefruit. "I told you there was no body," Dan said. He dragged his forearm over his forehead to get the rain out of his eyes as he bent down to reach into the coffin. "Only this." He removed the package and held it up.

"Is it . . . a head?" the gravedigger asked from ten feet away.

"Too small." Dan examined the heavy knots tying up the many layers of thick fabric. He tugged at the largest of the knots, then reached for the Swiss Army knife hanging from his belt. The fine steel blades snicked through the stout nylon cord, which fell away as the strands were cut. Dan was left holding what seemed to be nothing more than a bundle of rags. Carefully he began to peel back the wrappings, thinking of the men who had unwrapped mummies in Egypt. The last of the cloths fell away and Dan was left with a tough, springy object, about the size of a large, clenched fist. He held it up, heedless of the rain.

"Christ, Sheriff!" the gravedigger said faintly. "That's not . . ."

Dan felt the thing in his hands. Though the light was fading fast, he knew now what he held, and it made him queasy. "It's a heart," he said quite clearly.

"Shit!" the gravedigger said, and turned away to be sick over the back of a weathered tombstone.

Dan bent to pick up one of the cloths which had held the heart, and wrapped it around the organ again. Then he started across the cemetery to Dobbs's mortuary.

• • •

The workroom was deserted, as were the office, the study and the lavatory at the back of the building. No one sat behind the receptionist's desk in the front, and only one of the reposing rooms was open. Dan stepped inside that room and found, instead of a casket on the dais, a home-movie screen. There was a whisper of sound on the carpet behind him and Dan turned in time to see the door swing shut, and then, a moment later, he heard the unmistakable click of the lock. "Dobbs?" he called out, tentatively first and then more forcefully. "Dobbs! What's this all about?"

As if in answer to his question, a projector went on, and flickering brightness lit the screen. A hand-lettered sign announced the name of the film:

REVELATIONS

Disgustedly, Dan sat down. There were three quick, jerky shots of Potter's Bluff, the stores along Main Street and the high bluffs overlooking the ocean. It was a typical home movie—the pans were much too fast, the cuts abrupt and awkward, but Dan realized that the camera was following a course down to the cove at the north side of the beach. At one point the film showed two small figures in the cove—a man on the beach and a woman halfway up the rocks.

Then there was a group of people, unrecognizable in these grotesquely overexposed shots, standing around a beach fire. It took Dan about twenty seconds to recognize the center of the fire as a human being burning, and when he did, he felt hideously sick. Someone had actually made a film of that! Dan dropped the heart he had held, and it rolled a few feet away from him.

The screen was dark, and then Freddie's pleasant face with its small crescent scar filled it, smiling benignly.

Another hand-lettered sign announced:

TO BE CONTINUED

There was the sound of the film flapping

about the reel, and the light went off, leaving Dan with dazzled eyes, in the room.

"Oh, God," Dan murmured as he considered what he had seen. He became aware that he no longer held the heart, and was repelled by the thought of it. He made a swift, perfunctory search around his chair, but could not find it. Privately relieved, he stood up as he listened. Rain rushed down the windows, although the sound of it was muffled by the heavy draperies.

"Dobbs!" Dan shouted, although he did not expect an answer. He knew it was important to call out to him, for his own sense of control, but he also knew that somehow control had slipped away from him.

A minute went by. Two. There was a quiet click. The door was open. Dan stared at it, wondering if he dared remain in the reposing room, waiting. But there were too many questions. He strode out into the reception area and looked swiftly around. The door to the other reposing room was still closed, and when he tried it, it was locked.

"Dobbs!" The whole place was silent. Dan shivered suddenly, not entirely because of the cold and his wet clothes. He turned toward the front door. Four long strides took him out of the mortuary into the storm.

As his squad car drove away, the door of the locked reposing room opened, and Janet stepped into the reception area.

• • •

Freddie was checking the oil in Tubby Bass's Cadillac when the sheriff drove into the station and called his name. He looked up and was blinded by a flashbulb going off in his face. Dan shouted something Freddie didn't hear, then sped away. Freddie shrugged and went back to doing his job.

• • •

Back at the sheriff's office, Dan got on the phone. He had paid no attention to Betty's alarm at his soaked clothing, or her insistence that he attend to a number of minor matters. He sat at his desk, waiting for the long distance connections to be made.

"Providence Police Department. May we help you?" The faint rush on the line made the woman seem impossibly distant.

"This is Undersheriff Daniel Gillis," he began, and listed all his credentials. "I need immediate information on G. William Dobbs, B.S., M.S., M.D." It was all he could do to resist adding, "etc., etc."

"That would be the records division. I'll transfer you, if you'll hold."

"Thanks," Dan said, and waited to repeat his request to the next voice on the line.

This time it was a young man, and after Dan had told him all he had told the first person, he said, "I need information on this Dobbs. I'd appreciate it if you'd check for arrest records and/or convictions. He's working as the mortician here, and also serving as the deputy coroner. He has an M.D., as I told you.

He's lived here about ten years, so you don't need to check anything during that time."

"Very well," the man said. "How soon do you need this information, Undersheriff?"

"As soon as possible. We have . . . a difficult situation here, and . . . Dobbs's past, if he has one, might prove . . . embarrassing." Dan did not know what else to say. "Anything that you can give me, of course, will be treated with the greatest confidence. No matter what you come up with, if there is anything."

"We appreciate that, Undersheriff." The man cleared his throat. "Just to be certain, you want any arrest or conviction records of a G. William Dobbs, B.S., M.S., M.D. Will you give us an approximate age?"

"Fifty-five?" Dan said, uncertain of it himself. "Maybe as old as sixty. Something like that."

"Fine. You may expect a call from us as soon as the check is complete. Thank you for calling us." The phone went dead in Dan's hand, and he had the oddest sensation that he had placed himself in danger.

But he did not let himself be worried. He did not have time for worry. He pulled the Polaroid shot he had taken of Freddie from his pocket and looked at it, then went out around the partition and handed the photograph to Betty.

"What's this?" she said.

"I want this sent off to the police in St. Louis, special delivery. Indicate that this should be delivered to the Missing Persons Bureau." He saw the dubious expression in her eyes, and invented a plausible reason for his actions. "Look, we never did find out for sure if the man we buried"—he had a brief, terrible memory of the heart rolling away from him across the floor of the reposing room—"was LeMoir, and we never knew if he was traveling alone. So, send this along and if there is a record on the man, we might learn what actually happened to the guy who was . . . killed . . . in the hospital."

"But that's Freddie, the new man at Winslow's." Betty looked so calm, so reasonable, that Dan wanted to call the last two hours a dream.

"Yeah. It struck me as a little too coincidental that he should show up at the time the other man was killed. I know it's a long shot, but, damnit, Betty, I have to do something on this case or I'll end up climbing the walls."

Betty favored him with an indulgent smile. "I'll see that it goes out before I leave for the night. And you, Dan, should go home and get changed. You'll catch your death, running around with wet clothes on."

"I was planning to do just that," Dan said, starting for the door.

"Oh," Betty called after him, "I should have told you. Ernie Sutton called about an hour ago. He's back in the store and your film is ready. He's expecting you." She gave him one of her maternal smiles and waved him away.

• • •

"Gracious, Sheriff," Ernie said as he looked up at Dan. "You're soaked to the skin."

"It's raining out, Ernie." Dan said it flatly.

"Yes, lovely rain. I've always liked the rain." Ernie gave Dan one of his most cherubic smiles. "It's one of the reasons I live here. But I'm keeping you."

"That's right. Betty said you'd called—you have that film I left off . . ."

"Righto! Righto!" He beamed amiably at Dan. "I've got it right here." As he looked down, a fleeting look of alarm crossed his face as he caught sight of his hands. He thrust both of them under the counter. "It's ready."

"May I have it, please?" Dan asked wearily. "I have to head for home, Ernie. I want to get into dry clothes and make a few calls."

"Sure, sure," Ernie said, adding, "You might want to take a look at the new paperbacks I've got in. I haven't even unpacked 'em yet." He nodded toward a stack of books at the far end of the counter.

Dan sighed and went the few steps necessary to have a look at them, not wanting to offend Ernie.

While Dan glanced disinterestedly over the titles on the spines, Ernie brought a small paper bag from under the counter and set it down. He looked at the tips of his fingers. The skin was flaking, like old paint coming off a building. He rang up the amount on the register and put his hands out of sight again. "That'll be $15.40. You know how it is, Sheriff. Everything's going up."

Dan reached into his pocket and pulled out his wallet. "I think I've got the exact change," he said as he drew out a ten and a five. He fished in his pocket and got out a quarter and three nickles. "There you are."

"Good," Ernie said with more relief than would have seemed warranted. "I'm always short on change," he explained. "You know how it is."

"Yeah." Dan picked up the package. "Thanks."

"Any time," Ernie assured Dan, and his wide smile faded as the door slammed behind Dan.

• • •

By the time Dan had dried off and changed, his worries were nagging at him almost intolerably. He told himself for the twentieth time that he was making a total ass of himself, but he placed a call to Ed Thurston at the hospital.

"You're not busy are you?" Dan asked impatiently as soon as they were connected.

"Not at the moment, no. We've got a tricky coronary case in, but the nurse is with him, and that should be okay for the time being. If I hang up without warning, though, that's why." Ed sounded tired, as he always did.

"Good enough. I understand." He was holding the phone in one hand, pacing the length of the living room with nervous strides.

"Are you okay, Dan?" Ed asked after a moment.

"Yeah, yeah, I'm okay. It's not me, it's . . ."

"Hey, Dan, take it easy. Do I have to remind you that police work is a high-stress occupation? You've got to watch it. It sounds like you're running yourself into the ground."

"Into the ground," Dan repeated. "You know, that's kind of funny. Considering."

"Considering what? What is it, Dan? Tell me!" Ed sounded more concerned now; he spoke more slowly and kept his voice even.

"I warn you right now it's going to sound ridiculous. You're going to think I'm ready for a padded closet—"

"Good enough," Ed interrupted. "Get on with it. I'll recommend a shrink when I'm convinced you need one."

"That'll probably be two minutes from now." Dan stopped in the middle of the living room. "Okay. Okay." He waited, marshaling his thoughts. "Look, this is your professional opinion I'm asking, Ed, not a private speculation. Don't make allowances for . . . anything. Got that?"

"Sure."

"Yeah. Well. In your professional opinion is there any way *whatsoever* to . . . to reanimate people after death?" He took a deep breath and held it.

"That depends on what you mean by reanimate and death," Ed told him. "I'm not splitting hairs with you, I'm asking serious questions. You know that we now restart stopped hearts routinely. Of course, those cases are carefully monitored. And there are always questions about unplugging patients kept alive by machines. Is that what you're talking about?"

"I don't know. I don't think so. I mean, suppose someone has died, really died. They're sent off for burial, say. Is is possible for someone to . . . get them going again?"

Ed did not answer at once. "Well, you can get nerve responses with proper stimulus for some time after death has technically occurred. And muscle tissue can be made to respond with electric current. Massive doses of, for instance, insulin, can sometimes cause fairly startling results up to half an hour after death has occurred."

"Not longer than that?" Dan inquired hopefully.

"Not that I know of. But I haven't any idea what they're doing in laboratories these days. They may be able to prolong response if they can keep the nerve tissue viable."

"And would the dead person, if reanimated, be able to get up and walk around?"

"You have been working too hard, haven't you?" Ed chuckled in a kindly way, then paused when Dan said nothing. "Are you serious about this?"

Dan did not answer him. Instead, he said, "You remember what you told me when you finished testing those particles of human skin you checked out for me? They were for a suspected hit-and-run."

"Those? Sure. I said the body they came from had been dead for months." His tone was puzzled.

"Well, it hasn't been months since that accident happened. I got those samples from the bumper of my car. *I* was the one who hit someone, and it happened the night before I brought you the samples. The night before, not a month or two."

"Sorry, Dan, but it couldn't be."

Dan's knuckles whitened as he held the receiver more tightly. "Ed, I'm telling you it was. I was there. I hit someone. They got up and . . . ran away."

Ed sighed heavily. "Those samples weren't from that accident. Listen, maybe three months or so ago, Winslow was giving you a tune-up and scraped his arm on your grill. That could account for what you sent us."

"For Chrissake, I wash my car more often than that!" Dan set the phone down on the coffee table and leaned on the arm of a chair. "Ed, something's wrong here, very wrong. No one talks about it, but . . . corpses are disappearing in this town. One got up and left Dobbs's workroom, and another wasn't in his grave when the coffin was exhumed."

"That's possible," Ed allowed, "but you don't need to reanimate the bodies to take them. It's distasteful to consider, but there are necrophiles in the world, and they do make a habit of finding . . . what they need. It's more likely that you're dealing with a necrophile than that these missing bodies are being restored to life, I'll tell you that much."

"But could it happen?" Dan persisted.

"Is it possible, do you mean? Oh, remotely

possible. Very remotely. But even if you could reanimate the body for a time—say, several hours—there are a great many problems. For one thing, once the body systems stop, decay sets in."

"I know that," Dan said, trying to keep from yelling at Ed. "I simply want to know if it can happen."

"That's what I'm trying to tell you," Ed said. "Those who die of old age die because the body is worn out, like old machinery. Others have massive biological insults, and the body can't adapt. Disease does that. Those who die violently have great amounts of damage done to the body, so that the machinery can't function any longer. What I'm trying to say is that before death occurs, others things must happen. If it is possible to bring a body back to life, you still haven't explained how the reanimated person is going to respond to the original cause of death."

"Suppose the tissue could be restored—" Dan suggested.

"Not bloody likely," Ed cut him off. "If that could be done, we'd be using it on the living. Don't you think that any serious doctor would be overjoyed to restore his patients to health instead of burying them?"

"Sure, but—"

"It's a pretty dream, Dan, but that's all it is. Bodies are impermanent quarters at best and—Oh, shit!" The receiver slammed down and the line was empty.

• • •

Ten minutes later, Dan was headed back to the sheriff's office. He had left Janet's roll of film on the kitchen table. Unopened. Rain streamed down his windows, flicked away by the wipers. His vision was distorted by the water, and the few people he saw on the streets appeared oddly misshapen, like melting wax.

"What are you doing here?" Betty asked, sounding displeased, as Dan came through the door.

"I changed clothes," he told her. "And rain or no rain, I have work to do, and it's got to be done." He hurried around the partition to his desk, reaching for the top drawer of the nearest file cabinet.

"Dan, there's a message from Rhode Island. It's on your desk. It came about twenty minutes ago," Betty called out. "How long are you planning to be here?"

Dan picked up the message sheet and answered Betty remotely, "I don't know. As long as it takes."

"Well, I have to leave soon. It's after five, you know."

"Go ahead and leave when you have to." He sat down and turned on his desk light.

SUBJECT: G(AMMERA) WILLIAM DOBBS, DISMISSED 10 OCT. '69 AS CHIEF PATHOLOGIST, PROVIDENCE, RHODE ISLAND. EVIDENCE INDICATED SUBJECT MADE UNAUTHORIZED USE OF DEAD BODIES IN COUNTY MORGUE AND OTHER INSTITUTIONS. NO-BILLED BY GRAND JURY SUBJECT TO HIS IMMEDIATE RESIGNATION. CENSURED AND EJECTED BY RHODE ISLAND MEDICAL SOCIETY 30 NOV. '69.

AFTER A PSYCHIATRIC HEARING, SUBJECT RETAINED MEDICAL LICENSE. RESULTS OF THAT HEARING ARE AVAILABLE ON WRITTEN REQUEST. SUBJECT LEFT THE STATE OF RHODE ISLAND ON OR ABOUT 15 JAN. '70.

Dan sat tapping the paper and reading it carefully through three times. *Unauthorized use of dead bodies. Unauthorized use of dead bodies.* The phrase stuck out at him like tacks on a map. Slowly he got up, leaving the paper on his desk. He pulled open the file drawer and looked in.

"Betty?"

"What?" She was just starting to clear off her desk.

"Did you take the LeMoir file out today?" He had checked every current file and could not find the information on the man.

"No, why?"

"Do you know where it might be?" Dan did not want to accuse her, or make her think he was suspicious of her. Past experience had taught him that it would take a long time to convince her of his faith in her once he questioned her too closely.

"In the drawer," she answered.

"I've looked there."

"The top drawer of your desk?" She was slightly irritated. It was the end of the day, it was cold and rainy, and she wanted to go home, not spend extra time searching for a file.

Dan pulled it open and checked through the papers. "No. Not here. Any other ideas?"

"Did you take it home?"

"No." He slammed the desk drawer and began to open the other drawers of the file cabinets. He could not find the file for George LeMoir. "Was the office empty at any time today?"

"Of course not. I only went next door to the Post Office to mail that photo for you. No one came in after you left." She took her coat from one of three hangers in the little closet, and picked up her umbrella.

Dan knew the file was gone now, and that it was no longer in the building. He turned off his desk light, picked up the sheet of paper with the Dobbs information, and came around the partition again. "I've got to go out. I'll see you in the morning, Betty."

"No rest for the wicked, Sheriff?" she asked with the last of her humor.

"Something like that," he agreed as he started for the door.

• • •

Janet was not home yet. Dan pulled into the driveway on squealing tires and braked lurchingly to a stop. The kitchen was dark, as was the rest of the house, and Dan went through it without turning on the light. He had just entered the rarely used guest room off the dining room when he stopped. There was another sound in the house, the whirr of a machine turning on. It was not the familiar sound of the refrigerator or the rush of the heater, but a strange, stuttering sound.

A beam of light came on, striking the flimsy screen set up in the guest room and a moment later, a hand-lettered sign came on:

REVELATIONS
Part II

Dan took a step toward the screen, his shadow massive and menacing over the words, and then he stopped. From the fragment of picture, he recognized that this section of film was being taken at Jake Sutton's Hide-Away Motel on the outskirts of town in the best of the cabins. From the angle of the film, whoever was holding the camera was in the small loft, and was probably concealed from the couple who had just walked in the door. Almost against his will, Dan sank into a chair, out of the path of the light.

The man was tall and good-looking, obviously eager for the woman with him. He touched her shoulder as she paused in the shadow of the door, and his hand slid down over her breast as he spoke to her. Dan wondered what he might be saying. Apparently it was the right thing, for the woman went into his arms, her mouth open to his. It was only when she stepped away from the man and the light hit her face that Dan recognized her. It was Janet.

The anguish of his recognition brought him half-out of his chair. He could make no sound, so great was his shock and humiliation. He reached out and touched the screen, as if trying to verify what he was seeing.

Janet was taking off her coat, and then unbuttoning her blouse. She moved as if she had done this many times before. There was no hesitation, no awkwardness in her movement. Her face was subtly provocative as she turned to help the man undress. When she unbuttoned his shirt, she leaned forward and ran her tongue over his chest, smiling as he pulled her tight against him.

The camera spared Dan nothing. He saw his wife respond to the man's caresses, saw her perform acts with this unknown she had denied Dan. Naked, she clung to him in abandon, her hands drawing him toward her, over her, into her. One hand reached out to the side, out of the frame, and when it was back in view, Janet held a long butcher's knife. Her face was filled with joyous madness, her body rocked and surged with the man's above her, and her arm lifted the knife and struck it true and deeply into the small of his back.

The man on the screen jerked, his head coming back, his mouth open in a silent scream. Janet struck a second time, and a third, and each time the man wrenched and writhed like a gaffed fish. Janet's ecstatic expression did not change. Finally the man collapsed, his arms running red, his legs smeared.

The images on the screen wobbled as the camera was set down, and then, as the film went on, another figure came into the picture, a man who helped Janet roll the body aside so that she, slicked with blood and sweat, could step free of her victim. The man kissed her hand and turned back to wave at the camera. It was Dobbs.

Dan pressed his hands to his eyes and let out one terrible howl of agony.

Chapter 13

The door to Dobbs's Mortuary was ajar when Dan rushed up to it, prepared to break his way in if necessary. The reception area was unoccupied and the doors of both reposing rooms were closed. Dan could hear the gaudy strains of Berlioz's Symphony Fantastique coming from the workroom. He rushed toward the door shouting, "Dobbs! DOBBS! YOU BASTARD!" He flung open the door to the workroom and halted as the mortician turned toward him with a quizzical smile.

"What did you do to her, Dobbs!" Dan was finding it hard to breathe, and the ghoulish March to the Scaffold with its gleeful, fatal drums, rolled in his ears like thunder, shutting out words and thought alike.

"Good evening, Daniel," Dobbs said, indicating a folding chair which was set at the end of one of the tables. "I've been expecting you."

"What have you done to my wife!" Dan demanded, reaching out for the other man.

Dobbs stepped back out of range. "Be calm, my boy. It will all be explained to you. You must have patience. I've had patience, and so must you."

"Where is Janet?" Her name stuck in his throat.

"Dear Janet. She was my first, my true crown jewel, my seedling, if you like. It's an apt analogy, don't you think?"

"What are you—crazy?" Dan was suddenly overwhelmed by a sense of utter helplessness. He sank onto the folding chair and stared up at Dobbs. "Oh, God, where is she, Dobbs?"

Dobbs had opened his cabinet and reached under a stack of magazines to pull out a scrapbook. He handed it to Dan. "Have a look."

"Dobbs, if this is—"

"Oh, it's quite germane, believe me, Sheriff. Have a look at . . . my family album, if you will." He still wore that impish smile and he was humming along with the blaring trumpets.

Each page was filled with snapshots, and each was so horrific that Dan had to fight the gorge that rose in his throat. There was the man on the beach turning into a pillar of fire. There was Nils Uhri incinerated with his beloved boats. And there was an attractive young woman in the ruins of the boatyard, gasoline being spilled over her clothes as she was restrained by others. And there were others, many others, some with faces Dan knew.

"Look at them," Dobbs said dreamily as he came up to Dan. "Look at my children."

"Dobbs," Dan said when he was able to speak at all, "this is horrible."

"They had to be mutilated, of course. It allows me to preserve a certain anonymity, which is essential, don't you see? Families from the outside coming in to find out what happened—that would never do. I have to have them to myself. Also, it is a more challenging prospect, you understand. Anyone can restore someone who died in bed. No trick to it at all. But these, they so *needed* me. Only *I* could make them look as they *used* to look. That's a special art, Daniel. And I'm the best there is at it."

"And Janet?" His voice was rusty, as if he were suddenly very old.

"Janet. Yes. She was my greatest triumph, my first real success. I found her in her car, that Duster of hers . . . in Hollis Creek. She was dead. Her car had run off the road, and she had been knocked out. She had drowned, hanging there in her car, her seat belt holding her underwater. Ironic, isn't it?"

"This is insane." Dan closed the album and let it drop to the floor.

Dobbs did not notice. "Not her injuries, the bloating, anything, could hide how very attractive she had been. After Providence, I had decided not to risk experimenting again, but when I saw her, I knew she had to have it or go into the ground for good. I could not let that happen, not to someone so young, so lovely as Janet. And once I'd actually done it, I wanted to try it again. I had to prove to myself that it had worked."

On the record, the fanfare and drum roll announced the imminent execution of the dreamer.

"No," Dan muttered, unable to listen to Dobbs.

"She had been dead, but I was able to restore her. And all the others. Like poor Herman, who you hit with your car the other night. He came to me to get his arm fixed. He died in the sawmill, you know—but of course, you don't know—when one of the blades came off its axle and went flying through the air, spinning. That was a difficult job. He was quite dead when you hit him, but his restoration was fairly successful." He bent over and picked up the album.

"How? How?" This place, Dobbs, the record—they were all unreal to Dan, as if this were happening to another man, far away.

"There are those who might call it black magic. It isn't. I've made a medical breakthrough which could revolutionize . . . everything." He put the album back in his cabinet. On the turntable, the Witches Sabbath was beginning. "If there are doubters, if my methods are rejected, then I'll take my secret to the grave, if you'll pardon the pun."

"No."

"There are problems with the technique. It isn't perfect yet. There is this question of decay. Most of them will start to . . . fall apart if I don't touch them up a bit, oh, once a week. Janet, though, she's been my greatest success. She has gone as long as three weeks without any help from me. She gives me reason to hope."

"No. No." It had to be a nightmare, he told himself, and knew that it was not.

"I've always liked you, Dan. You're a good man, personable, reliable. Rare qualities in these uneasy days. I thought you could take care of her properly. So I gave her to you as a sort of . . . gift."

"No. No . . . no."

"I do what I can to give the others back their lives, as well as life, but it doesn't always work out very well. I've been trying various methods, to see how I can change that. Janet, though, she was different. She has her fear and love and sex and—"

"She's *alive!* If she weren't I would have known!" Dan's fists came down on the table beside him, and his eyes were hot and cold at once.

"I wanted her to be perfect. I want them all to be perfect. The others are like drawings, or sketches, but Janet is a fully realized masterpiece. Just think. She is safe from the predations of age and disease. She will never lose her beauty and her youth. Death has spared her all that, and asked nothing in exchange. Don't you see how fortunate she is, how fortunate they all are?"

Dan's fingers found his pistol without any prompting from his mind. He would kill Dobbs, he told himself. He would raise the pistol, pull the trigger and Dobbs would die.

"I wouldn't recommend it," Dobbs said as the Dies Irae theme brayed in the brasses. "You can try to kill me, Dan. You might come pretty close. But you won't do it, not the way you think. Go ahead. Shoot me. You'll only make me dead, but that won't kill me. You'll make me like the rest of my family." He took a step closer. "You can't possibly miss me."

Dan's hand was sweating as he lifted the pistol and aimed it, point-blank, at Dobbs's face. His arm trembled and every joint in his body ached as if he were being racked. His finger would not tighten on the trigger.

"Oh, dear. I was afraid you might feel this way. You're the most obstinately honorable man, Daniel. Perhaps I can provide you with motivation." He turned away and opened the door to the coat closet.

In horror, Dan watched Janet come into the workroom. Her face was set in a welcoming smile and she spoke to him with the demented enthusiasm of a television commercial for cake mixes.

"Janet . . ." Dan suddenly realized that Janet was not looking at him, but at some point over his head.

"Hello, Danny," she said brightly. "How did it go today? You're home so late, I've been worried about you. And listen, you won't believe what went on at school today. Paul Haskell is a maniac. He had *another* locker inspecion."

"Dear God," Dan said softly.

"It was ten minutes before lunch, and you know what those kids are like then. Everybody had to hit the halls and stand next to their lockers. They were mad as hell, and I don't blame them."

Dan looked up at her. "Janet, who was the man at the Hide-Away?"

"She doesn't remember, Dan," Dobbs said kindly.

"How could she not remember something

like that?" Dan was filled with revulsion as the imges rose before him again. Janet beneath the man, Janet stabbing him . . .

"But I told you. She's dead, Dan. The dead have no memory. That's one of the problems I've encountered, and I've been trying for years to find a way to fix it. As it is, the only memory they possess is what I manufacture for them."

"Anyway," Janet went on heedlessly, "what would you like for dinner tonight? Something quick, 'cause it's so late, unless you don't mind being hungry for another hour or so."

"She only appears to be alive, Dan," Dobbs went on sympathetically. "She does it better than the the others do, but it is only an illusion. I keep hoping to find the right way to restore them. That's the trouble. Brain activity ceases and nothing I can do is good enough to restore it completely. Memory is such a delicate thing. Even living people have trouble with it. The dead . . ." He shrugged.

"SHE IS ALIVE!" Dan screamed the words as he leaped out of the chair. He reached out his left hand, the hand that did not hold his pistol, and touched her chin, turning her face toward him. "Janet, Janet, don't talk like this. Don't listen to Dobbs." Inadvertently he tightened his hold on her. "We'll get it taken care of, somehow. I don't know what's wrong, but you'll get better, I promise you." He stared at his hand as he saw a patch of skin from her cheek loosen and crumble under the pressure of his fingers.

Janet did not notice this. She rambled on

happily, "You can have anything you want, but you might have to fix it yourself. I . . ." She stopped for a moment to reach up and pat her cheek. "I'll have to neaten up a bit, won't I?"

"Oh, Jesus." Dan stepped back from her, his body moving as if it were controlled by strings. He could not stand to look at her, and could not force himself to look away.

"If you want me to make dinner, well, you can have a minute steak."

One of the bottles on the counter fell as Dan backed into it. Dan bent and picked up the broken glass. Without warning, he lashed out at Janet, the shard of glass slicing through her upper arm.

"Or a big salad and an omelet." She did not bleed. She had not noticed the cut at all.

"No." It was a whimper now. Dan raised his gun deliberately. "Janet, baby, die. Please, please die." And he pulled the trigger.

The bullet slammed through her chest and she faltered. "What about pork chops? I can make beef stroganoff, if you're in the mood for something fancy." Her breath was whistling as she spoke, and she stumbled as he shot her a second time. "Of course, that comes out of a package." Like a windup doll whose spring has wound down, Janet fell silent. Slowly she looked down at the two neat holes in her upper chest, where a white substance oozed. Her bright expression faded, and with a look that was at once mocking and sad, she faced him. "Try again."

The third bullet caught her at the collar bone, and shattered it.

"Danny . . . bury me." There was very little voice left to her.

Dan was weeping now, his soul numb. He could not say anything to Janet as she tottered up to him.

"Bury me. Bury me, please."

"I—" He spun away from her, and found himself face to face with Dobbs. "YOU EVIL SON OF A BITCH!" He fired twice, directly into Dobbs's guts.

"Wonderful," Dobbs sighed blissfully as he slid to the floor.

When Dan turned around again, Janet had already left the room. He felt himself tremble, as if that were the last thing left to him in this terrible place. Dan heard the back door open, and ran out of the workroom after the sound.

On the turntable, the needle was stuck on the record, nine measures from the end of the piece.

G. William Dobbs lay on the floor staring up at the ceiling. He held one hand across his ruined abdomen, the other pressed against the leg of the table where he had fallen. Slowly he turned over, moving with care. He got to his knees, then reached for the edge of the table to pull himself erect. He leaned heavily on his hands, his button eyes inscrutable. Then he reached out for the turntable and pressed the reject switch. Abruptly the sound stopped. Dobbs smiled.

• • •

The storm had hit in earnest and the cemetery was filled with it. Trees leaned and soughed in the wind, the grass bent in long, silvery swaths. Only the headstones remained untouched, as they always had.

Dan had pulled his flashlight from his belt and aimed it into the rain as he searched for Janet. He shouted her name as he walked, and when at last he caught sight of her, he flung his pistol away.

"Bury me, Dan," she sighed at him.

"Janet!" He lost sight of her again, and shouted once more.

"Please," she wheezed, and at last he knew that she was looking for the open grave.

Dan's face was wet with rain and tears as he stumbled through the graves. He hoped he had chosen the right direction.

At last he found the grave where the burned girl was to have lain. He stood at the yawning edge of the hole and shone the beam of his flashlight into it. Rain silvered the light, and revealed Janet's peaceful, crumbling face. One of her hands was stuck in the earthen wall of the grave, as if she were trying to pull it in over her. Her eyes were fever-bright. "End it, Dan. Bury me."

"Janet!" All the emotion he had ever felt for her was in her name as he said it. He fell to his knees beside the grave and began to shove armfuls of earth in on her. Only when her face was all that was uncovered did he falter. Then he saw that the rain was washing her hair off her scalp, and he pushed the earth onto her.

Half of her face was covered and the other side was spattered with mud. Janet smiled up at Dan. "I love you," she murmured, and fell silent.

Dan did not stop now. He carried and pushed and kicked at the mound of earth until the grave was almost full. His flashlight was out, and there was only the dark and the rain to keep him company.

And then there was a hand on his shoulder. Dan crouched low and turned to see an arm with bones exposed by peeling flesh and muscles. The bony hand held a bouquet of flowers.

Ernie Sutton smiled down at Dan. "May she rest in peace," he said, and bent to place the flowers on her grave.

Dan looked up wildly to discover the cemetery was full of people. There was Agnes Whitestone, her pom-pom slippers wet and floppy, looking dejected and sniffing into a lace handkerchief. Beside her was Herman, his arm once more detached. He held two wild roses in his working hand. Penny Strickland was dressed for work in the bar, though her red cocktail dress was not sensible wear for this place, and time, and weather. Part of her exposed shoulder was cracking. Nils Uhri had lost three of his fingers, but he had brought a long garland of seaweed with him. And for once Harry Clemens carried a tub of carnations instead of two gas cans. There were more people, familiar people—the whole population of Potter's Bluff. Betty came up to Dan and put her hand on his arm. "She's the lucky one," she said in a scratchy tone. Dan saw that part of her throat had given way. Ed Thurston put an arm around Dan's shoulder. "I'm envious. She made it."

As Dan watched, paralyzed beyond any reaction, everyone he knew in town came up and left their token for Janet. Tubby Bass held his sagging jaw in place so that he could promise Dan that the town would see that she had a proper headstone.

One of the Rowen girls was in worse condition than most, and as she bent to place her flowers on the grave, one of her eyes fell out and joined the blooms as an offering.

At that Dan shrieked and broke away from the crowd. He ran wildly, stumbling, falling, back toward the mortuary. A murdered man was tolerable, but these creatures were not. He pulled the door closed behind him and choked back the laughter rumbling in his chest. He covered his mouth with both his hands and crept along the hallway like a naughty child returning late from play. It was only then that he noticed there was no music.

Now the workroom lured him, and he moved toward it with dreamlike intensity. He no longer knew why he was in this building, or what had happened to him ten minutes before.

• • •

G. William Dobbs was lying on the nearest table, hooked up to the blood excavation pump. The machine hummed contentedly and Dobbs hummed along with it. He turned his head as Dan came in the door. He waved easily and sat up. "Good. I was afraid you might be too late."

"She's buried," Dan said in a hideous voice. He stared at Dobbs, numb beyond all horror.

"I do enjoy these little chess games with you, Dan." Carefully he pulled the needles from his arm and reset the gauges on the machine. "Are you ready?" Dobbs was not alone—a stunningly beautiful young woman whom Dan had never seen before stood at the far side of the table smiling radiantly, unperturbably.

"Dan, this is—but I haven't given her a name yet. And of course you don't recognize her, do you? When you last saw this stunning creature she was lying in a ditch at the side of the road, burned beyond recognition."

Dan shook his head and took a step backward. His ankle and knee collapsed under him, and he looked stupidly down at them, at the end of the femur poking through rotten flesh and torn cloth. He reached out to cover it and the skin crumbled from his palm. His eyes were flat, he could no longer speak.

"Come on, Dan," Dobbs said indulgently as he came toward him. "Let me fix that up for you."